OVERTAXED

AND

UNDERAPPRECIATED

OVERTAXED

AND

UNDERAPPRECIATED

by

Cheryl B. Dale

J&H Press

Copyright Information

Copyright 2013 by Cheryl B. Dale
Published by J&H Press
Cover Art by Colin Beishir
Edited by B.L. Wilson

ISBN: 978-0-9853910-4-1

Other Fiction by Cheryl B. Dale

Romantic Suspense

Intimate Portraits
Treacherous Beauties
The Man in the Boat
Set Up

Paranormal Romance

The Warwicks of Slumber Mountain

Light Mystery

Taxed to the Max

www.cherylbdale.com
cherylbdale.blogspot.com
cherylbdale@hotmail.com

OVERTAXED

AND

UNDERAPPRECIATED

Chapter One

FIVE DAYS AFTER I burned the courthouse to the ground, leaving all the county employees homeless, so to speak, our esteemed county officials rushed to respond with their usual wisdom, foresight, and consideration.

They plunked down a secondhand, single-wide mobile home on one end of the shady square in Medder Rose, Georgia, and informed me that the grungy box would be my new tax office. No ifs, ands, or buts.

This second Wednesday in May saw the trailer well on its way to being transformed.

"What do you think, Corrie? Didn't I tell you it'd look better once we got it fixed up?" County commissioner Sam Blanken puffed his barrel chest out, pleased with his handiwork.

"Well." I adjusted my ponytail holder and tried to come up with sufficiently blistering words.

There were none.

Huge oaks, partly blackened but escaping total incineration, drooped branches like they were mourning this eyesore in their midst.

"We worked like dogs to get it up so fast. Had to call in a lot of favors and pull a lot of strings, but this is gonna be great." Sam put up a hand to keep me from speaking. "No, no, don't thank me."

Like I was about to. "I'll curb my enthusiasm."

The unadorned metal box looked exactly like what it was: a temporary tax office for a temporary tax commissioner.

Me.

I suffered no illusions about my position. My appointment by the county bigwigs after the old tax commissioner's death was a stopgap measure. Next year, Judge Hartley's nephew would graduate from the University of Georgia and could run for office.

The good ol' boys had big plans for him.

Not that those future plans were mentioned to my face, even by my daddy's best friend who had helped me get hired at the tax office in the first place and whose short rotund figure stood beside me now.

Sam jingled his change. "So? Be honest now. What do you think?" He waved at the, the *thing*, on its precarious perch of concrete blocks.

Wooden ramps led from the sidewalk to two doors facing us. Sad to say, the newly constructed ramps were the most attractive feature of the whole structure.

Be diplomatic, I reminded myself. *Don't call it tacky and ugly.* "I don't know if it'll work, Sam. Will it hold up to the wear and tear? An awful lot of people go through the tax office. I mean, everyone has to buy auto tags and pay property taxes."

Sam pooh-poohed my misgivings. "It's as sturdy as can be. It'll hold up to twenty people at a time, I bet."

I might be a reluctant tax commissioner, but I still ought to stand up for my workers and customers. "I thought I was gonna get a new double-wide like the clerk. Counting the two part-time people, I have one more employee than him."

Sam, paunchy face resembling a bullfrog, sounded like one, too. "Hon, the clerk's double-wide'll be another week getting here and then it's got to be set up. But you can be up and running tomorrow. Lucky the school board had this extra trailer tucked away."

Up and running tomorrow?

He wished. *Be tactful, Corrie, be tactful.* "I'm not sure this trailer will be big enough to hold us, much less all our customers."

Sam harbored no such misgivings. "Oh, yeah, it'll be fine. Come look at what Bert's done to the inside."

Bert Macroff was a frequent inmate of the county jail. According to my daddy, Bert sober wouldn't hurt a fly, but Bert drunk was another story. Liquored up, he demolished other people's property without so much as a by-your-leave.

Didn't matter. The commissioners forgave Bert much because he was an artist at his trade. His wainscoting and hardwood floors and solid bookshelves could—and did—grace mansions.

So whenever Bert was confined for one of his lapses, the taxpayers got their money's worth. Why, the sheriff once got an entire break area outfitted with cabinets, counters, and custom-made tables while Bert was incarcerated.

And the county offices weren't the only one to benefit. So did the public coffers. As a trusty—a county inmate trusted to work outside the jail without running away—Bert earned less than minimum wage. For his community service sentences, he made nothing.

"We was lucky Bert hadn't got halfway through his last six week sentence when the fire hit," Sam said. "We took him off the shelves he was building out at maintenance and put him right on redoing this here trailer. He can always do that humdrum stuff next time."

Sad to say, for poor Bert, there'd always be a next time.

But Bert wasn't my problem. This *thing* was.

The noonday sun peeked through the leaves of century-old oaks and glinted off Sam's bald pate as he stepped on a wide ramp. "Built sturdy enough to handle heavy stuff like wheelchairs." He jumped up and down to demonstrate. It bounced ominously, but Sam was already hurrying to unlock the door.

I moped after him.

Inside, the smell of fresh wood lingered. While Bert might be a binge alcoholic, he had indeed done a fine job on the high wooden counter that divided the mobile home lengthwise down the middle. Too bad its satiny finish looked out of place in such tawdry surroundings. Nobody had even tried to disguise the grubby metal walls and trim.

Sam slapped the counter proudly. "Solid birch. It'll hold up good. Now, people'll enter this door here, come right up to the counter so you can issue them their tags or whatever, and then they'll march right out the other door." He waved a pudgy arm toward the presumed exit. "Makes a little one-way circle so nobody runs over anybody else. Nice planning, huh?"

Right. Maybe six feet divided the counter from the back wall where one forlorn window did its best to entice daylight in. Six feet left us workers little room to maneuver. And the front corridor holding the taxpayers *might* be a yard wide.

"It's plumb cramped, Sam. Some of our customers are about as broad as this section where they have to stand. I don't know if they'll have enough room. Do you honestly think it'll work?"

Sam flapped a dismissive hand. "It'll be fine. You'll see. Behind the counter here—" he opened an inner door that had a hole where the knob should be, "—you got enough room to set up four computers. The clerks may have to be a mite friendly, but they can squeeze in. Then this door right here leads to your secure room."

"At least it's got a lock on it," I muttered.

Sam ignored the implied criticism and with a flourish, flung the aforementioned door wide open. "And looky what we got here!" he croaked. "Your safe."

Shock stopped me cold.

The battered vault, taller than my five feet five, was big and boxy. It looked like a Wells Fargo safe out of a bad western. A really *old* bad western. "Where'd that come from?"

"Sheriff had one at the jail he wasn't using. Combination's right here." He tapped a yellow sticky note on the front. "Sheriff says it's temperamental but you'll manage."

Not only was my office being stuffed into a tiny trailer, I wasn't even going to get a new safe out of the fire. This seemed plain-out wrong. Even if the fire was kind of my fault.

"Your tag plates go in here, too. Plenty of room." Sam's stubby form pivoted and flitted toward the other end of the trailer. "Now this here door leads to your office where you'll put your desk for paperwork and stuff. Good planning, huh?"

He didn't expect an answer. My age and experience offset any valid opinion I might offer. Not to mention Sam seeing me as Keith Caters' crazy daughter because of an unfortunate tendency toward mishaps.

But whether I agreed or not, this tiny box was where I was going to be stuck for...

"How long will it take to get the new courthouse built?"

Sam didn't miss a beat. "Well, it helped we had a plan we got ready back in 2008 when we thought the voters would approve that referendum—"

They hadn't.

People in Ocosawnee County don't like to spend money on frills like libraries and jails. Or courthouses. Now, ball fields and basketball courts and skateboard parks are another story. They're considered necessities.

"—so the purchase agent's getting the bid packages together to advertise. We'll choose a contractor when the bids come in, then whoever we pick'll get started. I'd guess a year, year and a half at most."

In your dreams, Sam. I'd seen the bid process at work. This dinky rattrap would be my workplace for at least three years. Could it get any worse?

Never mind. Like Daddy says, keep your mouth shut and your nose above water.

Back outside, a tractor trailer rig put-putted around the shady square.

I took a deep breath. "I bet that's my tag delivery." At least something was going right today. "The driver called this morning and said he'd be here around lunchtime. Do you have a key to that strong room so I can lock them up?"

With a magician's fanfare, Sam pulled out a ring holding about ten keys. "Right here. And this one's for your office. And this one is to the outside doors. The rest are spares in case you need to let someone open up for you or something."

"Thanks." I tried to drum up some gratitude. He had done his best. I guess. "Appreciate it, Sam. I better call the jail and get some trusties to help unload the truck."

Sam looked at me like I was crazy. "For a few measly tag plates?"

From experience, I knew the semi driver would not deliver the cartons any further than the back of his truck, but I did not snap at Sam for his ignorance.

Despite the fact he was putting me in a metal container related to a sardine can, I did not snarl.

Despite the fact he was giving me a used safe the sheriff should have consigned for scrap, I did not fly off the handle.

Instead, I smiled, showing my teeth. "We're getting more than a few tag plates because our entire inventory burned up in the fire, you recall."

Despite my good intentions, maybe a teeny edge of sarcasm did creep in, but I don't think I actually became shrill. Not then.

"And for your information, those boxes weigh over twenty pounds apiece. The driver won't move them any further than the tailgate of his truck because it's not in his job description. If you want to unload them yourself, I'll be *happy* to let you."

Okay, that *job description* might have come out a little loud. And the *happy* sounded downright manic.

Sam noticed. He stepped well away from me and whipped out his cell phone hidden somewhere in the fleshy folds that defined his midsection. "I'll call the jail. You flag that driver down. He's pulling over to where the courthouse used to be. He's missed us entirely. Looky there, he's slowed down. Too durn busy craning his neck at the burn site. Now he's going round the square. Imbecile." He croaked into the phone, "No, not you. You got any trusties handy I can borrow to unload some tags?"

As I sprinted across the square to catch the truck, a woman and young boy came out of the parks and recreation building situated diagonally across the street. The boy tugged at the woman's arm. "Hey, Mom, ain't that the lady that set fire to the courthouse and burned it up?"

I cringed but did not stop.

Technically, the courthouse fire was my fault, but I don't know how I could've handled the situation any differently.

When someone points a gun at you, you throw anything handy. In my case, it was a heavy lighted candle in a mason jar. I didn't have time to worry about what would happen to the office doused with kerosene by a maniac bent on murdering me.

Still, the resulting fire destroyed our ancient courthouse so that all its offices had to be relocated. That was why the new motor vehicle and property tax office was now a tee-ninesy mobile home with no room to turn around in.

By the time I flagged down the semi driver and he circled back and jockeyed his rig to where it blocked half the street, two trusties in detention center orange T-shirts had arrived. Each pushed a hand truck.

The driver came around and threw up the tailgate door. "You Corralie Caters, the tax commissioner?" He had a narrow, suspicious face that looked me up and down, and he smelled of grease or oil or something.

I allowed as how I was.

"These tags are for you then, but you got to unload 'em. My orders say ship to address. That means no inside delivery. And you got to pick the boxes up from the back of the truck. I'll stack 'em on the tailgate for you, but I don't take 'em no farther. It ain't my job. I can't be responsible for—"

"Yes, I know. You don't have to lift a finger outside your tailgate. We have people. See?" I pointed to the trusties.

He looked them up and down, too, before deciding it was safe to start shifting cartons.

Once he moved a stack from the cab end to the open back of his trailer, the trusties hefted the cartons onto their hand trucks and rolled them up the ramps. I crowded inside behind them to point out where to stack the boxes. "Right over here in the room with the safe."

Then I came back outside to help by taking down tag boxes from the tailgate. Once I got five or six in a stack, the trusties could slip a hand truck underneath, wheel it inside, and unload.

Sam supervised, which consisted of standing in the shade watching me stack while the trusties ferried cartons up the ramps. He did not offer assistance, but after a while he did stroll over to where I labored. "You ought to be able to open now you got tags. You think tomorrow morning?"

I tipped a stack of cartons so the trusty could slide his hand truck under them, and then wiped perspiration from my eyes. My morning shower was shot. "Sorry. No computer lines yet. Dyson says the State'll be here day after tomorrow to hook us up."

I had my fingers crossed since Dyson Sharmont, our IT guy, was one clueless dude. I knew why. Before the courthouse burned, the sweet stench of pot frequently hovered over his vicinity during working hours and doubt-less still did. "Maybe the State's people will show up Friday like they're supposed to and maybe they won't. You know how the State is."

"Great guns." Sam frowned at the boxes I kept stacking. "How many tags did they send you? Seems like an awful lot."

"We need a lot. I told you. All our inventory burned."

Sam joined me to peer inside the back of the semi's trailer. "How many boxes you got left up here?" he croaked at the less-than-energetic driver.

"For this county?" The driver topped off a stack towering over us and leaned on it. He had a toothpick in his mouth he rolled around. "These two piles is all."

Same gave him a thumbs-up. "Good deal."

The driver didn't crack a smile, but he did hold out a clipboard to me. "You got to sign for the delivery."

I signed.

As I handed back the clipboard, the driver glanced over my shoulder. His eyes and mouth widened. The toothpick fell out. "Whoa there, momma! That sucker's drooping big time! It's gonna go! Hey!"

Sam and I whirled in time to see my new office shudder.

Concrete blocks holding up the end with the tags gave way.

An ominous rumble ripped the air.

One resounding thud shook the ground as the mobile home settled lopsided, ramps askew. The one section of the trailer still resting on concrete blocks was the center. The end with the tags lay on the ground. The other side stuck up in the air.

The rumbling died away.

I stood frozen. So did Sam and the truck driver. So did the trusty outside at his hand trucks.

Then we heard the trusty inside yelling. "Help! Hey, somebody get me the heck outta here! What the *@#* y'all doing! These gol-darn boxes fell all over me and they're heavy as the dickens! Somebody help me! *Help!*"

Sam sighed without taking his eyes off the sad scene. "Yeah, I kind of thought that trailer looked like it was sagging on that end. Them heavy boxes must have overbalanced it. You ought to of had better sense than to put all them tags on one side, Corrie. You're gonna have to stow some in the office end to balance the load out."

Me? He *was the one who'd ordained that part of the trailer as the secure room!* I opened my mouth to tell him so but something slammed me in the back.

The next thing I knew, I hit the sidewalk. One side of my forehead hurt like anything where it rested on the concrete. Tag cartons lay scattered to the side.

That last stack of boxes. They hit me.

Sam's croak came from somewhere above me. "Good lord, man, you could have killed her. Whadda you thinking, letting them boxes slip like that? You gonna be lucky if you don't get sued for this."

He sure did sound far away.

He's fussing at the truck driver. Good. No, bad. Why isn't he helping me up?

"Hey, I didn't tilt those tags over on purpose!" The driver was downright whiny. "I was trying to see if anybody got hurt when that trailer tipped over, and the boxes kind of fell off by themselves."

Am I breathing?

A passerby in plaid shorts rushed up. "Stay right where you are. I've called nine one one."

"I'm all right," I got out.

Was that whimper mine?

Lord, my head hurt. And something was wrong with my

eyes. The red and green and yellow stripes in the loud plaid looked squiggly. And wasn't it still too cool for shorts? *I wouldn't wear shorts for another month. And his legs weren't that nice, either. If I had knees like that, I wouldn't wear—*

"Stay still," Plaid Shorts said.

"I'm okay." *I think.* "I may need some help to stand up."

Plaid Shorts went into full tizzy mode. "No, no, you stay there till the paramedics get here. Too dangerous to get up. We don't know how bad you're hurt. You lay still, don't move."

The truck driver, Sam, and Plaid Shorts banded together to keep me down.

I didn't feel like arguing. I sprawled, face sideways on the grimy sidewalk, and studied a crack in the concrete beyond my nose. Ewwww, yuck. How many people had spit where I lay?

Don't think about that. Look at the driver's brogans and Sam's paunch and Plaid Shorts' knees. Yep, he'd be a lot better off wearing long pants to hide those knobby suckers.

When two paramedics hopped out of their screaming truck, one rushed over to the trusty who'd been trapped— he'd managed to stagger outside and collapse beside a tilted ramp—and the other hurried to me. "Are you conscious, ma'am? Is she conscious?" he asked the others. "Has she said anything?"

Oh, shoot. Just my luck.

He looked like the EMT who'd helped get my toe out of the refrigerator grate a few months back. Or maybe he was the one sent out when the bald eagle dove through my windshield. Or maybe he was the one who showed up after the cow ran me off the road. Or...

Stop worrying about the wrong thing! Is he gonna recognize me, that's what I need to worry about.

He wasn't looking directly at me.

"My head is all that hurts." I touched my forehead gingerly, hiding half my face. "Here where it hit the concrete."

He stopped questioning the others and peered at me. "You that Caters girl, ain't you?"

So much for anonymity.

"Yes. This was not my fault. Those tag boxes fell on me and knocked me down."

"Uh huh." He asked me a few questions.

I answered with perfect lucidity, adding, "I'm all right. If you'll give me a hand, I can get up."

"No, you'd better stay still."

"I can stay still at home."

The other EMT abandoned the trusty to join his cohort. "That guy's okay. Shook up a little but nothing major. What about her?"

"She needs to go to the ER."

"No! Not the ER." I tried to sit up.

The EMT kneeling beside me pressed me back. "Look, ma'am, with your history—"

"But I'm all right. What history? I've never hit my head on the sidewalk before. This does *not* call for the ER."

Sexy Dr. Bennigan who usually manned the emergency room had regrettably seen me under similar conditions too many times, due to circumstances that were *not* my fault. Okay, maybe one or two episodes *were* my fault, kind of, but…

I refused to face him again.

"I told you how many fingers you were holding up and everything. I want to go home. I've got to go home." I might have sounded a little hysterical, but I so did not want to meet Dr. Bennigan.

The second EMT was already pulling out a stretcher and rolling it over.

"Hey, I said I'm fine!"

Plaid Shorts, who had been following the proceedings with interest, butted in. "Don't you remember that actress who got that head injury while she was snow-skiing? She didn't want to go to the hospital either. You know what happened to her?"

Who the heck was this nosy parker? He looked familiar but I couldn't place him. My head hurt too much and his loud shorts didn't help. He was darned meddling, whoever he was.

"That's right, hon," Sam chimed in. "I remember reading about her."

Plaid Shorts ignored Sam and intoned, "She died."

Died? Oh. Still…

"I don't think it's that serious. I feel pretty good except—"

Plaid Shorts pressed his case. "Do you want to die?"

I must have been disoriented or I would never have allowed the paramedics to lift me onto the gurney and strap me to it.

The crowd that had assembled around the ambulance gawked.

A boring day in Medder Rose makes me the star attraction.

Somewhere in the rear I saw a flash. Lightning. *Is it about to rain?* Another flash came, and a third as they put me inside.

Great. I'd hit my head and now a thunderstorm was coming. All I needed since I didn't have an umbrella.

The vehicle doors slammed shut.

Not that I needed an umbrella inside here.

Why do these things always happen to me? What have I done to deserve this?

Turned out the worst part of my day hadn't yet begun.

Chapter Two

NATURALLY, THE EMERGENCY room clerk called Momma because she's a nurse at the hospital. Naturally, Momma was on duty that afternoon. Naturally, she showed up in full maternal mode.

Almost before the aide settled me on the examining table, Momma trotted in. In fact, she bumped into the aide trying to leave and swept her aside without apologies.

A sure sign of her agitation because Momma's never rude.

Once in the curtained cubicle, she put her hands on her hips. "So you're back again. What is it this—?" She stopped in her tracks, mouth agape. "Sweet Lord in heaven. Your head. What did you do to your head?"

"I didn't do anything. The truck driver pushed some tags over on me and knocked me down. I hit my head on the sidewalk. This is not my fault."

"Never is." She moved over to touch my forehead over the right eye. When I winced, she did, too. "You've got a huge lump."

"I know. Leave it alone. It hurts."

"No wonder. It's bigger than a hen's egg. I don't know that I've ever seen one this big."

"What!?" I put up my hand and sure enough, the sore spot from earlier had burgeoned. "I have to go to Athens a week from Monday for the State tax conference. I can't go with a lump."

Dr. Bennigan—of course, it would be tall, dark, and

handsome Dr. Bennigan, lusted after by me and every other woman inside and outside the hospital corridors—came in about that time. "Hey there. I heard you were back to see us. We really must stop meeting like this. People are beginning to suspect something. Okay, what happened this time? Another cow? Another bird? No, no, let me guess. A monkey."

He didn't try to hide his blinding white grin as he touched my forehead. "Wow, look at that. The place we shaved to stitch up the bird attack has hair growing back on it. With that bump pushing them up, you can see the fuzzy strands."

My interest in Dr. Bennigan, despite his single status and resemblance to a certain hot movie star, cooled. I got enough snide remarks from Ethan Parters, my sort of boyfriend. Correction: my former sort of boyfriend because of those very same remarks.

"This lump is not my fault," I informed Dr. Bennigan. "I was knocked down and hit my head on the sidewalk."

"Hmmm, is that right? Let's see." He touched my head again and examined it while asking questions about blurry vision and all that before saying, "It's good the swelling is outside."

"Good for who?" I snapped. He wasn't the one who'd have to walk around with a lump the size of an egg over his eye.

His sympathetic expression would have worked if I hadn't spotted the lurking smile. "I know, I know. But when the swelling stays inside, the pressure can get to the brain and cause real problems. I think you're okay but we'll send you for an MRI anyway." He went to the door and called to an aide.

I thought of the newly delivered tags. Sam had reclaimed my keys as they loaded me on the gurney and assured me he'd see to righting the trailer and locking the tags up, but... "I need to get back to work."

I didn't trust Sam.

Momma said, "You need to do what Dr. Bennigan says."

Dr. Bennigan laughed. "Thanks for backing me up,

Jenny." He washed his hands. "Shouldn't take long. We want to make sure nothing's going on inside we don't like. I'll give you something for pain, too. Your mother knows what to watch for in case of complications."

"I'll watch her like a hawk," Momma said, and proceeded to do so.

My lump must have been fascinating because she couldn't take her eyes off it.

An aide came in. Dr. Bennigan told her what he wanted and started to leave. Then he turned. "Oh, by the way. Besides that lump, you're going to have a humdinger of a black eye for the next week or so. Don't let the mirror scare you."

With a cheerful wave, he vanished.

"Aiiigh!" I put both hands over my face. How could I go to Athens with a black eye and a huge lump? My first big conference as tax commissioner where I'd have to see all the other tax commissioners and their employees, including those I'd met at tag seminars before, not to mention all the big State honchos. And I'd look like I'd been run over by a freight train.

I peeked through my fingers. "I can't stand it."

Momma patted my shoulder, still focused on my forehead. "Now, now. It could be worse. I didn't call your father because my shift ends at four. You'll be done with your MRI by then so you can ride home with me. Then Daddy and I'll go back for your car when he gets home from work."

They could make sure the trailer with the tags was locked up tight, too. Sam Blanken wouldn't get billed by the State if the tags went missing.

I would. Personally.

I fretted about that as I waited for the ER staff to do paperwork and take me to the MRI section. I fretted some more as I filled out more papers and thumbed through a two-year-old magazine.

Once the technician settled me on my back on the narrow bench and warned me I'd have to hold perfectly still for several minutes while my head went through the cylinder,

I took the opportunity to calculate how much I'd owe if someone stole the tags.

Twenty dollars a tag plate, a hundred plates in a box. Two thousand dollars a box. Fifty boxes or so had been delivered so I'd be out of pocket…ten thousand dollars.

No, wait. I'd put that zero in the wrong place. A hundred thousand dollars.

I'd be out a hundred thousand dollars!

"Aighhh!" Shock jerked me upright. I bumped the other side of my head and half-toppled off the bench.

"I told you to be still!" the technician screamed. "Now you've ruined this test and we gotta start all over."

I needed to catch Sam and make sure he'd locked up that trailer even if it was still lopsided.

Finishing the MRI under the technician's glower, I slunk out and headed for an exit where I could use my cell phone.

Sam reassured me that yes, they'd got the trailer back on its blocks though it had taken six men to shift the safe and tags around so they could straighten up the trailer, but then he himself personally had locked up the tags—he'd made the trusties put half the boxes on one end and half on the other to keep it balanced as I should have done to start with, except being a woman, doubtless I didn't think of things like that but that was okay, he'd fixed it for me—and locked up the trailer, and he'd put the keys in his pants pocket so I shouldn't worry about a thing, and besides, wasn't the sheriff's office directly across the street from the trailer?

Who'd take a chance on breaking in with security like that? "Don't you fret, hon, your tags'll be fine," he croaked.

I ground my teeth and hung up. Why had I ever thought I could be tax commissioner? Every time one problem got solved, another popped up.

Brooding about whether I wanted the wretched job enough to go through the hassle of standing up to the good ol' boys and then campaigning against Judge Hartley's nephew, I went back to sit in the lobby and wait for Momma with a head that ached more and more. Probably from stress.

The receptionist, between answering phone calls and greeting people, gave me surreptitious, disapproving looks.

"What's the matter?" I finally snarled. "Haven't you seen a victim of malpractice before?"

She gasped and became engrossed in paperwork.

At five minutes past four by the clock over the admittance desk, Momma, her short form still in scrubs, bounced off the elevator. I was the first thing she saw. Momentary horror faded into a cheerful mask.

The headache that I thought couldn't get more painful, revved up another notch. "My bump's looking worse, isn't it?"

She took my arm. "Well, chickie, we expected it to, didn't we? Dr. Bennigan did say you'd have a black eye for a while, you remember. How do you feel?"

"My head's killing me."

She clucked. "Poor baby. Let's get out of here."

We went out to her car, a brand spanking new red Mustang convertible that she'd bought this week. Her last car, a late model, new-to-her BMW, got totaled in the courthouse fire. I'd borrowed it that fateful morning, though it was certainly not my fault a wacko picked that particular day to kill me and burn up the courthouse along with Momma's car parked beside it.

Momma had told me not to worry about her BMW, that she was just thankful I was okay, but I could tell she still halfway blamed me for its fate from little remarks she occasionally let slip.

Now she cast doubtful glances at my head when she thought I wasn't looking. "Do you care if we take a little detour so I can drop off some things for Miss Lavinia? She and Ophelia are having a tactical meeting at Barbara Prestotten's house. It's not much out of the way."

Of course I minded. I wanted to go home and hide. But I didn't say that because it wouldn't have done any good. Momma always did what she wanted anyway. "Sure."

She ignored my lack of enthusiasm. "Now if you feel too bad to stop, chickie, I'll take you home and come back even if it is a lot closer for me if I go by now. I'd skip it entirely but I worked on these financial reports all last week and promised Miss Lavinia she'd get them no later than today. They're important to our campaign."

The referred-to campaign was about to be launched by the local ladies voting league.

The Ocosawneean Dames for the Democratic Process had been around for over ninety years. They called themselves the ODD Pea Society in a less than obvious allusion to the Odd Fellow society, though Daddy's cronies called them the Oddballs. Anyway, the destruction of the century-old courthouse—for which they conveniently overlooked the part I played, preferring to blame the male commissioners who hadn't seen fit to keep up routine maintenance—had galvanized the organization to a fevered pitch never before seen in its history.

After persuading two of their number to run for county clerk and county commissioner in the coming year, the ODD Peas started raising money and talking up their candidates at every opportunity. They became frighteningly active.

Momma was a ringleader.

Sam Blanken and the other commissioners snickered when hearing about the ODD Peas' preparations. Our county had never elected a woman to any position, nor had the city of Medder Rose. County and city were both kept on a tight rein by a few men who refused to change with the times.

Even my appointment to tax commissioner had been a case of necessity: it was either me or grouchy Delores Kineely who everybody hated. The reason they picked me was because the good ol' boys figured I'd be easy to push around. They also assumed I would step down gracefully next year so they could get their handpicked candidate elected.

They didn't know it yet, but I hadn't decided whether or not I'd go quietly. I was kind of getting used to not having to kowtow to a boss's vagaries. And the job paid a heckuva lot better than auto clerk.

Yep, I kind of enjoyed being tax commissioner.

Except for all the stupid, unforeseen, hair-pulling, headache-causing situations that kept cropping up.

So I told Momma, "I don't mind stopping at Barbara's house, but if it's all the same to you, I'll wait in the car."

"Of course you will. I know you're feeling punk, baby. And I won't be but a minute, I promise."

I might be twenty-three, but to my momma, I would always be the baby of the family. I no longer bothered to object.

She let the Mustang's top down and pulled out two baseball caps, one saying NURSES EQUAL TLC and the other, BEST DARNED NURSE IN THE HOSPITAL. I gingerly fitted the one assigned to me on my head, careful to avoid my lump. Momma jammed hers on and whipped the car out of the parking lot.

Settling down once we were in the street, she drove sedately for about three blocks, till we hit the highway where the city limits stopped. Then she stepped on it. We sped through the verdant countryside and fading dogwood blossoms so fast the wind whipped unsecured fronds of hair across my mouth.

It was impossible to enjoy the freshly mowed hayfields and still colorful azaleas, or the newly planted impatiens and petunias blooming in different yards. They whizzed by in a kaleidoscopic smudge. And when we left the populated area and reached wooded acreage, leafy trees and shrubs became a green blur.

I almost forgot my headache, what with clutching my hat with one hand and the armrest with the other, worrying the whole time about Momma running us off the road. When we came to a four-way stop, she threatened to ram a rusty pickup that got there at the same time we did.

I cringed. She bluffed out the farmer driving and went on. Before I closed my eyes, I saw him show us a fist.

Or a hand. Or something.

After recovering from a sudden left turn, Momma resumed high speeds for about a mile till a white board fence appeared on the left. Then she slowed, following the fence to an entrance flanked on both sides by stacked stone pedestals. We drove through them, along rows of sweet-smelling magnolia trees down a twisting drive to a renovated two-story Victorian.

Barbara Ruth Prestotten *née* Dempsey, born and raised in Medder Rose, had acquired a law degree and two decades of success with a large firm in Atlanta. A second marriage to a high school sweetheart brought her back to set up her own office. She had agreed, when the ODD Peas asked, to run for county commissioner next year against the chairman.

In Ocosawnee County, we have three commissioners and they stay in office for six years. Every two years, one has to run for reelection. Whichever one is up for reelection automatically becomes chairman for his last two years.

It's a simple system and it works pretty well. *If* you don't mind the same group keeping an iron grip on the political structure.

Barbara Prestotten's candidacy, pulling support from Republican, Democratic and independent women voters as well as free-thinking men, flagrantly challenged the old-boy domination of the county. This made her a heroine in some circles and a too-big-for-her-britches female dog in others.

Momma pulled around the circular drive to a clematis-shaded veranda furnished with comfortable rockers and huge drooping ferns on wicker stands. At its wide steps, she stopped, so abruptly that the seatbelt had to keep me from hitting the dash.

"Oops. Sorry." She cut me a guilty look. "Still not used to these brakes. The ones in the BMW responded to the slightest touch and these take a little more pressure. I'm about to get the hang of them, though."

"Huh." At least we weren't still speeding. I took off my hat and used it to fan myself. The cloying scent of a gardenia over to the side made me a little queasy.

Momma got out. As she reached for a folder on the back seat, the front door of the house opened and Lavinia Pickardy, the president (some jokesters swear she was a founding member) of the ODD Peas, ran out.

Except that the phrase *ran out* does not do justice to Miss Lavinia's flight.

At ninety years of age, Miss Lavinia was seldom seen without either her trademark pearls or three-inch heels. This afternoon she wore both, along with bright red lipstick and a flowered post-Easter dress.

Oh, she was a sight to behold, tripping across the wide veranda and mincing in double-time down the steps to our car without falling on her face.

"Whoa." Admiration squashed my headache and nausea. Who knew Miss Lavinia could sprint like that?

Momma turned. "What in the world—?"

Miss Lavinia reached us and threw her arms around Momma. "Jenny, dahlin', thank God you're here! Ophelia fainted and Barbara's dead and I don't know which one to look after first."

She burst into tears on Momma's shoulder, without regard to the fact that her mascara would surely be ruined.

"There, there, Miss Lavinia," Momma said, unable to do anything else. With Momma barely five foot three, Miss Lavinia's tall frame was almost more than she could handle. One wild eye aimed in my direction brought me out of my stunned bemusement.

I opened the car door. "I'll go see what's wrong."

Miss Lavinia released Momma. "No, no, stay in the car, Corrie! There's a bear on the rampage out here. Maybe two."

Momma's eyes popped. "A what?"

I froze. "A bear?"

Miss Lavinia nodded energetically. Her white curls fell into disarray and she never tried to smooth them, a sure sign of her distress. "Ophelia and I saw the creature loping across the back patio. And another one in the woods, too. The one we saw was large and hairy and—" She threw up both hands. "Oh, it was awful! It's killed Barbara. Ophelia got sick. I thought she'd faint before I could get her set down."

Momma couldn't take in what Miss Lavinia was saying. "The bear was in the house?"

Miss Lavinia snuffled back tears. "It must have been, dahlin'. It mauled her. Barbara, I mean. Her whole head looks like… And so much blood…" A thought panicked her. She gripped Momma's arm while she looked around wildly. "Are we safe out here? It may be lurking."

"Come on inside, Miss Lavinia." I took her hand. None of this was making sense. Bears sometimes showed up in these parts but they normally avoided houses and people. And to enter a house? Was Miss Lavinia going dotty? "Momma, I can use a little help here." I softened my tone. "Please."

Momma, busy looking around for skulking bears, caught hold of Miss Lavinia's other arm. "Corrie's right, Miss Lavinia. Let's go inside and sit down. You've had a shock."

Maybe then we could find out what was going on.

Miss Lavinia resisted. "No, no. You've got to call for help. Ophelia started to, but then we saw the bear, and then she keeled over and it was all I could do to… Call for help, Jenny. We need help!"

Momma dithered, wanting to get Miss Lavinia inside but also wanting to call 911. My mother was the most competent nurse around, but any kind of emergency outside her hospital milieu addled her.

"Momma, let's get her inside." As Miss Lavinia opened her mouth to object, I added, "That way we'll be safe from the bears, Miss Lavinia. We'll call for help once we get in the house."

"You're right. So sensible, dahlin'. Like your father, bless him. Oh, I wish Keith was here. He'd know what to do." Miss Lavinia anxiously glanced right and left. "We might want to hurry."

Trembling, she leaned on my and Momma's arms, and went docilely enough even if she did keep acting like she expected a bear to pop up any moment and yell *surprise*. As we went up the steps, from somewhere in the woods behind the house came the faint noise of an engine roar.

Inside the Prestotten mansion, a large reception room held an antique settee and chairs, trimmed in mahogany and upholstered in wine-colored velvet. A matching mahogany sideboard stood near a marble fireplace. Heavy silver candlesticks sat on the mantel while a porcelain vase graced the sideboard. A plush carpet covered most of the hardwood floors, but heavy draperies drawn to the side allowed late afternoon sunshine to filter through white sheers. At the back, next to an open door revealing a billiard table in the room beyond, a staircase curved upward.

Too stiff and formal, if you asked me, but nobody did.

In this gothic backdrop Ophelia McEvans reclined, appropriately enough, on a dark blue fainting sofa beneath a window. Her eyes were open but dull, her complexion waxy.

"My goodness, Ophelia." Momma's nursing instincts took over. She rushed to kneel beside her patient.

I herded Miss Lavinia to one of the uncomfortable looking side chairs. "You sit right here while I check on Barbara."

"Oh, dahlin'," she said piteously, clutching at me, "it's too late for her. The bear's got her, I told you." She burst into a fresh volley of tears. "I don't know who we'll get to run for commissioner now," she wailed. "B-B-Barbara was the perfect person. A lawyer and everything. Such a good speaker."

If Barbara Prestotten was indeed dead, worrying about a replacement to run in the coming campaign seemed heartless. But, as I knew from firsthand experience, strong emotions can bring out the inane as well as the profound.

I patted her hand. "Where is she, Miss Lavinia?"

Looking every one of her years, she pointed over to pocket doors slid back. "In there."

Leaving Miss Lavinia, I peeked inside. A light Persian rug lay in the middle of more gleaming walnut floors. A grand piano took place of honor in a sort of round sunroom at the front, and toward the rear a cherry desk held a small laptop. Behind it stood a glass front bookcase.

The desk chair had swiveled around like someone had pushed it aside. Moving further in, I could see the figure lying behind the chair.

No wonder Ophelia had keeled over.

The entire head had been savaged beyond recognition. There wasn't any chance Barbara Prestotten could be alive.

Dark spots flickered. Though I heaved, I managed not to throw up. Instead, I closed my eyes until the nausea and dizziness passed, and my vision cleared.

She wore a speckled reddish-brown dress with a yellow background. No, the speckles were blood. The floorboards held similar stains though their wide splash was harder to make out on the dark wood. Some drops might have been on the cherry desk, too. For sure, the square blotter had blotches. The desk chair's cushions were spattered.

Barbara had died rising from her work on the laptop.

I backed away and returned to the others.

"Momma, you need to stay with Ophelia. Miss Lavinia's right. It's too late for Barbara." Then, with a shaky hand, I dialed 911 on my cell and waited. When I gave my name, their response was gratifying.

They've found out I don't call unless it's necessary.

Then the dispatcher's muffled voice said, "Yeah, it's that ditzy Caters gal again. Says she's at Barbara Prestotten's place and somebody's dead. Better get a car out quick. Who knows what's going on with *her* involved."

Ditzy! If I'd had time, I would tell the dispatcher who was ditzy. But I needed help. "Hurry it up. We've got one of the ladies who found her about to faint again. And the other one doesn't look so good, either."

Eight minutes later, I heard a siren blaring and a patrol car swerved to a stop at the steps. In tune with the rest of the day, my onetime kind of boyfriend was the deputy who hopped out.

Freckled-faced and eager, looking like a grown-up Huckleberry Finn, Ethan Parters rushed round the car as I went down to meet him. With his athletic physique, his uniform helped him pretend to be strong and capable.

I knew otherwise, having been confined in close quarters with him and several other deputies for a few weeks while my life was threatened. All of them had irritating quirks that left me pretty sure not a one was especially competent.

Ethan ran up the steps. "Corrie? Evie said you were the nine eleven caller. What are you doing here? Who's dead?" He noticed my face. "Man, what happened to you?"

Thanks to the trauma of seeing Barbara, I'd forgotten my headache. Thanks to Ethan's pointing out the lump, it started raging anew. "I had an accident. It's not important. Listen, is the sheriff on his way?"

"Corrie, Corrie." He sighed and shook his head. "You know what I think? I think you're accident-prone. Did you know some people are naturally bad luck magnets? I was reading an article in *Time* magazine the other day that explained all about—"

My mouth dropped. "You read *Time* magazine?"

"Dentist's office. Somebody before me got the *Sports Illustrated*." He waved a hand. "Anyway, it said that certain people have all sorts of weird things happen to them. Like you. It gives this explanation that makes a lot of sense. Seems some people are naturally prone to—"

I closed my mouth. He rambled on. This was why I was no longer sure I considered Ethan a friend, much less a boyfriend.

Focus on the problem at hand. "Look, Ethan," I interrupted his far-out theories. "You've got a crime here. Barbara Prestotten is dead. Somebody or something killed her."

That yanked his attention from my battle scars. "Killed? Barbara Prestotten? Something killed her? What kind of something?"

I shrugged, led him up the porch steps. I wasn't about to tell him about Miss Lavinia's bears. "In there." I pointed.

He didn't stop at the pocket doors but went inside and felt for a pulse. When he came back into the reception room, his face was pasty. "Yep, she's dead."

"I told you that." I don't know why I bothered to hang out with him. Yes, I did. We were two of the few unmarried people our age left in Medder Rose. Most people bolted as soon as they finished high school.

Of course, lots of them, like Barbara Prestotten, came back to live.

Or die.

I shivered, tamped down queasiness. "Well? Is the sheriff on his way?"

"Yeah, I, I…" Ethan's shoulders shook convulsively. He

held up one hand as if to tell me to shut up, put the other over his mouth, and rushed out the front door.

"Hunh." At least I hadn't thrown up.

Maybe the sheriff would get here soon. Ethan might look capable, but Sheriff Duval, or Duke, as his friends called him, actually was.

Thankfully, he showed up less than two minutes later. In pretty good shape for being fifty-something, he looked like a film good-guy sheriff. He wasn't wearing his usual Smokey hat, but tall and big-shouldered, he exuded professional know-how.

The atmosphere immediately calmed.

The first thing he did was escort me and the other women out to the veranda.

Ophelia McEvans, by this time, was able to walk. He asked if she needed to be carried, but she whispered she did not. He personally settled her diminutive form and Miss Lavinia in white wicker rockers as two more officers arrived with bags and kits of some kind. "This way," he told them, and they all disappeared inside.

Momma and I sat down, too. Nobody said anything, but the four rockers went back and forth. Over their creaks, we heard the vague murmur of voices.

Another man in a business suit showed up, nodded to us, and went inside. Then the EMTs arrived. They trooped inside, too.

I could have told them it was too late to revive Barbara, except one looked familiar and I didn't want to draw attention to myself.

When the sheriff and the Suit came out, Sheriff Duval introduced him. "This is Detective Ogarty. He'll be working the case." He looked at me. "You called it in, Corrie. Can you tell us what happened?"

Where should I start? "Momma had to drop off some things on the way home from work."

He stared at my lump. I said in answer to his unspoken question, "No, my face has nothing to do with what happened here. I got knocked—never mind. That's a different thing entirely. When we got here, Miss Lavinia came running out and told us Barbara was dead. Miss Lavinia's the one you need to talk to."

"That's true," said Miss Lavinia. She sat in the rocker next to me, rocking, her head resting against its high back and her eyes shut as if to blot out memories of the afternoon.

I didn't blame her. I wished I hadn't insisted on seeing Barbara.

Miss Lavinia wet her lips. "Ophelia and I came over to discuss her candidacy. Barbara's candidacy. She has, um, had, agreed to run for county commissioner, you know."

"I do know." Amusement crept into the sheriff's words.

Momma stiffened. We both knew the good ol' boys were laughing up their sleeves about the ODD Peas' intentions.

Her eyelids still closed, Miss Lavinia didn't notice and went on before Momma could spout off. "Barbara said she was coming home after lunch and could meet us here at four-thirty. Ophelia and I got here a little early, maybe quarter after. The screen was closed, but the door was open. We rang the doorbell but when she didn't answer, we went on in, thinking she was most likely upstairs. We called out, but she never did answer. Then Ophelia saw the piano and we walked over to admire it."

Her eyes fluttered and opened. A sparkle showed some of her natural cheerfulness had revived.

"It's a real grand, and it's so wonderful to know people still play them nowadays when most of the time it's all these keyboards and yowling guitars and electronic thingamajigs. My parents made me and all my brothers take piano lessons from Miss Mary Paul Lennox when we were little, and I had every one of my children take them, too. Not from Miss Mary Paul because she was retired by then, so I used Mrs. Elizabeth Palus O'Mally, who's dead now, too. Ruth Cumberman's daughter teaches, though, and I'm so glad we still have someone in town who does. If more people played a musical instrument—"

"Yes, Miss Lavinia, I agree. Completely," Sheriff Duval cut in without a smidgen of impatience. "When you went into the next room, what did you see?"

During Miss Lavinia's little ramble about pianos, Detective

Ogarty's eyes had grown so big the whites stood out against his caramel skin.

Has to be his first encounter with Miss Lavinia.

"What do you mean, what did I see?" Miss Lavinia frowned. "Why, the piano. I just told you that, Duke. Weren't you listening? When you were a little boy, your momma always did complain about your mind wandering, but I'd have thought you'd have outgrown it by now. Especially considering your profession and all."

Ogarty, rapt under Miss Lavinia's spell, didn't crack a smile. Sheriff Duval lost a tad of composure. "Yes, ma'am. I, um, I did hear you. But afterward, was that when you found Ms. Prestotten?"

Ophelia, silent to this point, whimpered and put her fist to her mouth. Her complexion that had regained some color under Momma's ministrations, turned waxy again.

Momma, seated next to her, patted her arm. "There, there, Ophelia. Watch what you say, Duke. You're upsetting her."

Miss Lavinia didn't look too good herself. She leaned back and rocked determinedly.

The sheriff apologized.

Miss Lavinia, mollified, went on. "We turned to go back to the living room and, and... We saw Barbara by the desk. And that's when we saw the bear, too."

"Bear?" Ogarty was surprised into speaking.

Sheriff Duval turned his head toward me and raised a brow.

I shrugged.

His forehead creased. "What bear was this, Miss Lavinia?"

"The bear out back." Miss Lavinia spoke with assurance. "You can see the patio from the French doors behind where Barbara...where she lay. The bear was loping across it like he'd come out of the house and was leaving. He disappeared into the woods out back."

"A bear. Loping out of the house." Sheriff Duval gave a sideways glance toward the openmouthed Ogarty. "You're sure it was a bear?"

Miss Lavinia stopped rocking and glared.

"Duke Duval. Do you think because I'm old I can't see?"

"No, no, Miss Lavinia. That's not what I meant. This bear. Was it a black bear? Or brown?"

"Black. Oh, land, it must have been three feet high, maybe four." She scrunched up her face, remembering. "I don't think it was full grown. It must have been a cub. The other one in the woods must have been the momma."

"The other one?" Detective Ogarty once more forgot his deference to his superior's questioning. "There was more than one bear?"

Miss Lavinia resumed rocking vigorously. "We didn't see the second one as well because of the leaves and all. But it was reared up, taller than a man. I could barely make out the top of it through the trees. Dark with some kind of tan markings. Then it and the baby one disappeared in the woods. That's when I heard Jenny drive up and I came out to warn her."

"Tan markings." The sheriff stroked his chin. "Mrs. McEvans, you saw these bears, too?"

Ophelia McEvans nodded weakly. "The cub. And something was shaking the tree branches in the woods, but I'm not sure what. I didn't see…I can't… It's all been such a shock."

"And no wonder." Momma patted her arm again.

Sheriff Duval and his sidekick didn't speak for a few minutes. I could guess what was running through their minds.

Bears. Momma Bear and Baby Bear. So where was Papa Bear?

I'm delirious. I need to go home and go to bed.

"Tan markings," the sheriff repeated after some pondering. "Don't know of any kind of bear with tan markings."

An angry flush heightened Miss Lavinia's rouged cheeks. "Maybe it had dead leaves on its head then. I don't know. The thing was hidden in the edge of the woods. You need to get some people to search for them, Duke. If an animal would come into a house and maul a woman to death like this, heaven knows what it'll do next. It might even be mad. Do bears get rabies?"

"I don't know, ma'am," Sheriff Duval said meekly. "But we'll get right on it. Detective Ogarty here might have a few other questions for you before you leave."

He beat a hasty retreat into the house.

I hopped up and caught him in the reception area. "Sheriff, what's on the other side of those woods?" I kept my voice low so Miss Lavinia and the others wouldn't hear.

"Best I can remember, the Dodgins' farm and the back of Wild Honeysuckle State Park."

"I heard a car or truck start up as we came inside. Not close, but back through the woods somewhere. Do you think if somebody was parked on the other side of them, maybe at the farm or in the park, they could have left this house without us seeing them when we drove up?"

"Bears aren't licensed to drive cars."

Smart aleck. "No. They aren't. They don't get into houses and tear up a woman's face without leaving traces behind, either. Like overturned furniture and ripped up curtains and generally one big mess."

"You noticed that, did you?"

"Kind of hard to miss."

He nodded. "Don't bring it up. No need to get Miss Lavinia and the others more upset than they are."

No need to give Miss Lavinia another chance to jump on him, was what he meant.

But I agreed. I had imparted my puny observations to the proper person. Sheriff Duval might have a messy personal life, with all his divorces and flashy girlfriends throwing hissy-fits in public, but he did know his business. Maybe.

After speaking with Detective Ogarty, who was brief in his questioning and never once mentioned a car in the woods, we were allowed to go.

"We'll be calling each of you separately to get a statement later on," Sheriff Duval told us in dismissal.

He had Ethan drive Miss Lavinia and Ophelia McEvans home since they were so shaken.

Momma insisted she could drive us.
I wasn't so sure about that, but I wasn't given a choice.
Thank goodness the day was almost over.

Chapter Three

"DADDY'LL BE WORRIED to death." Momma turned the car into our drive, so sharp my elbow bumped the door. "I got so upset I forgot to call."

Built more than forty years ago, our home was a boxy two-story in a quiet neighborhood a few miles out of town. It had housed me all my life.

Once I'd dreamed about my own apartment but until recently, I couldn't have afforded it. Now that I was tax commissioner and made enough money to rent my own place, I didn't want to.

I'd come to terms with not being an adventurous type.

To calm Momma's fretting, I said, "We're not that late."

"I should have called him," she muttered, pulling into the garage. "With everything that happened, I didn't think about it. He'll be out of his mind with worry."

"He knew you were going by Barbara's house tonight."

I did not add, though I might have, *Daddy never gets upset when you're late because you're always late. Now if we were talking about an unplanned overnight absence, it might be different. He might notice.*

I simply said, "I'm sure Daddy isn't too concerned."

We went inside the utility room that led from the garage into the hall. "Keith?" Momma called. "Keith!"

"Back here," came from the kitchen.

I passed the hall mirror and shrieked. "I can't go to Athens looking like this!"

Mother, intent on assuring Daddy we hadn't been

kidnapped or murdered, said in passing, "You'll look better by then."

"Not with my luck."

"Keith, you won't believe what happened to Corrie." As she went back to the kitchen, she mumbled, "And that bald spot was almost starting to look decent."

Like I needed to be reminded.

I touched the place where the stitches from the eagle attack had been. Some brown strands were growing back in, but they didn't help my looks since the lump was right beneath them. This new bruise covered that whole quarter of my face.

My mouth trembled, but I couldn't cry. I was too old to cry.

What was happening? Why did all these awful things happen to me? Was Ethan right? Was I really a bad luck magnet? Was there such a thing?

"Don't be silly. Ethan's a dork." I pulled myself together and gave Momma a few minutes to explain to Daddy why I looked like I'd been in a car wreck. When I didn't hear any outcries of worry or concern or fear for my well-being coming from the kitchen, I figured it was safe to go on back.

The kitchen was steamed up and filled with the enticing smell of baking chicken.

Daddy, closing the oven door and holding a potholder in each hand, didn't try to hide his shock at the sight of me. "Good grief, chickadee." He put down his potholders and hurried over to hug my shoulder. "You look like you been in a barroom brawl."

"On the losing side," came a voice from the rear.

I spun and confronted Bodie Fairhurst, my one-time fiancé who had jilted me right smack in front of the altar. He stood at a cutting board on the kitchen counter, holding a chopping knife and a partly diced tomato over a big bowl of lettuce bits dotted with sliced cucumbers, celery, carrots, mushrooms, cheese, green peppers, and heaven knew what else.

Long and lean and entirely too good-looking for his own

ego, Bodie stared at my forehead with the same fascination Momma had earlier displayed.

To add insult to injury, my cat Bill wound languorously around his feet.

"What are you doing here?" I no longer loathed the ground Bodie walked on, but I saw no need to be extra friendly.

Sure, he'd apologized for walking out of the church on me. He'd explained he could see I wouldn't be happy leaving home for Atlanta where he'd taken a job, and decided a clean break was best. However, despite my accepting his apology, one cold fact remained.

He had jilted me. Even if he was right, and I wasn't ready to get married and move away from my family and Medder Rose, he had still jilted me. At the altar. With over two hundred people, nearly all of them local, present to witness my humiliation.

He dragged his eyes away from my lump. "I heard about your accident and caught your dad as he was leaving work."

"What? How'd you hear about it? It only happened this afternoon."

"Maura Czerny called me."

"Maura Czerny." This was not good. Maura Czerny was the new editor of the local newspaper. I'd heard she'd been dating Bodie. "How'd Maura Czerny find out about me getting hit?"

"One of the staff photographers happened to be going past when you fell."

I remembered the flashing lights as the EMTs loaded me up in the ambulance and clapped my hands over my face. "Aighhh."

That hadn't been lightning I'd seen. Those had been camera flashes. Newspaper cameras.

"That's just great," I mumbled from behind my hands. "That's just peachy."

I would probably be on the front page of the paper. Bad enough that everyone in town knew I was responsible for burning down the courthouse. Now everyone would blame the trailer fiasco on me, too.

I pulled myself together and uncovered my eyes.

Bodie, his chopping knife motionless, offered a peacemaking ploy. "I drove your car home."

"I got him to drive your car home," Daddy said at the same time. "Saved Momma and me a trip back later to pick it up."

"I'm meeting some friends up at the pool hall tonight." Bodie stared into my eyes, carefully not ogling my lump. "One offered to swing by and pick me up in a little bit."

"In that case, you're having supper with us," Momma said.

Bodie tried to protest. "Oh, no, Mrs. C. I can't impose on—"

"You aren't imposing one bit, Bodie. I won't take no for an answer."

Still holding my gaze, Bodie raised his brows inquiringly. A slight curve of his lip promised his signature smile, the one that turned me all weak-kneed. From his wide shoulders to his narrow hips to his long legs, Bodie possessed a lot of things that turned my knees weak.

Not that I let him see how he affected me.

"You're making the salad so you can see we got plenty," Daddy said to him. "I thawed out one of the chicken casseroles. If you don't stay, we'll have it three nights in a row. Believe me, one night's plenty. It's pretty heavy."

Momma reared her head back. "I thought you liked my chicken casserole."

"I do, I do. But it's a mite heavy now it's getting warm weather, with all them noodles and sour cream and cheese and, uh, tofu and, and Chinese peas and, and, uh, things like that. Point is, there's plenty for all of us."

Crud. I was hoping it was the chicken broccoli one I liked. Guess Daddy couldn't tell which one was which in the freezer.

Although Momma did have a habit of deliberately mismarking stuff.

She eyed Daddy suspiciously. "Things like what?"

"You may as well eat with us," I told Bodie ungraciously. "Now that you're here."

Bodie let loose the promised smile that turned his eyes into blue slits between sooty lashes. "In that case, I'd love to stay, Mrs. C. I wouldn't ever turn down your chicken casserole."

"Aha." Momma sniffed, mollified. "You see, Keith? Bodie doesn't think it's too heavy."

She didn't see Daddy roll his eyes before he started setting out plates.

I leaned on the table so my knees wouldn't give way.

Bodie went back to dicing up the tomato.

Nobody tried to pump me about the murder. "Did you tell them?" I asked Momma.

"Tell them what, baby?"

"Momma." I couldn't believe she'd forgotten.

"Oh." She remembered and got all lively. "Oh, Keith, the most awful thing happened after Corrie's accident. We stopped by Barbara Prestotten's on the way home from the hospital so I could take her those financial calculations, the ones I've been working on for the ODD Peas all week and…"

It took her twenty minutes, in fits and starts and with expert interventions by Bodie when she got off track, to tell about Barbara's murder.

I guess since Bodie was formerly with the GBI, he knows the knack of interrogation because he went about it in much the same way Sheriff Duval had.

"—and poor Ophelia still looked like a ghost when Ethan drove off with her and Miss Lavinia," Momma concluded.

Bodie looked skeptical. "Did it look to you like a bear attacked her, Corrie?" He had finished making the salad and now sat across from me at the kitchen table.

I snorted. "No."

"Miss Lavinia said she actually saw the bears," Momma objected.

Daddy sprinkled garlic on the buttered Italian bread. "I'm sure Miss Lavinia's eyes aren't what they used to be."

Mama bridled. "Ophelia saw them, too. And Miss Lavinia may be old, but she's not senile. If Cap Fanville had said he saw a bear, you'd have believed him, and he's as old as Miss Lavinia."

Daddy realized belatedly he shouldn't have expressed doubts of Miss Lavinia's sighting and started trying to smooth things over. "Now, honey, I never said Miss Lavinia was senile. No sir, that wasn't what I said at all. All I said was—"

Tired of the subject, I went into the den and collapsed in front of the TV. I hadn't sat down long enough to find the remote before Daddy dragged Bodie through. "We're going down to the basement for a minute so I can show Bodie the new computer I got last week. Call me when the buzzer on the stove goes off." He said to Bodie, "I'm still having one little problem with my email setup. I bet you can help."

I risked a glance. Bodie winked at me. "Right behind you, Mr. C."

It was almost like old times.

Not that I cared.

Bodie Fairhurst meant nothing to me anymore.

At supper we sat around the table, conspicuously avoiding the subject of Barbara Prestotten's death. Instead, we talked about Momma's work with the ODD Peas, my new temporary office, and Bodie's unsuccessful job hunt. He had handed in his resignation to the Georgia Bureau of Investigation a few weeks ago and moved back to the county from Atlanta.

Some people said the GBI had requested he resign. Others whispered his resignation had something to do with drugs. I knew he'd been placed on administrative leave, but as for the rest... I didn't believe a word of it.

Bodie would never have anything to do with drugs in any context. I'd never even known him to drink more than two beers at one time.

Since I was no longer part of his life, I didn't ask Bodie about the rumors and he didn't volunteer to tell me. He didn't mind relating particulars of his job search, though. "Lonnie at the tire place said he could use me. I reckon I've laid around long enough, but I'm not sure how good I'd be at changing tires all day."

"Sherry's husband Caleb is looking for a car salesman,"

Momma said. "Why don't you try him? Be a lot easier. We'll put in a good word for you."

"Will you? I might take you up on that. Would you put another helping of that casserole on my plate, please, Mrs. C.? This is the best thing I've eaten all week."

Momma preened.

Laying it on a bit thick, I thought, as he scarfed up his food like he was half-starved. Especially since he'd been living at home since going on administrative leave. "Has your mother stopped feeding you?"

His smile flickered. "I don't get home for dinner much since I moved into an apartment."

With Maura Czerny? I don't know why my heart dropped.

"Oh, you've moved out?" Momma asked, in all innocence. "Where'd you move to?"

"Rented an apartment in town, down the street from the high school. The Mint Gardens."

My heart started beating in place again. Maura Czerny lived in a condo on the lake.

Not that it mattered.

Daddy forked up a bit of casserole stoically.

I ate mostly salad and garlic bread.

We finished up with Churn Dash ice cream, Mocha Madness, a flavor Daddy picked up when Momma sent him grocery shopping last weekend by himself. It tasted okay but was nowhere near as tasty as Chocolate Drowned Cherries or Pecan Cream Pralines or the good old standby Nellie's Hand-Cranked Vanilla.

As we finished, Bodie's cell vibrated. He looked down at it. "My ride's here."

He texted back and took a last bite of Mocha Madness.

"Thanks for supper, Mrs. C., Mr. C." He pushed his chair back. "I'm sorry to eat and run, but I better go while I have a way home. Maura doesn't like being kept waiting."

Any calm I'd attained during dinner evaporated.

My parents clucked and fussed and walked him out. I dawdled over the dregs of ice cream and let the blahs kick in.

For some reason, Momma and Daddy never had soured

on Bodie. Probably because they weren't the ones he'd jilted.

Bill hopped on the table, heading for Bodie's ice cream bowl. "Oh, no, you don't." I whipped the dish out of his way. "Get down from there."

He mewled, a thin wail that no self-respecting cat would let loose.

Bill was not a self-respecting cat though. He was skinny and scraggly and prone to hairballs. If I put a diaper on him, he'd look very like the Bloom County cat he was named for. Hard to comprehend how the cute kitten I got on my ninth birthday could turn into such a sad specimen in a mere fourteen years.

"I said get off."

He put on his pitiful face and fastened his unwavering stare on me.

"You're not getting any. Chocolate isn't good for cats. Forget it." I picked him up and set him down on the floor and started cleaning up dishes.

Momma and Daddy came back in. "I'll do that, chickie," Momma said. "You go on up to bed. A good night's sleep will make you feel better."

No argument from me. I picked up Bill who, still miffed at not getting ice cream, was pretending to be reluctant to go upstairs, and carried him with me. As we left, I heard Momma chattering to Daddy, "That newspaper woman's a pretty little thing, isn't she? Do you think she and Bodie'll make a go of it? She looked like she could eat him up, did you notice?"

"No, I didn't," Daddy said. "She's a little old for him, ain't she?"

"Oh, for goodness sake. She's thirty-two and Bodie's about—" was the last thing I heard Momma say.

Twenty-seven, I finished in my mind. *Bodie's twenty-seven.* Almost four years older than me.

Bill and I went on upstairs. I didn't want to hear about Bodie Fairhurst and his romantic affairs. Especially I didn't want to hear about them from my own parents.

After getting into bed and settling Bill under one arm, I

pulled out a half-finished Deborah Smith novel set in our north Georgia foothills. I usually enjoyed her books, but tonight my mind kept wandering.

When I was growing up, I didn't recall much crime in Ocosawnee County, but retirees and refugees from Atlanta had discovered our area a few years back. Consequently, the population had almost doubled. Maybe all the growth was the cause of more and more incidents like this latest murder.

Which was definitely a murder.

Miss Lavinia's opinion notwithstanding, no bear had killed Barbara Prestotten. And there were no signs of anyone ransacking for valuables. Her laptop computer sat on the desk in plain sight while those large silver candlesticks remained untouched on the mantel.

No. Not a robbery. Someone had murdered her, either deliberately or in the heat of anger. Who in Barbara's life could have hated her so? My contact with her was pretty much limited to saying hello when we occasionally passed in the courthouse halls, so I had no idea of her friends and enemies.

On TV and in movies, her husband would be Sheriff Duval's first suspect. Two or three years ago, she had married local banker Paul Prestotten who, according to Daddy, was her high school sweetheart. In any event, she'd abandoned a successful legal career in Atlanta to move back here. Though a second marriage for both, only Paul had children.

If not the husband, how about his kids? How old were they? Old enough to murder their stepmother?

Momma said Barbara had been forced to set up her own office in Medder Rose because none of the male attorneys wanted to take her in. Momma also said a lot of people switched to her for legal work because she charged less.

"And she'll listen to you," Momma had added. "I mean, she looks at you and listens while you talk, instead of pretending she's listening and not just waiting for a chance to tell you what to do."

Anyway, Momma and Daddy used her to draw up their wills and my uncle Frederick got her to do a deed for him and other folks followed. Could one of the local attorneys be annoyed enough to murder the competition?

The pain pill made me light-headed but I managed to finish my book before turning off the lamp. Bill nestled under my arm and purred before we both conked out.

Chapter Four

THE NEXT MORNING, I got up, looked in the mirror and screamed.

That woke up Bill who, lazy animal, was trying to sleep in. To his satisfaction, I went back to bed where we started a Graeme Smith funny fantasy on the eReader and dozed most of the day.

My best friend Sherry Bartovich interrupted when she called to check on me, as did my part-time employee Miss Ruby Bromfield, my full-time employee Lucy Coffee, and several more people.

Though the newspaper wouldn't come out till Sunday, news of my fall had spread across Medder Rose like a stomach virus.

The following day, which was a Friday, I didn't have the luxury of hiding in bed. The State IT guy was coming that morning to set up our computer lines for access to the State's tag computers.

I showed up at the trailer bright and early, in time to meet Sam coming out.

"Wasn't sure you'd make it in today so I let Dyson in and left your keys with him," he rasped, gaping at my forehead. "I'll check back at lunch to see if you need anything. That's some lump, sugar. You ought to sue that truck driver."

"Don't have the energy or the money."

When a girl wearing skin-tight jeans and a large hobo bag over her shoulder walked up, we both swiveled our heads.

She was near my height, maybe five feet five or so, but forty pounds heavier. More if you counted the makeup.

Bleached blonde hair around a narrow purple streak fell past her shoulders while earrings—four studs circling each ear and two pendants in each lobe—sparkled in the early May sunshine. They matched the tiny gem in one nostril. A skimpy top revealed most of a rose tattoo on the top of her left breast and some kind of leafy vine twined around her right bicep. A gold ring glinted from her exposed navel. Black polish adorned fingers and toes peeking out of strappy heels.

We infrequently see people like her in our small north Georgia town. I tried not to gawk.

She was doing a little gawking of her own at my bump. Then she caught herself and looked me in the eye. "Are you the commissioner?" Her tongue had a small gold ball in it. My teeth hurt when the metal clacked against hers.

Sam stuck out his chest and thumped it. "I'm the commissioner."

Her round face mirrored confusion. "I thought Corralie Caters was a woman."

"Oh. You want the *tax* commissioner," Sam said dismissively.

For some reason, the tax commissioner, even though it's a duly elected post and brings in most of the money spent to maintain the county, is a redheaded stepchild when it comes to respect from the other politicians.

"I'm a *county* commissioner." Sam hooked his thumbs in his belt loops and looked important.

"I'm the tax commissioner," I said.

She shifted her attention from Sam's belly back to me. "My name's Kayleena Tustenson. Someone told me you need an auto tag clerk."

You could say that. The person who'd run the tax office for thirty years was now awaiting arraignment. I had been besieged with inquiries about the job the past week. Most of the people in the county either wanted me to hire them, or else knew somebody they wanted me to hire.

Sam, disinclined to leave, openly eavesdropped.

I took a deep breath. Honesty is always the best policy. "I do have a vacancy but lots of people are interested in it." I could have added, *Candidates who look much better than you, girl*, but restrained myself.

"I want to apply anyway." The tongue stud didn't clack this time, but did cause a slight lisp.

I tried not to lisp back out of sympathy. "Well…"

"I've been a temporary tag clerk down at Gwinnett County for the past two years, but I've moved up here to be near my boyfriend. I need a job and I know tags."

"Gwinnett?" That called for rethinking the situation. Gwinnett County claimed several hundred thousand people as opposed to the twelve thousand populating Ocosawnee County. "You've worked tags in Gwinnett?"

She nodded. "I was trying to get on full-time. They don't like to hire you unless you temp first. But then I met Georgie and he's up here. So here I am."

She waited expectantly.

Young, about my age. The flagrant tattoos suggested she might be a bit on the rough side, but that was not necessarily bad. You couldn't be timid and deal with our type of public.

I evaluated her appearance against her experience, and experience won. Hands down. "Go see our personnel manager. The ad closes out Tuesday so you need to apply before then. I'll get back to you as soon as I can."

She cast a doubtful eye at the mobile home. "So how do I find personnel?"

"Good question." I'd been too busy trying to get my own office set up to worry about other departments from the courthouse. I looked at Sam.

So did the girl, blinking eyelids shadowed purple to match the streak in her hair.

Sam knew where personnel was. "In with us commissioners, along with accounting, zoning, and purchasing. At the old Piggly Wiggly two blocks over. We still got some reworking to do, but Rick's office is pretty much set up for business."

Trust the commissioners to find a decent home for themselves and their cronies. No single-wide or even a spacious double-wide trailer for them. No, sir.

Nor for Judge Hartley who, after the fire, had immediately rented a brand new structure built by the city for future offices (the mayor was an old childhood friend) and turned it into courtrooms. The old guard would look after themselves and everyone else could be hanged.

Never mind. I was getting the knack of politics and would soon be playing the game with the rest.

After Kayleena got directions to the former Piggly Wiggly building, she turned to leave, but her bag slid off her shoulder. When she bent to pick it up, her top parted from the low-cut jeans and bared an expanse of ivy tattooing from her waist to her crack. Once she stood and adjusted her hair, a heart tattoo on the back of her neck made a brief appearance.

Wow. That was one tough momma. Rick had better give her the county policy on tattoos and body piercings. I didn't want to be the one telling her.

Sam watched her walk away. "You done the right thing, getting her to put in an application, Corrie. Got to let everybody apply. Don't want to run afoul of the law, no matter what type trash want to work here. But don't you worry. Dick Beaufort's picked out somebody nice for you. His cousin's girl graduated high school early and can't find a job."

My hackles rose. I wasn't about to hire some giddy teenager over a woman, however marked up she might be, who had two years hands-on experience in one of the largest counties in Georgia.

I made myself take a deep breath. *Be diplomatic, Corrie. You're a politician now. This is a county commissioner you're speaking to. He approves your budget.* "I'm not sure somebody right out of high school is the best fit."

"Oh, she'll be fine. Not that much to selling a tag, is there? Take the money and hand 'em a plate." He waved a dismissive hand. "Or decal or whatever. Any idiot can do it."

A red haze blinded me.

I'd give anything to witness Sam dealing with someone trying to buy an auto tag with an out-of-state registration and nothing else. He wouldn't have the faintest notion how to follow a title's chain of ownership on a multi-transferred vehicle to see what was a legitimate transaction and what wasn't. And he'd never be able to process the paperwork for inheritance or repossession or title bonds when a title of record couldn't be found.

Oh, yeah, I'd pay good money to see Sam Blanken explain to customers that they couldn't buy a tag because the title was in someone else's name, or they didn't have insurance, or the VIN—vehicle identification number—on a bill of sale or insurance card was wrong and there was no record of any such vehicle being manufactured anywhere in the country.

In fact, I'd love to see Sam Blanken handle an irate customer threatening to punch him out, period.

I kept my mouth shut, though.

Gosh, this learning to be a political animal was hard.

Oblivious, Sam checked his watch. "I better go." He started toward his EMC pickup—the electric co-op was real good about letting him off to see to county business whenever he needed, Sam had once confided—but turned. "I nearly forgot. Rick wants to see you about them job applications. He's got a few ready for you to look over. Dick Beaufort's cousin's gal is one of 'em."

"If I have time, I'll go pick them up."

At the moment, I was more concerned about what our pothead IT guy was doing inside our tin can office.

Surprise, surprise. Dyson was actually working. One computer with monitor and printer had been installed on the counter and sat winking at me. Dyson, a fat roll oozing over his jeans waistband, sat on his haunches on the floor in the process of unpacking another monitor. How he was going to get up with all those extra pounds I didn't know.

Not my problem. "Hi, Dyson. Got my keys?"

"Sure thing." He hauled himself up by using the counter top.

As he dug in his pocket, I inhaled discreetly. Yep, there was the telltale odor. Not strong like he'd been caught smoking. Just a faint scent from an earlier joint that might be clinging to his clothes or maybe his new beard that hid his baby face.

Maybe he wasn't stoned completely.

Dyson didn't notice my sniffing as he found the keys and burped. "Here. State called and said they'll be here at ten. I'll have these hooked up and ready to go by the time they get wires run."

"Good."

He nodded toward one end of the trailer. "I got an extra computer I need to set up in the room by the server, but there're too many tag boxes in the way." His eyes looked bleary, but then they always looked bleary. "Why don't you move all of 'em on this other end where the safe is? There's plenty of space for 'em there. Then you could get you a desk for that room and put the computer on it. Maybe use it for your office."

I showed my teeth. "What a good idea. Too late now."

He shrugged chunky shoulders but didn't comment on my black eye.

Maybe it didn't look as bad as I feared. I *had* plied the bruised part with makeup this morning and draped some hair over as much of the lump as I could.

Dyson went back to work while I started shuffling tag boxes so that they were in some kind of order.

I had to separate out motorcycle tags first because they're smaller than regular tag plates. Then I sorted out trailer tags, prestige tags, college tags, and other special tags so I could put my hands on whichever plate the customer needed.

Lugging boxes back and forth from one side of the trailer to the other, while making sure I didn't overbalance either end, got me hot and sweaty.

Dyson and I were both finishing up when the State guy, a nerdish, older man with wiry arms, arrived. He sang out, "Good morning!" at the door.

I answered in kind.

He gasped as he saw my face, and then hastily looked away.

Guess the bump did still look bad.

"You the tax commissioner?" No longer cheerful, he pointedly stared at his tool case.

"I am."

His eyes stayed down. "I'm here to hook you up."

"Good. Dyson!"

"Wiring's right back here." Dyson led him into what was supposed to be my office.

As they worked, the State guy's hushed voice floated out. "What happened to her?"

"Who?"

"The tax commissioner."

"I dunno. Did something happen to her?"

"Man, she's got a bump on her face the size of Texas and that black eye covers half her face. She got a domestic problem?"

"Black eye? She's got a black eye? Cool. Never thought she was the partying type. Guess you don't never know about people."

Good grief. Dyson must have enjoyed a big weekend himself if he hadn't noticed my bruises and black eye this morning.

Dyson.

I thought of the tax digest due to the State by August.

That digest, the list of every piece of property in the county and its value, was my responsibility. State law said the tax commissioner had to present it, accurate and complete, to the State Revenue Department on time, or face stiff penalties.

But Dyson was the one who'd be downloading data from the assessors' computer system to ours where we could compile it and print tax bills. How in heavens name could I depend on a pothead who didn't notice a bad injury when it was staring him in the face, to make sure the digest was accurate?

"Who else do I have?" I muttered. "I sure don't know anything about putting a tax digest together."

While Dyson and the man from the State worked on computer things, I called the purchasing agent to ask about the chairs and other furniture we'd ordered. Sheila Aldren, the secretary for the commissioners and other bigwigs, answered his phone.

I explained I needed the purchasing agent to see when to expect delivery of our furniture.

"He's in a meeting. Why don't you check with the office furniture place yourself?"

She gave me the phone number, and I called.

The local supplier in turn assured me their truck would be out first thing Monday morning, and we went over the list of ordered items. When he came to the large desk with filing drawers on each side, I said, "Forget it. It's too big. I need a little one, maybe even a table. No longer than four feet and about two feet wide. Oh, and skip the executive chair, too. It'll take up too much room. Give me a plain desk chair."

Maybe I could squeeze the table and chair into what was left of the room that was supposed to be my office.

The office supply salesman promised he'd find something that would work.

Then I called Miss Ruby Bromfield, one of our part-time workers, and Lucy Coffee, our full-time employee, to let them know they could report for work Tuesday morning.

By the end of the day, my computers were up and the printers working. I checked them out, found I could indeed issue tags and collect taxes, and broke into a happy dance.

The State man and Dyson left together. The State guy still avoided looking at my head. I don't think Dyson ever noticed the condition my face was in, even though the State guy had pointed it out.

Never mind. The important thing was that Tuesday, a little more than two weeks after the fire, the tax office would be open for business as usual.

Chapter Five

ON SATURDAY, SHERRY Nuckles Lowman Bartovich, my best friend since preschool, dropped by the house. I had my eReader on the front porch swing so she had a good view of me when she bounced up the steps.

Her mouth and eyes circled. "I heard it was bad, but oh, Corrie."

"It gets worse. Dr. Bennigan was the one in ER."

"Dr. Tall, Dark, and Handsome? Oh, no. And he saw you looking like this? You poor thing." She dropped down beside me.

The swing jiggled side to side till I used both feet to stop it.

I laid my eReader down on my lap. "Like Daddy says, that's the way the cookie crumbles."

She spent a moment in silent sympathy, then, "When are you going to Athens?"

"A week from Monday."

"It'll be better by then."

I lifted one brow, conserving energy.

"It will," she consoled before getting to the real reason for her visit. "Listen, what happened to Barbara Prestotten? Some people are saying a bear ate her, but other people are saying Miss Lavinia's lost her marbles. And some are thinking it's mighty lucky for Dick Beaufort she died. As many people as he's PO'ed lately, Barbara had a good chance to win his commission seat in next year's election."

I guffawed. "Dick Beaufort? Come on, Sherry. You

ought not to spread rumors. Next thing you know, people'll be saying he did her in to save his precious seat."

"Okay." She pushed and the swing started creaking. Sherry has big hair, big boobs, and a big smile with an outgoing personality to match her looks. In short, she's the perennial cheerleader.

"Strike Dick Beaufort for murderer. I've got a better suspect anyway. Wait'll you hear what happened. You know Caleb's car lot is right next to Arvin Smelting's office building?"

"Uh huh." Sherry's husband Caleb was a successful used car dealer.

"Caleb says Sheriff Duval went in and talked to Arvin Smelting yesterday for a long time. A real long time."

"You're kidding. Arvin Smelting?"

Arvin Smelting is the richest man in the county and the most disliked. He throws out renters for one month's unpaid rent and forecloses on loans as soon as people get behind. Some people say he's a multimillionaire. If true, it does him little good because he has no friends. The only people who have anything to do with him are ones who haven't learned what a backstabbing skinflint he is.

Sherry beamed. "Yep."

"Arvin Smelting." I tried to link him with Barbara. "I can't imagine why the sheriff would be talking to him about Barbara's death."

"No?" Sherry's mascaraed eyelashes fluttered. She tried to hide a smirk. "Listen to this." She stopped the swing in mid-arc.

I caught myself before I fell out.

Sherry didn't notice. "Barbara Prestotten was representing Ike Hansfeldt against Arvin in some kind of land dispute."

I scrambled back into the swing. "Who's Ike Hansfeldt?"

"You know. He owns Quick Change Alley."

The oil place. I'd visited it with my dad once or twice but couldn't place this Ike fellow right off. "Okay. And?"

"Well, Ike's got an offer, a big offer, on acreage his grandfather left him alongside the four-lane at the corner of the new technical college they're building. He wants to sell, but Arvin claims an acre allowing access to Ike's land belongs to him."

"So?"

"Arvin says the Adams family that he bought it from gave the Hansfeldts a right of way back in the fifties. They never actually deeded that one acre over to Ike's family. So the only access to the property belongs to Arvin."

"Arvin's not going to kill anybody over one measly acre."

"No normal person would, but you know what a moneygrubber he is." Sherry pursed knowing lips and started us swinging again. "The thing is, Barbara's secretary heard him and Barbara arguing last week. According to Jasmine, they got pretty loud. Arvin accused Barbara of legal malpractice. Barbara said she'd sue him for slander if he repeated that in public. Arvin stomped out of the office threatening to get her disbarred and run out of town."

That was news, but not hard evidence. "So Arvin pitched a temper tantrum. Sounds like him. That doesn't mean he murdered her though."

"No, but Jasmine also said that the morning she was killed, Barbara got a package of old papers from one of the Adams descendants out in Texas. Later on, Barbara talked to Arvin and made an appointment to see him Thursday morning. But she died Wednesday afternoon. Obviously, those old papers were proof backing Ike's claim."

I thought about it. "Not necessarily."

"Okay, Miss Doubting Thomas, how about this?" Sherry gave one big push and inspected her fake French-tipped fingernails as we swung. "Caleb said the sheriff was over at Arvin's office for at least half an hour or longer yesterday. And he also said Arvin didn't look happy when he came out after the sheriff left. Came out dragging his butt, is what Caleb said."

I shrugged. "Still doesn't mean anything."

She let out a sound of disgust and stopped the swing again. "I'd prefer Arvin Smelting did it instead of some maniac going around killing people at random, wouldn't you?"

I thought about it. "I guess so. What about Paul Prestotten?"

"Giving a speech to some bankers in Los Angeles. Left Tuesday morning and didn't come back till after the sheriff contacted him. Ethan says he's alibied."

"Alibied? Is that a word?"

Sherry threw up both hands and gave the swing an impatient push with her feet. We wobbled side to side before getting straight. "You know what I mean. And one of his children lives in France and the other in Alaska. They've got alibis, too. So it's not anything to do with Barbara's marriage. It's either a random killing, or Arvin did it."

I hated to give up the husband theory. "Could have hired a hit man."

"Oh come on. Why? They were practically honeymooners, hadn't been married but a couple of years."

"Maybe he found somebody he liked better."

"Uh uh. It's Arvin. Gotta be."

After that, we talked about the Athens trip. "You'll have such a good time," Sherry squealed. "I love Athens."

Sherry loved everything.

I didn't. In particular, I didn't love driving long distances to socialize with a bunch of people I didn't know. "I have to travel by myself and stay in a motel by myself and everything. I'm gonna hate it."

"You'll be fine. Think of it like a vacation. It'll be fun."

"Tax classes fun? Yeah, right."

"Hey, you won't be in class at night. And it's Athens, remember? Home of UGA? Party school of the south? Maybe you can find yourself a graduate student. Or a cute professor. I'd go with you if I didn't have to work."

Sherry had got on at the landfill as mail clerk *cum* secretary a few months ago. She had no leave time built up and wouldn't risk her position by calling in sick. She'd worked too hard and too long to get hired by the county to throw away her future.

Like any future in a job that included dealing with an irate public and bosses that blew hot or cold, depending on the current political climate, could possibly be good.

Right.

Poor Sherry hadn't worked for the county long enough to learn that.

**

LATER THAT DAY Ethan called. I talked to him while shaking out my newly washed clothes and putting them in the dryer.

He was bored. "Don't guess you feel up to going bowling."

"Nope."

He sighed. "Figures. First Saturday night I've had off in three weeks and nothing to do."

"Why don't you see if Rayla wants to go?" I tried not to sound catty. After hanging out with me a couple of years, Ethan had become infatuated with Rayla Cothrew, onetime jail secretary with augmented breasts, recently promoted to deputy. Divorced and looking, Rayla was several years older than Ethan and not at all suited to him.

Ethan, once he'd caught her scent, didn't care.

"She's working. How about I rent a movie and get a pizza and come over?"

I opened my mouth to say no, but decided what the heck. Maybe I could pump him about Barbara Prestotten's murder, assuming he knew anything. "Sure. Nothing gory though. Get a comedy or something. Make it a large pizza, too. Maybe two. Momma's going over to Miss Lavinia's, but Daddy'll be here."

Ethan did know something about the murder investigation.

Before we put on *Casino Royale* (Ethan knew I'd overlook the violence in favor of ogling Daniel Craig), we shared a large supreme pizza with Daddy. When Daddy got up to get a beer for Ethan and himself, I asked, "Has the sheriff figured out what happened to Barbara Prestotten? I heard Arvin Smelting's been questioned."

"Yeah, I heard that, too." Ethan thanked Daddy for the proffered bottle. "One thing we know, it wasn't a bear killed her. Shotgun blast straight to the face. Duke and Feldon think she must've took both barrels."

"Double-barrel shotgun." Daddy shook his head in

disbelief as he twisted the top off his bottle. "My word. Some people are plain rotten. How could anybody do something like that?"

My daddy had one of the best hearts around and hated to believe the worst of anyone.

"Of course," Ethan added, "we won't know for sure till the autopsy report and all, but the sheriff and Feldon ought to know what they're talking about."

Duke Duval had been an Atlanta detective for twenty years before coming home and running for sheriff. When he won, the first thing he'd done was bring in his crony Feldon Whittonfeld from the Atlanta force as chief deputy.

Some kind of surgery had put Feldon out of commission for several months, but last week he'd started back working half days.

Ethan was right. Both Duke and Feldon had seen enough crime in Atlanta to recognize what was happening in Ocosawnee County.

"So they don't think the bear's important?" I asked.

Ethan shrugged, took a swallow of beer. "Probably not. Miss Lavinia may very well have thought she saw one, but it don't seem, uh, it doesn't seem pertinent."

Pertinent. I bet the sheriff had used the word and Ethan had picked it up.

"Do they know when she was murdered?" Daddy asked.

"We got it narrowed down." Ethan wiped his mouth with the back of his hand and trailed pizza sauce from one cheek to the other. "She left her office at twelve-thirty sharp and stopped by the new Piggly Wiggly on the way to her house not long after. Bought some cold stuff. We saw it in the refrigerator so it looks like she went straight home. Probably got there between one and one thirty."

I would have let him run around with sauce all over him, but Daddy handed him a paper napkin. "Better wipe the pizza off your face before you get it on your clothes."

"Thanks, Mr. C."

"When did Miss Lavinia and Ophelia McEvans get there?" I asked, trying to put Ethan back on track.

"About four fifteen, best we can tell."

"That's what they said," I murmured. "And found Barbara dead."

Ethan rubbed his face and, satisfied it was clean, crumpled the soiled napkin. "Coroner thinks she was killed closer to two than four but says not to hold him to it."

One more piece of pizza sounded good so I helped myself. "Does the sheriff seriously suspect Arvin Smelting? I heard Arvin had some pretty heated words with her last week."

Ethan shrugged, took another swig from the bottle. He avoided my eyes. "Dunno anything about that."

About to take a bite, I held the pizza slice away from my mouth. "You know something."

He shook his head. "No. No, I don't." He got up. "Are we through here? Want to put the movie on?"

My pizza got put down. "Come on, Ethan. Spill."

"Nothing to spill." He eyed my hips. "You putting on some weight, Corrie?"

I didn't remain speechless for long. "So what if I am?"

He took a step back. "Not that you've put on much, I mean. And it looks good on you. You've always been kind of skinny and ten pounds or so helps fill–"

"I haven't put on ten pounds!" I jumped up and stalked into the den before I realized he'd changed the subject.

In the past, Ethan had been pretty free with inside information, but despite my best efforts this night, he wouldn't say any more. Either he didn't know anything or else the sheriff had held a come-to-Jesus meeting with him about blabbing.

One thing I'd wangled out of him by virtue of his transparent face, though. Sherry was right. Arvin Smelting was definitely a suspect.

Chapter Six

TUESDAY MORNING, AFTER receiving our furniture and copy paper and calculators and other office supplies on Monday, we opened up to the public for the first time since the fire.

My lump was visible but smaller. My eye and its surroundings were less black, turning purple in places. I slathered on makeup and brushed some bangs down, but still looked like I was practicing for Halloween.

We weren't very busy that morning because no one knew we were open but after lunch, word got around. People started drifting in.

Most customers had heard about me falling, thanks to the local Sunday edition of the paper that ran a front page picture showing me being loaded into the ambulance and an inside page devoted to one column of print and a lot more pictures.

Me sprawled on the ground amid tag boxes.

Me being helped to sit up by the EMT. Me with one eye drunkenly closed.

Me with open mouth protesting the proffered stretcher.

Me being thrown on the proffered stretcher.

Me raising a hand to touch my lump.

And finally the back of the ambulance speeding away.

I was big news.

"Good for voter recognition," Momma had ventured when she saw my expression as I read the paper that morning.

"Yeah, if people don't mind voting for someone they remember sprawled out in the street like a wino."

The end result was that most people coming into the office knew about my fall and sympathized. The few who didn't generally asked Miss Ruby or Lucy about my scars in low tones I wasn't supposed to overhear.

Ruby Fay Bromfield looked exactly like what she was: a sweet lady who wore her white hair in a bun on the back of her head, Amish-style. At seventy-four, her short plump form moved slowly and her computer skills were slightly above minimum, but her mind was sharp and her memory better than mine. She might be a little nosy, but she was dependable. She came to work on time and didn't goof off. And if you got her tickled, she whooped with contagious laughter. Some folks came by and told her jokes just to hear that laugh.

Miss Ruby was also disconcertingly honest. When customers asked about my face, she was prone to blurt, "Didn't you see Sunday's paper?"

The standard answer was an indignant, "That rag? I stopped reading it years ago."

"That's too bad." Miss Ruby's nasal twang carried through the whole trailer and out the door. "If you subscribed, you'd know the tax commissioner got a bunch of tag boxes dumped on her by some idjit delivering 'em and had to go to the emergency room. Paper had pictures and everything. You ought to go get you a copy before they sell out. Or at least look at the online edition. They're in color there."

Lucy, newly widowed and still grieving, tried to be more circumspect. "An accident," I heard her murmuring over and over. "No, she's fine now, just bruised up a bit."

At five, we had four people still in line, but we finished them up so I could lock up at five twenty. As we counted our cash drawers, I asked Lucy about joining a gym with me. "I'm out of shape, and it'll do you good to get out of the house."

Ethan's words about my weight gain rankled, and Lucy, whose husband had died from poison meant for me, could use some socializing.

Miss Ruby, ears always pricked, looked up from straightening her currency. (Bills count faster when they're turned the same, with heads on one side pointing in one direction.) "Been eating too much Churn Dash ice cream?"

I stiffened at the overt attack. "Maybe."

Miss Ruby looked me over. "Now that you mention it, you do have a little potbelly starting. How much you gained?"

"Not much," I said defensively.

Miss Ruby opened her mouth.

Lucy hurried to deflect further interrogation. "You may be right about me getting out more, Corrie. All I do is think about Briant and cry when I'm home by myself. We could go to that gym between my house and town. It isn't much out of your way."

"Trim With Fitness?" I asked.

"Ain't that the one that's got a beauty shop and gym and ice cream parlor all together?" asked Miss Ruby.

"Yep, Trim With Fitness," Lucy said to me. "And yep," she nodded at Miss Ruby, "it's got a hair styling shop in it. Not an ice cream parlor, though. It's a health food café. Has a yogurt bar."

Miss Ruby clucked. "I wouldn't eat in it. Not with it being in a nasty place like a gym. And I don't think I'd get my hair done in a place like that either."

"No worse than eating in a bowling alley," Lucy said.

"Well, now, I don't know 'bout that. You kind of expect a bowling alley to—"

The debate could go on forever. "You're right, Lucy. That's not much out of my way if I take a different route home. What's it cost?"

"I don't know but I think county employees get a discount. Lots of the deputies use it."

Lucy agreed to check on costs, and we decided if it wasn't too expensive, we'd start working out together.

Like Miss Ruby, though, I didn't think I would ever get my hair cut there. As for eating in the health food café— well, I wasn't big on health food anyway. I took after my daddy. Meat and potatoes and green beans were more my thing.

We put our cash drawers in the safe and locked up. The second-hand safe was ornery. It took several tries to figure out I had to slam the door at the same time I swung my hip against it to make it close.

But by six, I left for a class at a college in the next county.

I was in my third year working toward a business administration degree. At the rate I was going, I'd be about sixty when I finished, but with Daddy's urging, I persevered.

That night, I had a final exam in business accounting. A weekend's review left me pretty comfortable about passing, and taking the test gave me no reason to feel differently. I should end up with a high B in the course, or with luck and lenient grading, a low A.

On my way out of class, I ran into Professor Jeffrey Random buying a pack of crackers from the vending machine near the exit.

I'd dropped his Business Statistics class early because I was about to fail, not because I didn't like him. Extremely shy, he was cute in an endearing Jimmy Stewart kind of way. Lots of coeds had a crush on him. I'd tried to flirt with him, but he was oblivious. I think females frightened him.

Today, he walked on crutches and had one arm in a sling because he'd broken an arm and a leg in an accident at the courthouse shortly before it burned.

An accident, I might add, which had nothing to do with me.

He saw me and dropped his crackers.

I hurried to pick them up. "Here you go."

"Thanks, Corrie."

After his fall from a balcony into the lobby, I had gone with him to the hospital where, still in shock, he confided why he was in the courthouse. He wanted to get records on Billy Lee Woodhallen, our local hooligan.

Most people, including me, tried to stay out of Billy Lee's way. Professor Random, tracing his origins, didn't have that option. Adopted as a baby, he at first hoped Billy Lee might be his natural father. But after confronting Billy Lee in person, he hoped Billy Lee wasn't.

In fact, Professor Random was so horrified at the idea of

being related to Billy Lee, he decided to abandon his research altogether. Then he found out Billy Lee's deceased older brother was a better paternal candidate.

Now the professor was hopeful again, and determined to find out whether the older sibling really was his father.

While we stood in the college hallway, I asked how he was coming in his quest.

He shook his head sadly. A strand of brown hair fell over one temple like Hugh Grant's did in *The Englishman Who Went Up a Hill.* "Billy Lee refused to give me a DNA sample. He won't even talk to me. I hired a lawyer, and she was working on getting a court order to make him get tested. But then, she got killed last week."

"Barbara Prestotten? She was helping you get DNA from Billy Lee?"

He nodded. "I guess I'll have to start all over with a new lawyer." A worried, earnest face beseeched me. "Do you think I could get her records on what she'd done for me?"

"I don't know."

"Who should I ask? The sheriff?"

"I'd guess her heirs. Maybe her husband but I'm not sure. I expect the probate judge will get her will soon and then you can find out who's in charge of her estate. Does Billy Lee know you're trying to get a court order?"

"Oh yes." His spaniel eyes grew wide. One agitated crutch wiggled in the air. "I ran into him at the grocery store last week. He cursed at me, told me I wasn't getting any of his family's land no matter how hard I tried to prove I was a Woodhallen. I assured him I didn't want any of his land or anything else, but he wouldn't listen. I thought he was going to hit me."

"Sounds like Billy Lee."

Professor Random set his shoulders. "I'm not giving up. No matter what he threatens. I want to know where I came from." The hand not holding crackers brushed unsuccessfully at the errant strand of hair. "Do you know of another good lawyer?"

"Not one I'd recommend for something like this. I'll talk to my folks, though, and see if they know someone."

As I went out to my little Hyundai, my mind started jumping.

So Billy Lee had threatened Professor Random. Had he done the same with Barbara Prestotten?

Not that I thought he would have murdered her.

But Billy Lee was reputed to be the toughest man in the county. I'd recently discovered he ranked close to Arvin Smelting in wealth, too, although his money was mostly tied up in inherited land and businesses which explained why he was so adamantly opposed to DNA testing.

If the professor proved his father was Billy Lee's brother, he could likely claim a big chunk of the Woodhallen estate.

Would Billy Lee kill to preserve his inheritance? He was rough, occasionally getting cited or arrested for fights. He'd done some time in prison when he was young, too, but no one knew exactly why. Current rumors tied him to arson and drug-dealing for the Mexicali Mob, a kind of Hispanic mafia supposedly operating in north Georgia.

"I don't know that for sure, though," I argued with myself. "Nobody ever proved Billy Lee burned down that charity building or that he has anything to do with drug running."

One thing I did know. Billy Lee had saved my life. If he hadn't come along and rescued me when I was locked up in the courthouse attic, I'd have died in the blaze.

***

ON WEDNESDAYS, we usually worked a half day. But when I got to the trailer this Wednesday, we had a long line waiting. I counted over fifty people, about what I expected since we'd been shut down for close to three weeks.

I gave Miss Ruby and Lucy the bad news. "No leaving at twelve thirty today, ladies. We can count on working overtime. May as well plan on sending out for lunch, too. It's going to take us till then to tend to the people already in line.

"Yep." Miss Ruby pointed out cars still prowling for parking spaces. "And more folks are bound to come now they know we're open."

After I unlocked the doors, people crowded inside.

Two customers wanted to pay late taxes on their land, and both of them argued with me about having to pay interest and penalties.

I prevailed. Taxes had been due the end of last year and should have paid on time. The office being closed had nothing to do with their late property tax payments.

Landowners were the exception though. Today most customers wanted auto tags or decals for mobile homes that had been due May first. All of them were edgy, raring for a fight if we charged late fees. The first of May (the deadline for mobile homes) and their birthdays (deadlines for tags) had come and gone while Ocosawnee County was without a tax office. Now they were late paying so everyone was scared I'd penalize them.

They calmed down when we waited on the first few customers and word circulated that no, any people who had birthdays while the office was closed would get a free ride on tag penalties, and so would those customers renewing their mobile home decals after the due date while the office was closed.

I helped Miss Ruby and Lucy at the counter, trying to work the line down. No matter how we labored, it got longer and longer, till it eventually stretched halfway around the square.

As predicted, the big turnout meant no question of closing on time so we ordered lunch delivered. Our sandwiches arrived about eleven-thirty, and we took turns sitting in my "office" to gulp them down before returning to the combat zone.

The line ordered in, too.

Miss Ruby noticed when she got up to take her fifteen minute lunch break.

"My land." Her nasal voice penetrated every corner of the trailer as she stood on tiptoes to look out the front doors that stayed open because people in the queue kept shoving their heads inside to see how long it would be before we got to them. "Look at them idjits partying in the street."

She pulled out the crate she used at the computer for her

feet—her legs were too short to reach the floor comfortably—and climbed up to look. "That better not be my car they're setting on!"

At her squawk, I stood up and moved to where I could see out.

There they were.

People spread out eating pizza and drinking sodas on parked cars in front of the trailer, laughing and talking and flirting as they waited their turn at the counter. They looked like they were at a family reunion. Some had even brought lounge chairs and set them up in the shade.

"Your car's across the road, Miss Ruby," I said. "Nobody's on it. So far."

Miss Ruby took a good long look. "Hunh. Like a blooming circus," she muttered as she toddled over to my office.

As the afternoon wore on, we tired.

Miss Ruby, normally sharp as a tack, revealed her weariness by getting louder. Sometimes she sounded like she was calling hogs. Lucy, not fully recovered from the death of her husband a few weeks back, said less and less. She took on a pallor like she was ready to collapse.

"Okay," I said grimly, when the line eventually thinned. "That's it. We were supposed to close at twelve thirty today and it's after two. We're not waiting on another soul after we finish this group. I'm going out to stop anyone else from getting in line. Y'all work down the people who're left."

To get outside, I had to exit from behind the counter and go through one of the two front doors. While trying to squeeze between Miss Ruby's customer, a man weighing at least three hundred pounds, and Lucy's customer, a woman nearly as large, somebody reshuffled their stance.

I got caught between the woman's hip and the man's butt.

"Hey!" The man tried to see who was goosing him, but the tight space for customers combined with my hundred and twenty-four—well maybe twenty-nine—pounds between him and the fat woman, didn't give him room to turn.

"Excuse me, sir," I said. "Could you move over a bit, please? I need to get out."

"I can't," he said plaintively. "I'm slap against the wall as it is."

I turned as best I could to the woman on the other side.

"Somebody's crowding me over here," she barked over her shoulder, "but I'm almost through. If you gimme room so I can leave, then you can get out, too."

"Hey, you dimwit," another woman waiting her turn said. "Stop squeezing me. That's my ass you're feeling up."

"Sorry, sorry," a man in line at the door behind her mumbled.

"I bet you are, buster. Keep your hands to yourself 'lessun you want a big fat lip."

The obese man wedged against the wall coughed. "Air. I need air." He took a big gasping breath. "I'm squashed between the counter and the wall and you. I can't breathe. You've got to move."

I squeezed myself back behind the counter.

The large woman got her tag decal, scowled at me as she rotated one baby step at a time, and left. The fat man had regained some color.

I scooted past him and got behind the last person in line. "Sorry, folks, we're closing," I told each new would-be customer straggling up.

They did not take the news well.

"I asked off work to get my tag today," one grizzled man in coveralls complained.

"Sorry, but we close at twelve thirty on Wednesdays. It's two hours past that now."

"Well if that ain't the government for you!"

"If you want to leave your form and check—"

He didn't stay to listen, but spat tobacco on the ramp as he stomped off. "Taxpayers count for squat around here, don't they? See what happens come election, missy. You sure ain't gonna get my vote."

Can't win them all.

A well-dressed woman burst into tears when I stopped her. "But I've got to get my tag today. I can't come back tomorrow because I'll be out of town."

"Sorry. We normally close at twelve thirty on Wednesdays.

If you want to leave your form and check, we'll mail the decal to you."

"But I'll have to pay penalties," she blubbered.

"Not if you leave it today."

"Oh." Tears vanished and she sashayed away, muttering to herself about arrogant county workers.

A teenager rushed up with tag prebill in hand. "My mother said y'all were open and for me to come down right down and I hurried as fast as I could, but a wreck at Fiddlers Meadow held me up over twenty minutes. My birthday's today and if I don't get my tag, I'll be late." He gulped for breath.

"Come back tomorrow morning. I won't charge late fees if you come back tomorrow morning first thing. Ask for me."

He was the one person who left happy. I turned away three more annoyed people before the last tag buyer departed the trailer. When I locked the doors, it was heading toward three o'clock. Miss Ruby, Lucy and I gave a concerted sigh of relief before we began counting drawers.

For a few minutes, nothing but the clinking of coins and rustle of bills filled the air. Then we had another ten minutes of clacking calculators and stacking of checks. Once we balanced our receipts against the computer, we shoved money and checks into envelopes, then put the envelopes and our cash drawers into the safe.

By the time I found the right combination of hip and shoulder to close the cantankerous vault and then got the secure room locked up, it was three thirty.

"Corrie, I hate to ask you," Lucy said as she turned the key on her tag drawer and I retrieved my purse, "but I need a ride. I left my car so Ike could change the oil and it's ready to be picked up. He closes early on Wednesdays, but he said he'd meet me there if I let him know what time. Would you mind taking me by?"

"Not a bit. Won't be much out of the way at all."

After locking up the trailer, Lucy and I set off.

She had fallen into a funk with her husband's death, but I saw signs of the vivacious woman I'd hired emerging as we chatted. Her earthy kind of sex appeal would make it easy for her to attract another man.

At least I hoped so. I sure hadn't had much luck after Bodie jilted me. But then I was the quiet type who enjoyed my own company. Lucy liked to socialize.

This gym thing would help her.

Chapter Seven

HEADING OUT OF town, we passed Trim With Fitness.

The sign jarred Lucy's memory. "I meant to tell you what I found out about the gym. County workers do get a discount." She told me the cost, adding, "We can pay month by month with no contract, and it's got an inside pool besides all the machines. When they aren't using it for water aerobics, we can swim in it."

My enthusiasm for physical exercise had kind of cooled, but Lucy sounded so excited I hated to back out. "Sounds good."

We decided to sign up the next day after work.

Quick Change Alley, the oil change place, was near Lucy's home, on the same side of town as Barbara Prestotten's house. We passed by the new Piggly Wiggly—it being only three years old—where the dead lawyer had made her last purchase, but turned off before reaching the road that led to her driveway.

Our route led us past Wild Honeysuckle State Park that abutted Barbara's back yard.

Could the mystery car I heard that day have been in the park? Not that it was any of my concern. I'd told the sheriff and he knew his job. Let him check it out.

"Over here. On the left." Lucy pointed to a former gas station converted to an oil change place. "Pull up in front."

When I did, she got out and a muscular man in neat khakis and golf shirt emerged. Curly blond hair was pushed over to one side.

"Hi, gal," he said to Lucy in a pleasant baritone. "Your car's all set."

"Hi, Ike," Lucy called over the car hood since he'd approached on my side. "I sure do appreciate your coming back to work so I could pick it up."

"No problem. I stayed a little longer at the gym and came back on my way home."

Lucy turned back and bent in the open car door. "Thanks a lot for the lift, Corrie."

I barely heard her.

Ike looked familiar. Real familiar.

Plaid Shorts! I barely stopped myself from crying out the nickname accusingly. "Ike?"

He saw my look of recognition and stopped, puzzled. Then his face cleared and he came on up to my window. "You're the woman those boxes fell on the other day. Saw in the paper you were Keith Caters' daughter. The tax commissioner."

"I sure am."

"You okay?" He looked at my head. "Oooh. Guess not."

"It doesn't look so bad," Lucy said loyally.

"It doesn't hurt anyway." I didn't want to do it, but the politeness drilled in me all my life by Momma kicked in. "Say, Ike, thanks for stopping and helping." *You buttinski. If it hadn't been for you, I could have gone on home without having my picture spread all over the newspaper.*

He waved a hand. "Aw, that's okay. I was in town paying my water bill and saw the whole thing happen. I had to help out. Anybody would have done the same."

I curved my mouth upward, bad as I hated to do it. "Well, I appreciate it." *Not really, but I'm a politician now.*

"Forget it. Come on in, Luce." He started inside with Lucy trailing along, both chatting like friends.

I noted the back of him in his coveralls and heck, he had a great body. Tight rear, slim waist, wide shoulders.

Knobby knees, I reminded myself as I pulled away. A glimpse of him and Lucy in the rear view mirror showed them laughing together, the first time I'd seen Lucy laugh since her husband died.

Hmmm. He hadn't been wearing a wedding ring. I started back the way we'd come.

Lucy didn't know about the knobby knees. Maybe she'd find out life was worth living after all. Ike had to be okay financially, with his own business and all, so he'd be a good match. And hadn't Sherry said he was about to sell some land for a lot of money? Make that a great match.

As I neared the park, dreaming of fixing Lucy up with Ike and his oil change place and possible fortune, a familiar crew cab pickup came toward me.

My first thought was *Billy Lee Woodhallen*!

My next thought was *No, can't be him.*

Billy Lee lived in the far north of the county and this was southeast of town.

When the black truck met my car, sure enough, I spotted the sullen face of Billy Lee hanging over the wheel. He held an arm up to hug a passenger leaning over him from the back seat.

Or was he trying to fend the passenger off?

We eyeballed each other, but our vehicles passed before my brain processed the fact that the passenger trying to get to Billy Lee was black and furry. He also had his snout open as if about to...

It looked like a bear.

Couldn't be a bear.

No way.

In my rear view mirror, I saw the truck turning into the park on two wheels.

Without a conscious decision, I whipped my Hyundai around in a movement Momma would have been proud of and raced back toward the park entrance.

Once inside, the road forked. I chose the right side and rode around for some time before the ambling circle brought me back to the front entrance.

"Shoot. He must have gone the other way." I headed down the left fork.

A few minutes later, I came up on the four-door pickup parked in a graveled camping area.

I didn't see Billy Lee. Even when I got out and walked

over to the picnic table beside his truck, there were no signs of him or the bear.

If it was a bear.

My eyes must be playing tricks on me. Surely that couldn't have been a bear. Maybe a woman with black curly hair?

Oh, yeah? With a snout like that?

I spent a few minutes looking around, trying to see where Billy Lee and his passenger might have gone.

Was that someone talking? From somewhere beyond a sapling thicket, a familiar voice started yelling. I headed in that direction.

"You goldanged miserable fleabag, are you trying to kill me? Stop! Come back here! No, go back that way! THAT WAY! Stop it! STOP IT RIGHT THIS MINUTE!"

Apprehensive, I walked down the trail a little way before I found them.

Billy Lee Woodhallen cowered on the ground, cornered at a tree.

A bear leaned over him, trying to eat him.

I screamed.

Billy Lee saw me and rolled his eyes in disgust. "Oh, gawd, just what I don't need."

The bear stepped back, or tried to. It seemed to be connected to Billy Lee.

No. Not a bear.

A dog.

A big black dog.

A big black dog on a chain.

Billy Lee half-lay, half-sat on exposed tree roots of a white oak a couple of feet in diameter. The dog had wrapped its chain around Billy Lee and the tree but was straining, trying his best to bound toward me.

All its leaping around tightened the chain holding Billy Lee prisoner.

"STOP IT, goldammit! Hold still, you stinking bag of shit!" Billy Lee's face flushed with anger.

Or maybe the chain choking him was cutting off blood circulation.

He managed a scowl. "Well? What do you want?"

Nope, he could still breathe. I opened my mouth to answer, but the dog tried to prance and the chain continued to squeeze the breath out of Billy Lee.

He let out a choked sound, then squawked ungraciously, "Long as you're here, come get this dam—dadgone dog off me."

"Okay." I moved forward tentatively. "Does it bite?"

"Naw, he don't bite. He's stupid, is all."

I caught hold of the chain, but it was wrapped too tight to unwind. "I'll have to let him go before I can get this untangled." The clip on the collar was a quick release one.

"No! Don't do that! Don't—!"

Too late. The dog, freed, leaped up and down, and shook himself in a frenzied fit before running toward the woods.

"Now you done it." Billy Lee heaved a resigned sigh. "Well, undo this golda—confounded chain and get me out of here."

As my fingers worked, so did my mind. So this was why Miss Lavinia thought she'd seen a baby bear. The dog was big and black and furry like one. "Why don't you use a leash?"

"Ain't long enough. The chain lets him roam around while we're here."

Uh huh. I bet the dog had been roaming the day Barbara Prestotten died. Roaming off the chain like now.

Billy Lee got impatient. "Ain't you through yet?"

"I'm working on it."

Billy Lee mumbled to himself about how some people couldn't use the brains they were given and were natural klutzes and couldn't be trusted to do the smallest thing, and other stuff I didn't pay much attention to.

I was too busy struggling with the kinked chain and thinking.

Billy Lee might look dumb and act mean, but I knew for a fact he was smart enough to marry a bright woman who I doubted would put up with any of his guff. He was also smart enough to save my life.

If the dog had been running around when Barbara died, what had Billy Lee been doing here in the park?

When I finally freed him, he grabbed the tree and used it to leverage himself up till he got on his feet.

Billy Lee is big. Maybe six and a half feet tall and built like a tank, with tree trunk legs and hands as big as hams. People claim he's used them to beat up more than one person though I don't know that for a fact. I did see him hit one of our assessors in the nose one time, but I don't think he intended to. It was the heat of the moment.

So despite his size and reputation, Billy Lee didn't scare me.

Not too much.

Once upright, he straightened his navy work shirt and pulled his jeans out of his ample butt and adjusted his crotch and belt. Then he hawked and spat on the ground and worked his shoulders like they were cramped. At last, he looked around and went over to pick up a black baseball cap and perch it on his round noggin.

Large orange-tan letters over the bill proclaimed FAT MAN CLUB.

I remembered the bear. "I don't hear your dog."

He shifted his eyes and muttered something under his breath. I figured he was saying something derogatory about my letting his dog loose since all I could make out was, "...know somebody like her'd come along and now I got to go look for the goldarned stinking..."

Yep, his dog had to be Miss Lavinia's bear. I'd bet a nickel the vehicle I'd heard drive away last Wednesday had been his crew cab truck.

Billy Lee walked back toward his pickup and stopped at the rustic picnic table.

I followed, not afraid, but not exactly at ease, either. How should I put the question to him? *Say, Billy Lee, do you know what your dog was doing last Wednesday afternoon?*

Billy Lee sat down on the bench. He might have been eating lemons, from his sour expression. "I'll let him run a bit, I guess, now that you turned him loose. Once he starts running, can't catch him till he gets tired anyways."

His beady suspicious eyes inspected me up and down, came back to rest on my forehead. Lingered. "Heard you got hit by a truck. Lucky you're still alive. You looking for me, for some reason?"

Caught off-guard by his direct question, it belatedly occurred to me I should have come up with an excuse for chasing him down. "Oh. Er, yes. Yes, I was." Inspiration struck. "I wondered how your injuries are doing."

Billy Lee had been wounded in the leg and shoulder while rescuing me from the lunatic who intended to burn down the courthouse with me locked up in it and blame the fire on Billy Lee since everyone knew, though it was never proven, he'd torched a charitable organization a few years back.

Billy Lee foiled the scheme by finding me. Unfortunately, we got caught before we could escape and Billy Lee got shot pointblank when he refused to walk into the vault and be roasted.

"Doing fine," he growled, like he didn't want me anywhere around.

The dog pranced back about then. Close to three feet high at its shoulders, he ambled over and sat down by my foot. Trusting brown eyes aimed up at me. His tongue lolled.

He didn't look like he'd bite.

"Hi, fella."

He didn't growl so I put out a hand. He sniffed and licked and we were friends.

"Nice dog. What kind is he?"

"Newfoundland."

"Hmmm. I thought Newfoundlands had droopy ears."

"Yeah, yeah, yeah. Had some kind of ear fungus when he was a puppy. Told the vet just to bob 'em off."

I stopped myself from asking how the dog felt about losing his floppy ears. "He's pretty furry for the heat. What's his name?"

"Doc."

"Doc?" Hmmm. Billy Lee didn't seem the fairy-tale type. "Like Doc in *Snow White and the Seven Dwarves?*"

His lips sneered. "No, dumba—uh, no. Doc for Dr. Doolittle."

Wow. How many facets of Billy Lee were there to ponder over and marvel at? "So you're a fan of Dr. Doolittle?"

That brought out a few choice syllables Momma wouldn't care to hear or have repeated, ending with, "...no. The dog belongs to my girls. They named him Dr. Doolittle 'cause he's black. Like Eddie Murphy. *They're* the ones watch them kind of movies."

"Oh." That did make sense in a warped kind of way. "So you're bringing him to the park for an outing?"

He let out another huge sigh. "Jeez, what is it with you? No, I *ain't* bringing him to the park for an outing. He's a guard dog. He watches out for the girls. He rides with us to ballet and back every Wednesday. Don't have time to drop 'em off and go home before it's time to go back and pick 'em up again. And I sure ain't gonna set there with all them pansi—I mean, I ain't gonna wait at dance class for 'em to get finished."

Light dawned. "I see. So you and Doc come over to the park until they're done with their lessons."

"That's about the size of it."

"Okay." I waited a moment, unable to think of anything else to say. "Guess I'll go on home then. I saw you turn off and since I hadn't caught up to you since the courthouse burned down, I thought I'd see how you were doing. After getting shot, I mean."

Good grief, that sounded coherent. Not.

I took a big breath. I didn't want to say it but I needed to. "I'd have burned up if it hadn't been for you. Thank you, Billy Lee."

To his credit, he looked embarrassed. "Yeah. Well, my leg's getting well and my shoulder, too. You better remember you owe me come tax time."

"Got to collect what's owed regardless of any personal feelings," I said. "Sorry."

"Understand that. But how about watching them assessors a little closer? That young cockadoodle deliberately run my values up this year, I'm pretty sure of it."

The county employed two assessors, and Fred Bauers was middle-aged. "You talking about Calvin Dredger?"

"Yeah."

"Did you appeal within the deadline?"

"Dam—darned right I appealed. Right away. 'Cepting I figure Fred Bauers got a grudge against me and won't do nothing even when he knows I'm right."

Well, I wanted to say, *you* did *bust poor little Fred Bauers in the nose when all he did was ask you to calm down.* Instead, I trotted out the old standby. "I'll check on it."

"You do that." He got off the table and picked up a stick, trying to entice the dog closer.

Doc wasn't buying a friendly game of chase-the-stick as long as Billy Lee held it, so Billy Lee eventually had to throw it. The dog ran over and picked it up, but instead of returning to Billy Lee, he cavorted toward the woods again.

"Doc!" Billy Lee bellowed. "You get back here!" He took off. "You hear me? You come back here right now." Billy Lee was heavy, and his stout legs weren't fast enough to catch Doc. Doc waited till Billy Lee got almost to him before bouncing off again.

Billy Lee roared, "I'll kill you, you miserable excuse for a dog! You get back here. I'm putting that short leash back on you and you'll never get off it again. See if you do."

Doc disappeared into the woods.

I checked my watch.

According to the time Billy Lee entered the park today, his girls' class must start at three thirty. Drawing from my own youthful dance lessons, I guessed he'd pick them up at four thirty. That put him and his dog right smack in Barbara Prestotten's back yard about the time Miss Lavinia found her body.

Billy Lee's stocky form through the leaves might have looked like a bear. The letters on his hat might even be what Miss Lavinia took for tan markings on her bear's head.

Miss Lavinia hadn't been imagining things.

Wait till I told Ethan.

On the other hand, maybe I should tell the sheriff in person. I didn't think Billy Lee shot Barbara Prestotten, but he had a motive, kind of, with Barbara handling Professor Random's case trying to get Billy Lee's DNA.

Then again, if Barbara died closer to two than four like the sheriff thought, Billy Lee couldn't have killed her.

My mind whirled, trying to work out the timetables. I had to shake my head to clear out all the whens, thens, and wheres.

Better let the sheriff figure the timetables out.

As it happened, I saw Ethan that night when I stopped by to pick up some ice cream at the Piggly Wiggly, and told him about Billy Lee's dog that looked like a bear.

He pooh-poohed my theory. "Aw, come on, Corrie. A dog? Kinda reaching, aren't you?" He did promise to tell the sheriff, but I could see him, as he drove away, snickering.

Chapter Eight

ON FRIDAY, RICK Pelling, the personnel officer, gave me a few applications that I went over during the weekend. Dick Beaufort's relative turned up among those applicants but Kayleena Tustenson did not. Tuesday was the cutoff date for applying so Thursday morning, I went by his office to get the rest of the applications.

Rick, drinking coffee from a ceramic mug decorated with the county logo, insisted I sit down. He did not offer me a cup. He steepled his hands and produced a patronizing smile. "I know you've never hired anyone before so…"

"I hired Lucy."

"Yes, but she was actually a transfer and we could prove it was an emergency situation. We didn't have to be quite so concerned with legal niceties." Rick was small and thin, with pale gray hair that matched his pale gray eyes. He blinked them behind wire spectacles and laid a hand over the applications like they needed protection from me.

His desk, I noted while thinking of my tiny table stuffed in a tiny room between tall stacks of tag boxes, was new and large and gleaming under a few piles of paper. A nice wooden desk, maybe cherry. A round table of the same wood sat in the corner with four chairs upholstered in gray.

To match his eyes, maybe? I mentally slapped myself. *Don't be catty.*

I tuned in to what he was saying. "—so that's why I want to give you a quick do-and-don't procedure for interviews."

He took a sip from his mug.

I couldn't resist. "I thought you had my new hire already picked out. Do I need to do interviews?"

He choked on his coffee. "Of course you have to do interviews! The county has to be very circumspect." He calmed down, brushed a stray drop off the golf shirt that had the county logo on its pocket. "You don't know how careful we have to be in hiring people, naturally, being new to the job like you are. Here's what you do. Pick at least three candidates to interview. Make a chart. Grade each candidate on appearance, personality, education, things like that."

"Experience?" I asked helpfully.

"That's right." He settled back in his plush executive style chair. The roomy office, besides its new furnishings, had pictures and certificates up on the wall like he'd been here for years. In one corner sat a tasteful five foot tall palm that Sheila, no doubt, had to keep alive.

His surroundings today were far removed from his old space in the courthouse with its battered furniture and soiled carpet.

The fire hadn't been a total write-off for some of us.

He went on, oblivious to my building discontent. "Like I said, choose three or so candidates, make up your check list and weight each item on it, percentage-wise. Education, personality, appearance. I imagine appearance is pretty important in your office and so is personality. Maybe give each of them forty percent or so."

"We do need agreeable people."

"Right. So weight those categories high and then grade each interviewee. You can always mark up the one you want to hire in different areas." He gave me a complicit smile as he peered at me over his spectacles. "Understand?"

I gave him a toothy smile in return. "Perfectly."

Experience would account for sixty percent, appearance ten per cent, personality ten percent and education twenty percent.

That should do it.

"Oka-a-ay." He pushed the pile of applications toward me. "Now that you understand that part, let's go over some more stuff. You can't ask any personal questions at all. Nothing about age, religion, family, children—"

Resistance to my baser nature was futile. *Oh, Rick, Rick. Such an easy target you make.* "Sexual orientation?"

He literally blanched. "No! No, don't even ask if they're married or in a relationship. We could be sued if you—"

"Teasing, teasing. I've heard some of this from Momma." I neatened the stack of applications and picked it up.

"Ah. Okay." He tried to relax, but I could tell he was still scared I'd get the county in trouble. "Well, then, once you make your choice, she'll need to come in for drug tests and paperwork."

He wanted me to interview three of the best candidates in his office so he could oversee things, but I sweetly declined, saying I wouldn't dream of inconveniencing him. In the middle of him arguing his point, I walked out. When I got back to the trailer that was the tax office, I sorted through the applications.

Out of two hairdressers, three preschool teachers, one former accounting manager, three former accounting clerks, one former IRS employee, two former warehouse inventory managers, one high school graduate with no work experience except an afterschool job at the local drugstore but who was Dick Beaufort's cousin's daughter, and Kayleena, I picked out three people and called them in.

Yes, the cousin's daughter was one of them. No way I could get out of interviewing her even if I was pretty sure she'd be a washout. I was learning to work the system.

By busting my butt, I managed to interview all three by two o'clock that day. By two fifteen, I'd made my choice. Since I phoned Rick, I couldn't see his face when I told him, though I would have liked to.

Nothing but silence came over the line.

After I neatly piled up the applications and interview notes of the losers, I put a pen back in the pencil holder. Then I straightened my stapler and paper clip holder.

"So." He cleared his throat. "Kayleena Tustenson. Have you already told her she's hired? Because if you haven't, I might point out—"

"Yes. I've told her."

"You do know Dick Beaufort recommended one of the girls?"

"I interviewed her, but she would burst into tears the first time a customer yelled at her. She jumped out of her chair when a car backfired outside. Besides, Kayleena's experienced in titles and tags, and I need her tomorrow."

He sputtered about paperwork and drug tests and background checks.

"She's worked for Gwinnett County," I pointed out. "You can start all that going but I need her right away. I have a mandatory tax commissioner conference in Athens next week—" Okay, mandatory might be stretching it, but the State auditor had stressed I needed to go. "—and I've got to have someone who knows about tags to leave in the office. Lucy isn't trained for much except renewals yet and Miss Ruby is slow. Maybe with someone experienced like Kayleena beside her, she can hold the fort while I'm gone."

"Let's discuss this before—"

"Oh, and you need to tell her the county's policies on tattoos and body piercings and stuff like that. Thanks a bunch for all your help."

He was still talking when I hung up.

By two forty-five, I had informed Kayleena she was hired and that I needed her tomorrow morning and that she should report to personnel immediately for drug tests and paperwork.

I spent what was left of the afternoon trying to figure out how to run reports and balance them against three days' worth of proceeds. I'd never balanced before because our bookkeeper had always done it. Since she was no longer available, she couldn't teach me. I'd have to learn on my own.

It took till seven that night to get a handle on the accounting part. Making up bank deposits would have to wait until the next day. I was beat.

Friday morning, Kayleena came in wearing a modest shirt and skirt, with her tattoos discreetly covered and displaying one set of earrings and no nose or tongue stud.

She still sported the purple stripe in her hair but that seemed like a pretty good trade-off for the tattoos and body bling.

She got a cup of coffee and sat down at the counter where, after stashing her purse in a drawer, she checked out her supplies.

So far, so good. Since she'd worked in a large county where all kinds of weird problems arose, I figured she was as knowledgeable about tags as me. Maybe more so.

To make sure, I kept an eagle eye on her for the first hour or so. She might be abrupt with customers, but she did indeed know her motor vehicle stuff. Lucy and Miss Ruby would have someone to help answer their jillion or so questions every day while I was in Athens.

Things were looking up.

After lunch, I went into my so-called office, shut the door, and worked on bank deposits for Tuesday and Wednesday. When they were ready, I balanced Thursday's receipts and got that deposit ready, too. Disbursements to the state, schools and county would have to wait till I got a handle on this part.

Then I called for a deputy escort who turned out to be the skinhead I'd disliked ever since a killer had been after me and he'd been one of my 24/7 guards. Naturally, he made me sit in the back like a criminal while we rode to the bank and back. By then, daylight was waning and the clerks were clearing their counters.

I told Kayleena how lucky I was to get her.

She shrugged, but seemed pleased. "I'm the lucky one. My boyfriend told me it's impossible to get on at the county."

"Right now it is. A lot of people are looking for stable jobs. A few years back, you couldn't hire a person to work here because private companies paid a lot more. Guess times have changed."

"Yeah. My boyfriend Georgie says business where he works is off, too."

A late customer came in about that time so I didn't have a chance to ask what Georgie did for a living. Kayleena greeted the older man pleasantly, but not effusively.

I approved. You can't get too close to people in our business. Be a little too friendly with them and first thing you know, they want favors. Illegal favors.

When I started working as a tag clerk, I had nightmares about processing a fake title or issuing a tag for a stolen car and being hauled off to jail. I'd settled down a lot in three years, but people still expect us to overlook little things and sell them a tag.

Little things like no valid title. No insurance. No registration or even a bill of sale.

Kayleena seemed able to handle that part of the job okay so I could go off to my first conference as tax commissioner without worrying too much about the office. With Kayleena to take care of tricky tag problems and Miss Ruby to lock up the vault—I needed to show Lucy how to close it; Miss Ruby would never be able to handle that bump and lift movement of the hip it took— and office every day, I could concentrate on learning whatever it is tax commissioners are supposed to know.

On the way out, I whistled a happy tune.
This job might not be too bad after all.

Chapter Nine

THAT WEEKEND, AS the conference in Athens neared, I got more and more nervous over traveling alone.

Athens, home of the University of Georgia, was a big city compared to Medder Rose, and I had no experience with cities other than visiting them to shop or take vacations. Someone else always drove.

Momma was off Tuesday and Wednesday, so on Saturday I caught her as she was leaving for her thirty-six-hour shift and asked her to go with me.

"You can sightsee while I'm at the conference and at night we'll go out on the town. They say Athens has lots of good places to eat."

"Sorry. The ODD Peas need me. With Barbara dead, we've got to come up with a viable candidate for commissioner."

This called for tougher tactics. "I've never stayed in a motel by myself before. Do you reckon it'll be safe for a woman alone?"

That should get her.

She was always warning me not to walk on dark sidewalks and to watch out for panel vans parked next to me and stuff like that.

Momma was distracted. "It's a hotel. A nice hotel, according to Peg Nardstrum. They're big Bulldog fans. They go to all the football games, so she knows all about the hotels down there. Anyway, you'll be fine. By the way, have you heard any more about Barbara's murder?"

I shook my head. "No, Ethan isn't talking." I used my

pitiful look. "Athens is a long way to drive by myself. I've never driven that far. What if I get lost?"

Momma's brow creased. She picked up her travel mug of coffee. "I can't believe Duke doesn't have a suspect. It's been well over a week."

I tried again. "What if I have a flat tire or a car problem? What if somebody carjacks me? I hear they've got all kinds of crime in Athens."

"I know he's looking at Arvin Smelting, but what about Dick Beaufort? Dick kicked up a ruckus when he found out Barbara was running against him for commissioner. Threw his pencil jar on the floor and smashed it. Sheila saw him."

I gave up. "Momma, Dick Beaufort has a whole year before he needs to worry about somebody running against him."

"Just the same, the sheriff needs to start asking where some of these people were when Barbara got murdered. If he doesn't watch out, Duke might find himself running against somebody who's more..."

She went off, a short figure in scrubs and baseball hat, muttering.

Sunday, I complained about Momma's attitude to Daddy while he lay back in his recliner and watched the race on the huge thin TV he and Momma had given themselves at Christmas.

"I'll have a long drive by myself and I'll have to stay in a hotel room by myself. I've never stayed in a hotel by myself in my whole life. Don't you think Momma should come along to keep me company? She's off Tuesday and Wednesday."

Daddy had no sympathy. "Time to grow up, chickadee. Put on your big girl panties and suck it up." He reared up in his recliner. "Aw, no, come on, Kyle. You already wrecked Kasey. Now you going after Joey, too?"

"He couldn't help it. He got squeezed."

"Hanhh. Seems to always happen when he's closing in and wants by, though, don't it?"

When he lay back and picked up his beer, I tried my pitiful expression on him. "I don't know how to get to Athens or how long it'll take me or anything. I need somebody to drive me."

Daddy didn't move his eyes off the television. "Take you about three and a half, four hours, depending on traffic. Google a map. Or you can borrow my GPS. Best way's to skip Atlanta and go through Gainesville." He waved his beer as the TV crowd roared. "Way to pass, Carl!"

Talk about modern day lack of parental nurturing.

Monday morning, after opening up the office and making sure nothing needed my immediate attention, I left the office keys and written instructions with Miss Ruby. "Anything comes up and you don't know what to do, call the State. I'll have my phone, too, but I doubt they'll let me have it on in class. I'll try to check in at breaks."

"Oh, don't worry 'bout us. We'll call the State if we can't figger something out." Miss Ruby smoothed my instructions out and carefully put them under her four-leaf clover paperweight. "You have a good time, you hear? Don't you worry about a thing. We'll be fine."

"That's right," Lucy seconded. "Your head looks lots better, too. You have to get real close before you can tell it's still a little puffy. I bet nobody'll even notice."

I touched the diminishing lump. "I used makeup. Lots of makeup."

Kayleena inspected it. "That always helps."

The voice of experience.

When I left about midmorning, Miss Ruby and Lucy both hugged me goodbye. Kayleena was with a customer, but she waved as I went out the door.

I didn't want to go. Nor did I want to drive three or four hours by myself on strange roads. With my luck, I'd get lost and never be seen again.

Sure enough, even with Daddy's GPS, I missed a turn in Jasper and wandered around for an hour before I found my road again. In Gainesville, I got turned around after a late lunch when the fast food parking lot exited onto a one-way street heading the wrong way.

That time it was not my fault. The darned GPS kept telling me to make a U-turn and go right, which I did. I kept ending up back at the fast food place I'd eaten at. When I decided to trust the signs saying Athens was straight ahead, the GPS squawked but I didn't pay any attention. After another thirty minutes or so, it found its brains and put us back on track.

About six, I got to the outskirts of the college town and cheered up. Driving by shopping malls and big box stores, I reached the old part of Athens and came out, exactly as the revitalized GPS predicted, at the Classic Center, site of the conference.

Since the unintended side excursions in Gainesville and Jasper meant I arrived later than expected, the day's registration was open for a bare half hour more. I parked and ran inside.

A bunch more latecomers milled around the tables, but I found the line labeled A-H and gave my name to the pleasant woman manning it. She marked me off her list, handed me a plastic bag, and I grabbed it and left.

Its contents could wait till check-in at the hotel.

The Hilton Garden Inn turned out to be an elegant, multistoried hotel with an indoor pool and hot tub. It was prettier than its pictures on the internet, but I was sure Mr. Jethro, the deceased tax commissioner whose place I'd taken, had booked his room there because of the convenience. The Classic Center stood directly across the street.

Safe in my room, I called Momma to let her know I had arrived without mishap. Unconcerned, she went on and on about the dinner the ODD Peas were hosting at their clubhouse later in the summer to raise money and the difficulty getting the larger stores to donate to the campaigns and the vain attempts to find another candidate to take Barbara's place and some other fundraising problems.

I could have been kidnapped and murdered, and she'd never have noticed. Put out, I hung up abruptly. She could have shown a little excitement that I was safe and sound.

Dumping the contents of the conference bag out on the king bed, I plopped down and examined the goodies. A T-shirt proclaiming the conference and its dates, a mug with the same information, a small calculator, and a packet of paperwork, including badge and food tickets.

The schedule included a general welcome by several people whose names I didn't recognize and classes including: Stealthy Internal Controls, Sensitivity Training for Outspoken Clerks, Cowing Delinquent Taxpayers, Dealing with Obstinate Personnel, CAVEAT—What the heck was that all about?—Title/Tag Twitter, A Sparkling Tax Digest...

Aha. That was one class I'd make it a point to attend. The State expected our tax digest in a couple of months, but I didn't have the slightest notion of how to put one together.

All I knew about a tax digest was that it listed every piece of property in the county and its value as determined by the assessors. And it was the basis of tax collections.

How we got tax bills from it was something of a mystery.

For not the first time, the realization I was in over my head weighed heavily. I fell back on the overstuffed pillow and closed my eyes. This wasn't going to work.

I snapped them open again.

Yes it would! I was *not* in over my head. I had made it to Athens, hadn't I? Despite getting lost in a couple of places, I had navigated the side roads and braved the traffic and arrived at my destination on time. All by myself.

The feeling of empowerment was heady.

I am woman, I shall overcome, I am the champion!

Getting up, I put my shoes back on with renewed confidence.

Now all I had to do was to get through tomorrow, Wednesday and part of Thursday, and I could go home the same way I'd come.

Except without getting lost.

Maybe.

I fetched some ice and a root beer from the vending machines, hung up my clothes, laid out my toiletries and figured out how to operate the TV. The room service menu lay on the desk ready for my supper order. My eReader was loaded with books. I could read, eat, rest up for tomorrow and not leave the room.

Because who knew what might happen if I went out by myself? Athens was a pretty wild place, with druggies and lunatics running around all over. Nothing like Medder Rose.

As I mulled over the menu, my cell phone rang from somewhere in my purse.

Daddy calling to check I'd made it all right. Unlike Momma, *he* cared what happened to me. Digging my cell out from under tissues, crackers, hairbrush, mascara, dental floss, and other feminine musts, I pressed the talk button. "Hey there."

A well-remembered, molten chocolate voice on the other end said, "Hi, Corrie. How're you making it?"

The rush of pleasure vanished. "What do you want, Bodie?"

"I thought you might like to have somebody to eat with."

Why would he think I'd want to eat with him tonight or any other time? I said smugly, "Sorry. I'm in Athens."

"I know. By yourself. That's why I thought you might want someone to eat with."

His words struck me dumb. Then my brain started working again. "You're in Athens?"

"Yeah. Is that a problem?"

What could I say?

Once showered, I put on clean underwear and redid my makeup, taking special care over the fading bruise. After using lip gloss, blush and mascara, I put on one of the nice pair of pants packed for class and added a new summer top. Hair, being thick, long, and glossy—my best feature—merited close attention. It went up, with some brown tendrils loosened to dangle by my chin in a casual manner that didn't look like I'd fixed it especially for Bodie. A pair of leather sandals and I was ready to go down to the lobby when he called.

On the other hand, I might dawdle a few minutes. It wouldn't hurt Bodie's ego to wait ten minutes or so.

In the event, I didn't have to decide. He showed up at my door without calling.

"How'd you know my room number?"

"Got a friend working the desk."

A female, I bet. No sense in digging. I didn't care. No sense in letting the no-good dog get too familiar with my room either. I grabbed my purse, and we left.

Turned out he'd driven over Saturday to visit a fraternity brother who worked for the University.

"I was going back this afternoon, but I talked to Caleb and he told me you were coming in today," Bodie said as we walked down the street to a nearby restaurant he recommended. "I decided to stay over one more night and see if you wanted to eat dinner with me."

"I was thinking about skipping dinner and going down to sit in the hot tub."

As he held the door to the restaurant for me, one of his sexy smiles said he knew perfectly well I was lying. Darn him.

"You can soak in the hot tub when we get back. If I'd brought my trunks, I could enjoy it with you." He put his hand on my back to guide me inside. "Too bad I didn't."

My knees quivered but I pulled myself together. I would be a fool to get in too deep with Bodie Fairhurst.

A big fool. I'm sooo not going down that road again.

In the restaurant's dim interior, I peered around.

Hmmm. I didn't know about this. Sure, the waiters dressed in tuxedos and the maître d' had a haughty air about him and the ceiling was nice, one of those old ones with curlicues and things. But still, the subdued lights and nice architecture couldn't hide the fact that this was an old building. A really, really old building. The kind with rats and cockroaches.

"We'll eat upstairs," Bodie told the maître d' without consulting me.

I wasn't sure I wanted to eat here at all. Death from food poisoning might be painful.

The maître d' summoned a smiling girl in a long black skirt who led us up worn steps to a dark hole that held a bar and a lot of noisy people. The girl put down menus and silverware on a table for two crowded against the wall and vanished.

Surely the health department would have inspected the place. They wouldn't let it stay open unless it passed inspection. Still...

"The county's paying for my meals," I told Bodie. "If

you want to go somewhere a little nicer, I can afford my part."

His eyes crinkled. In the dark, all I could see was double thick fringes of lashes. "Look at the menu, Fluff—Corrie."

When I looked at the menu, I forgot to be annoyed that he'd nearly called me by the old pet name. "Ouch. I'm not sure I can afford these prices." What would the county say if I turned in an expense report listing this much for one meal?

Our server, a cute guy most likely waiting tables while going to school at the University, got our drink orders—mine sweet tea and Bodie's a draft beer—and recited the chef's choices before rushing off.

None of those specials sounded inexpensive, either. Surely the menu held something cheap I could have. I squinted at the ornate script.

Bodie read my mind. "I'm paying for mine, remember? Have a salad. Salads aren't too bad."

In the end, I opted for one of the more reasonable items, a Wild Mushroom Hamburger with fries. If the county administrator checked my expenses, I didn't intend to land in trouble for going on a spending spree the first time county business took me out of town. The newspaper had covered me enough lately.

"Want some oysters for an appetizer?" Bodie asked. "My treat."

I shuddered. "No."

He didn't try to hide his amusement. "Figured not. You never try new things, do you?"

"That isn't true. It depends on—"

"How about some fried dill pickles? Or unpeeled shrimp?"

I wavered at mention of fried dill pickles.

Before I could say yea or nay, Bodie said, "I know the perfect thing. Garden egg rolls."

I agreed with relief. By that time our cute server had set out our drinks and was waiting expectantly for my choice. He hid his sneer pretty well at my hamburger order.

Bodie got the Fresh Catch Thibodaux with cabbage salad

and dirty rice. The kid liked that better and swirled away, leaving me to face Bodie over the small table with nothing to say.

Bodie didn't realize that. "How's Mrs. C. doing on finding a replacement to run for Dick Beaufort's commission seat?"

Our knees accidentally touched. For the prices they charged in this place, you'd think they'd give people more space. "She's working on it."

He nodded. "Miss Lavinia asked Mom about running."

"You're kidding!"

"Nope." He held up his right hand to testify he was telling the truth.

Unbelievable. Bodie's mother is the definitive southern belle, if such a thing exists any more.

Mr. Fairhurst owns some kind of plastics plant outside of town that makes something to do with electronics, but his wife has never worked a day in her life, so far as I know. She plays tennis three times a week, golf once a week, and bridge once a month. Besides the ODD Peas, she belongs to the Ocosawnee Women's Club, the Ocosawnee Garden Club, two neighborhood reading groups, the First Baptist Church, the hospital auxiliary, and, along with her husband, the Ocosawnee Country Club. She also serves on the boards of the county library and the local theater group.

And she constantly flits off to New York to see Broadway shows, or to St. Croix to escape the Georgia winter, or to Vail for a ski vacation. Usually *sans* Mr. Fairhurst.

In my opinion, she isn't the brightest bulb in the chandelier.

Okay, maybe my opinion is flavored by the fact she was dead set against Bodie marrying me. Still, with her fake blonde hair, she's the stereotypical dumb blonde.

I'd never voiced my opinion of Bodie's mother to anyone and didn't start now. "Is she going to do it?"

Bodie shrugged. "She's considering it."

Marvels would never cease.

Our server brought a small loaf of bread, still warm, to the table. I used two of the real butter pats. The first bite melted in my mouth. "Ohhhhh." I closed my eyes in bliss.

"Figured you'd like the bread," Bodie said complacently. He knew all my weaknesses.

The egg rolls were spicy which he hadn't mentioned, but they weren't overly so, and disappeared before our entrees came out. My hamburger was better than the ones Daddy made.

This place wasn't so bad.

Inevitably, the conversation veered to Barbara Prestotten's death. Like Sherry, Bodie had heard Arvin Smelting was a suspect.

"Evidently, Arvin doesn't have an airtight case against Ike Hansfeldt when it comes to the right of way between their properties. When he brought suit, I bet he figured Ike would fold or settle so as not to lose the sale. Arvin didn't count on Ike hiring Barbara. Now he's gonna be out the legal fees and if Ike finds another attorney and wins—which he'll do from what I hear—the deal with the developer will go through and Arvin'll be out even more money."

"Hmmph." I touched my temple that was thankfully almost back to normal. "Ike was the one who made me stay on the sidewalk when those tags fell on me. He even called nine one one. I'm never getting my oil changed in his shop again."

Bodie burst out laughing. "You hold a grudge, don't you?"

I eyed him, remembering the two hundred friends and family gaping in the church as Bodie walked out on me. "Yes."

He could tell exactly what I was thinking. He leaned over the table and touched my fingers. "Come on, Corrie. It wouldn't have worked. Not then. We were both way too immature."

I snatched my hand away from the heat of his. "One of us most certainly was." Was he hinting that it might work now?

No way.

I shoved back my chair. "I'm through eating."

As we brushed by the maître d' stand, a couple stood with backs to us. I caught part of the man's profile before we passed. It looked familiar.

We got outside before I realized why. "Wasn't that Dick Beaufort back there?"

"Didn't notice. Want to go back and see?"

"No!" Besides, if it was our county commission chairman, that didn't look like a wife with him. His or anybody else's. Not with that tight red dress and fishnet stockings. Dick's wife, if I remembered correctly, was kind of plump and favored tent-like clothing.

All the way back to the hotel, I wondered what he was doing in Athens with a strange woman. Then I forgot about Dick when Bodie came up to my room without invitation.

He looked around. "Nice."

"Don't get any ideas."

"*Moi?*" His grin was lopsided, but he was serious. "No, don't worry, Corrie. I wanted to tell you…" He cleared his throat. "I'm kind of…kind of seeing Maura Czerny."

I shrugged. "So? Should that mean anything to me?"

He searched my features. "No. Guess not."

I hoped my face didn't give me away. "Okay, then. Thanks for going to dinner with me."

"My pleasure."

At the door, he turned back with a low laugh and what I recognized as the *what-the-hell* glint in his eyes. "For old times' sake," he murmured and before I knew it, he swept me into his arms.

I let him hug me. Hard. I let him kiss me, too.

Actually, I kissed him back. My traitorous body melted against his as if we had never been apart. My mouth opened involuntarily to let his tongue flick mine, to lovingly touch each tooth the way it used to. I felt each muscle, each bend, each familiar part of him as we molded ourselves together.

My annoyance was forgotten, anger thrown to the wind.

He was the first to pull away. He didn't look happy as we stood opposite each other, both of us breathing heavily.

"Sorry, Corrie. That won't happen again."

What did he expect me to say? "Darn right it won't."

I shut the door on him and wished I didn't feel like crying.

Chapter Ten

IN CLASS THE next morning, while the State's deputy property tax director discoursed on procedures and regulations, it was hard not to fall asleep. I did my best to listen, but my eyelids kept wanting to close. At least till the deputy director started getting interrupted by irate tax commissioners.

They wanted to argue. With her and then among themselves.

The arguments got loud. Tax commissioners are politicians, after all, and they do like to hear themselves talk.

Some were indignant. "How can you charge a man penalties and interest if he never received a tax bill? That ain't right."

Others were inflexible. "Taxes are due. Everyone knows they have to pay their property taxes every year. Whether the post office loses the bill or not. In my office, if they don't pay, I charge interest beginning the day after the due date. No matter what excuse they come up with."

Some were conciliatory. "Well, I had a soldier overseas email me because he wanted to pay, but…"

The few vocal ones got to trying to outtalk each other and I, like the silent majority, swiveled my head back and forth to see who was saying what in an attempt to stay awake.

Once the interruptions got taken care of, things settled back down. A fat woman two seats down from me started snoring so hard her skinny friend had to nudge her awake.

Twice.

Not that I didn't commiserate. These were the most boring classes I'd ever been to, bar none. Compared to them, my college courses looked like *Raiders of the Lost Ark*. There were lots of things to learn, lots of information I needed to know, but I'd never stay conscious long enough to hear what was being said.

Break came about the time my eyelids closed and my head began to droop. Maybe some outside air would revive me.

Outside, the smokers had taken over the patio. I wandered over to a shrubbery-backed stone wall at the outskirts where fresh air might still be available, and sat down within earshot.

A middle-aged woman waved her cigarette, swirling gray smoke around her. "The thing is, if an employee's dishonest, you won't know it till it's too late. My accounting clerk was jiggling figures and making receipts match deposits but I didn't find it out for a whole year."

She jabbed her cigarette to emphasize the *whole year* part. "And then the reason I found out was because my cousin whose tax payment got voided came in and wanted to know why he'd received a notice for unpaid taxes when he'd paid 'em. Showed me the receipt, too. When I got to investigating, I found out what she'd been up to, the hussy."

Another woman chimed in. "Oh, honey, that's nothing compared to what happened to us. The GBI came in when our former tax commissioner diddled with collections. Chained up the office and took him off in handcuffs. It was awful."

An older man nodded. "The deputy before me stole money, too. 'Bout killed the tax commissioner because they'd gone through school together and were best friends, had babies at the same time, raised the kids together, and everything. She..."

Good grief. Would I have to contend with dishonest employees on top of everything else? I thought of Miss Ruby. I could trust her, I knew. I didn't worry too much about Lucy being honest either. But Kayleena...I didn't know anything about Kayleena other than she was experienced.

No, no, I shouldn't worry. Rick would have called

Gwinnett County, and done a background check. If she'd been up to anything in the past, a record would have shown up.

Wouldn't it?

Great, now I had something else to stew over.

At lunch I sat with a fiftyish tax commissioner and his deputy from south Georgia, along with an older tax commissioner from north of Atlanta and four of her people. The tax commissioners, Marvin and Henrietta, were buddies from previous conferences, but they included me in their conversation and made me feel right at home.

Henrietta had known Mr. Jethro, my tax commissioner who'd been murdered. "Such a nice gentleman." She oozed sympathy. "I so much enjoyed hanging out with him at these things." Her eyes misted. "He was a really nice dancer."

I took a second look. Yep, older woman, but still attractive. Maybe twenty or thirty years younger than Mr. Jethro but that wouldn't have mattered. Mr. Jethro liked the ladies. After his wife died, Mr. Jethro had squired a lot of widows and divorcees around Medder Rose, sometimes two and three at a time. Guess these tax meetings let him expand his boundaries.

I missed Mr. Jethro.

After lunch, Henrietta asked if I'd like to go to dinner with them that night.

Marvin seconded the invitation. "One of my county commissioners says I gotta try this place outside town, so me and Henrietta here are taking our deputies. We got room for a fifth if you want to come."

Happy not to eat room service food alone in my room, I accepted.

Marvin, Henrietta, and I met that night in the lobby to wait for the deputies to pick us up. The Hilton, Henrietta mentioned, was reserved strictly for us tax commissioners because of its convenience to the Classic Center. All other personnel were housed in places further away.

"Makes it kind of inconvenient, us here and our people off somewhere else," Marvin grumbled. "Can't keep an eye on 'em. No telling what they might get into. Although I don't never worry about Rupert getting into anything. He's a good ol' boy."

He carried a box under his arm. Not until we moved outside to wait for their deputies did I see that the box was a twelve pack of beer. As he held the lobby door open for me, I also realized he'd started his evening festivities early.

Scenting danger in his yeasty breath, I opened my mouth to plead a headache, but before I could utter a word, an SUV pulled up.

"Here's Rupert and Bob. Whoa, boy!" Marvin hopped out in front of the SUV and put out a hand like a crossing guard.

Luckily, the Envoy had good brakes.

"Get right in here, Miss Flossie." He opened the rear door. I continued to have second thoughts about the whole thing, but Henrietta scrambled in, laughing and exclaiming she was starving. Her deputy, the aforementioned Bob, crowded me from the back.

Maybe it would be okay.

I climbed in.

"Hurry up, Marvin," Henrietta called. "People are trying to check in and we're in the way."

We piled inside, Marvin beside the driver and me stuffed between Henrietta and Bob. Bob wasn't overweight but was tall, with a sturdy build, and took up a good portion of the seat.

For about fifteen minutes, we rode while Marvin and Henrietta chattered. She and Bob clung to the back straps. Wedged in the middle, I swayed with the flow and tried not to clutch at Bob's thigh.

Marvin, jovial in front, turned around to offer us beer. Henrietta took a can, but nobody else did. When Marvin finished his, he threw the empty out the window and popped open another.

Great. I was going to dinner with an alcoholic who was also a litterbug. At least he wasn't driving.

We rode some more. Marvin sang, "Glory, Glory to Old Georgia." Henrietta talked nonstop. Bob and Rupert grunted now and then. I didn't say anything.

Marvin opened some more cans. Henrietta made her one last.

If she was worried about the length of time we were taking to get to the restaurant or the number of beers Marvin kept downing, she never let her concerns show.

Instead, she chatted about the banquet Wednesday night that was to have a Hawaiian motif, which was a really nice idea, and how she enjoyed dancing at these things because there were no places to dance in her home town, even though it was really a nice town but somewhat provincial, and I really needed to come see her sometime because I'd have such a nice time.

She'd see to it personally.

I hoped my eyes weren't glazing.

She moved on to describe her hotel room and how nice it was, and then she talked about her little dog and how she wished she could have brought him, but she had the nicest pet sitter who stayed in her house and played with Snookie and made sure he got outside every four hours. And wasn't I enjoying being in Athens? Athens was such a *nice* place to visit.

I smiled and nodded.

Bob remained pretty quiet. So did Rupert, up front at the wheel. Marvin kept drinking and singing.

Henrietta pulled out a picture of the pooch and told me his age, weight, and serial number. "See his haircut? I've got the nicest groomer and she says Snookie is the nicest…"

My smile became forced, but I made appropriate noises.

A sharp turn put us on a road winding through woods on either side.

Woods? This couldn't be right. Where the heck was this place?

"Ahem," I ventured, "is it far now?"

Silent Bob may have muttered, "God only knows," but his mumble was indistinct.

"Maybe not," Rupert said. "The directions say that was the last turn."

"Almost there," Marvin said jovially.

Fifteen minutes later, through woods getting blacker and

thicker, we pulled up in a parking lot with no cars in sight. A long low building was dark. The place looked deserted.

"Wha's going on here?" Marvin was disgruntled. "Rupert, get out and see what that blankety-blank sign says."

His deputy climbed out and came back to report, "It's closed, Marv. Sign says it's closed on Mondays and Tuesdays."

"Must be closed on Tuesdays," Marvin said, not hearing the last part.

"Well for goodness sakes, Marvin," Henrietta said without exasperation. She may have giggled. *Does this woman never get upset?* "Didn't you ask if it was open tonight when you called to find out where it was?"

I'd have screamed, but I didn't know these people that well so I clamped my teeth together and seethed.

Everyone else took our bad luck in stride. We turned around and rode back the way we'd come while Marvin and Henrietta discussed the nicest places to eat, which places would be too crowded, where we were heading, where we were...

Where we were, was lost.

"Don't you have one of those navigational thingamajigs?" asked Henrietta.

Rupert admitted he didn't. Bob had one on his cell—I saw him looking at it—but he couldn't make Marvin let him direct us.

"Naw, I know where we going," Marvin kept saying.

Bob pocketed his cell. He looked kind of disgusted. My sentiments exactly.

After passing through an area of Athens that didn't look particularly safe, we came to a section with bright lights and neat stores. At Henrietta's insistence, Rupert pulled up to a convenience store. Refusing help, she jumped out and went inside to ask directions.

Bob checked his phone and tried to convey to Rupert our whereabouts. Again.

Marvin kind of half-listened. Until Henrietta came back to report on the cashier's helpfulness. "She was the nicest thing, even wrote the directions down for me. Now where did I put them?" She patted her slack pockets and searched in her purse before she ended up giving Rupert oral instructions from memory.

"There y'go, Rupert," Marvin said. "Just do wha' the li'l lady says."

Bob put his cell away and sank back in his seat.

We rode around some more. I believe we went in a few circles. I know I saw the same building at least three times.

At ten o'clock, we got back to the old part of Athens near the Classic Center.

Marvin, despite imbibing the whole time, had not quite lost all his wits. When we stopped at a red light, he waited until it changed to green before he threw an empty can at a pedestrian waiting to cross.

Clipped the man on a shoulder.

"Woo hoo! Dead center!" Marvin brayed.

Understandably annoyed, the pedestrian pulled a gun.

Marvin snapped upright. "Hell's bells! You shee that? Shtep on it, Rupert! He'sh coming after ush! Whash he doing with a gun! Don't he know he can't wave gunsh around?"

We three in the back cowered against the seat.

Rupert stepped on it.

"Can you b'leeve that sucker pulling a gun on us? He ought to be arreshted, that—" Marvin looked back. "Fashter, Rupert! He's gaining! Don't shtop for that light! Don't shtop!"

The yellow light changed to red, but we went through anyway.

Henrietta pointed at something we whizzed by. "Isn't that the restaurant?"

Rupert made an illegal U-turn and parked us in front of the place where Bodie and I had eaten the night before.

In a No Parking zone.

I pushed Bob out and slid out right behind him. My legs shook but held me. "I, um, I think I'll walk on back to the hotel. I'm not hungry anymore."

"Oh, naw, don't pay any mind to Rupert'sh driving!" Marvin said. "He ain't had but two wrecksh in the lash year.

Come on in and I'll treat you. Put you on my expensh account."

"Oh, thanks. That's, uh, sweet of you. But actually, I'm not hungry a bit. In fact, I feel a little queasy. Prone to carsickness, you know."

I scooted off without waiting to hear more.

In a few minutes, Henrietta and Bob overtook me. "We saw the guy that Marvin hit coming down the street toward us," she explained breathlessly. "He recognized Rupert's Envoy so we thought we might ought to disappear."

All three of us hightailed it for the Hilton.

At the back entrance, Henrietta swiped her key card and held the door for us. "I'm going to the bar and get a sandwich. You two want to come? It's a pretty nice place to eat."

How in heaven's name could the woman be so chipper?

Bob said, "Sure."

Were these people crazy? "I don't think so. I'm not hungry anymore."

Translation: *I'm going up to my room and hide in case the lunatic with the gun finds out where we're staying.*

***

THE NEXT DAY was a continuation of the first day's classes except even more boring, if possible.

The biggest difference was that everyone was abuzz about one of our number who had been arrested for public intoxication and littering and maybe simple battery. Seems whoever it was had attacked a policeman, but the grapevine said the anonymous tax commissioner had bonded out and left town.

I kept my head down and pretended to know nothing.

The class on digest submission was taught by Jerri Sinclair, the auditor who'd gone over our county tax books with me when I first got appointed tax commissioner. She wore a pretty fuchsia blouse that looked good against her milk chocolate complexion and a narrow white skirt that showed off her cute figure. A white bead necklace and earrings completed her ensemble.

My dress pants, black blouse and crystal drop earrings

looked dowdy in comparison, especially since the pants were a little tight. I made a mental note to buy clothes before next year's Athens conference.

As Jerri preached, I paid close attention but to no avail. Half of what she said went right over my head. I would have to get help before preparing the county digest for the State.

When she finished her speech and everyone got up to leave, she motioned for me to stay behind.

After dealing with some inquiries from laggards seizing the opportunity to vent to a captive State revenue person and who were understandably reluctant to let her escape, Jerri managed to extricate herself and pull me off into a corner. "How're you doing?"

"How do you think I'm doing? I've figured out how to balance receipts against the work done. I'm trying to figure out how to pay the funds out. And I have to get a digest ready by August with no clue as to how to do it. I've found out from a class today I can be sued by my clerks if I don't give them adequate protection and a customer attacks them. I've also learned fake titles are roaming around that we have to be on the lookout for. And to top it off..."

I bit my tongue. Better not go into details about my harrowing evening. I might be arrested as an accomplice.

Jerri eyed me suspiciously. "You weren't out throwing beer cans at off-duty policemen last night, were you?"

"I don't drink." Not much anyway. I tried to look indignant and like I wasn't lying.

Her mouth twitched, but she patted my shoulder. "You'll be fine. Call me if you have questions. I mean it. You still have my card, don't you?"

"I'm holding on to it like a life preserver."

She laughed in my face. Why shouldn't she? She didn't have to roll up her sleeves and do the actual work. *I* did.

After a social hour that night where everyone had to stand around and make small talk with a lot of strangers, we went into the banquet room. The Hawaiian theme that circled plastic leis around each place mat had let everyone wear bright tropical shirts and sundresses (except me; I never got the memo on the dress code). Awards of some kind were given and announcements made and speeches orated. The main dish turned out to be some kind of stuffed chicken, surprise, surprise.

Then the Swinging Medallions, a regroup from the sixties when some of these people were young and hip, came out and played oldies-type music. The lights dimmed, people lined up for the cash bars, and the dance floor got busy.

I tried to disappear in the crowd, but Henrietta saw me and grabbed me when the line dancing started and made me go dance with her. Jerri Sinclair was on the floor, too, along with a few other State instructors and what looked like half the Dekalb, Fulton and Gwinnett tax offices.

Let me tell you, those women knew how to move. I followed their lead as best I could and ended up having a pretty good time.

Maybe being tax commissioner wouldn't be too bad.

The final day of the conference saw lots of hangovers and people hogging the coffee pot at the continental breakfast. Not many attended the question and answer sessions because most everyone had left. By eleven thirty that Thursday, when the last class scheduled to end at noon elicited no more questions, we were dismissed.

I had checked out before coming to class so I, too, made my exodus from the Classic Center and Athens.

I had survived my first State conference as tax commissioner.

Home to the hills!

Chapter Eleven

THE OFFICE WAS fine. Nothing awful had happened while I was gone.

In an unusually roundabout way, Miss Ruby complained about Kayleena's language. "Not that it bothers me," she said earnestly, "but she orten be talking like that in front of customers. I don't think she means anything. She just don't know no better."

I promised to speak to Kayleena about toning it down. Other than that, things seemed calm.

At lunch Friday, Lucy and I went to Joanie's Vittles. Sheriff Duval came in with a deputy. "Ladies," he said, taking off his Smokey-type hat before sitting down at the table next to ours.

I hitched my chair back against his. "Did Ethan tell you about Billy Lee Woodhallen's dog?"

He looked over his shoulder at me and grinned. "Yeah, he did. Thanks for the tip."

I was dying to find out more. Had he questioned Billy Lee? Was the dog in Barbara Prestotten's yard? Did he think Billy Lee had anything to do with the murder?

I didn't want to ask in public, though.

Maybe I could get Ethan alone and see what he knew. Except this was Friday. Darn. Ethan wouldn't be off this weekend after being off last Saturday.

Besides, since he seemed to be clamming up on me, Rayla Cothrew might be more communicative. She and I had reached a certain rapport during the time she babysat me when I was under police guard. Maybe Rayla was off duty tonight, and we could go bowling or something.

After lunch, I went back to the office and continued trying to balance for the four days I'd been gone. I'd checked Kayleena's work first thing that morning and to my relief, her money was a dollar short one day, a dollar over the next, and right on the mark for the other two. Wondering about her honesty had bothered me more than I realized.

Billy Lee showed up about four o'clock. "Need to talk to you," he growled.

Now what? *Oh, lord, the sheriff's questioned him and he's found out I squealed on him.*

"Um, okay."

He acted as if he were waiting for me to come out from behind the counter or to invite him back.

Miss Ruby goggled at him till he glared at her. "Private-like."

She pretended to be busy checking over her titles, but turned her good ear our way.

Miss Ruby didn't miss much.

"I don't have any place to talk privately," I said.

He looked around. "Them commissioners stuck you in this little bitty trailer while they renovated the old Piggly Wiggly for themselves?"

"I don't mind."

"Huh. You ought to." He looked around again. "Well, come on outside, then."

Reluctantly, I went out. He turned his back on the sheriff's office and jail across the street, leaned to one side, and spat. "Let's walk through the square."

We took the tree-lined sidewalk leading away from the trailer and toward the obligatory Confederate soldier statue gracing the middle of the square. This was a copy since the original statue had been toppled right after being erected in 1883, brought down by a mob egged on by people who complained he looked like a Yankee.

I couldn't see how anybody could tell a statue was a Yankee. What did a Yankee look like, anyway? "I wonder what made people think the first statue looked like a Yankee."

"Huh? What Yankee?"

"Never mind."

Billy Lee didn't share my curiosity. He had other questions in mind. "Why'd you tell the sheriff I was over at Barbara Prestotten's the day she got killed?"

"I didn't tell him." That wasn't a lie. Honesty made me add, "I mentioned you having your dog at the park to Ethan. He may have said something to Sheriff Duval." *Especially since I specifically instructed him to tell his boss.*

"Well, I don't appreciate your repeating my business."

"Sorry. I didn't know it was a secret."

He stopped in front of a three-foot diameter oak that let small patches of sunshine dapple the ground. His round face turned red. "Everybody tries to pin stuff on me that ain't my fault. I never had nothing to do with that woman's death and I don't appreciate being dragged in on it. Makes me look like a suspect."

"Well, you were close by about the time it happened."

"Maybe." He looked cagey and pulled up his jeans a notch. "Maybe not."

"Come on, Billy Lee. Miss Lavinia saw a bear. You've got a dog that looks like a bear. Tell me the truth."

He stuck his wide thumbs under his belt. "I already told the sheriff. Yeah, me and Doc might have been at the park and maybe Doc did run away and maybe I did chase after him. But I never went in that house. I never even come out of the woods. I saw Doc nosing round the yard and I called to him, and he came and I caught him. So there, Miss Know-It-All."

"So what difference does it make if the sheriff found out you were at the park? You didn't see anything else while you were there, did you?"

"Like what? Somebody running around with a shotgun yelling *I did it! I did it! I killed her?*" He snorted. "I tell you same as I told Duke. I didn't see nothing and I didn't hear nothing. Nothing happened when I was at the park except old Doc ran through the woods and ended up in that yard."

"I'm sure the sheriff believed you," I said.

"Huh. Little you know. I tell you, anytime anything goes

wrong in this county, it's all my fault. The nosy fire marshal gets run off the road, I'm responsible. The sisters' charity shop gets burnt down, I'm responsible. Some cow takes a dump in a flower bed, it's my bull! Hel—heck! If I'm not nowhere near the vicinity, it's still my fault."

He stood and smoldered, and meditated on being so sorely put upon.

I said, "Sheriff Duval's got to find a murderer. You can't blame him for following up any leads he gets."

"Huh!" Billy Lee spat. "Course, now, I feel sorry for the woman. Even if she did put ideas in dimwits' heads about taking people to court and all."

That could only be an oblique reference to Professor Random trying to make him take a DNA test. Maybe he might spill more if I probed. "You think she talked people into suing?"

"Hel—heck, yeah." He took his thumbs out of his jeans so he could wave his ham hands around. "One of them big Atlanta lawyers like she use'ta be? She thought she could send a legal-sounding letter and make us honest people shit our—"

He donned a virtuous expression. "But that ain't no nevermind. She's gone now and I won't speak ill of the dead. But I don't know nothing about what happened to her. And next time you see me out somewhere, I wish you'd mind your own business."

"I didn't—"

A parks and rec worker in the county's green uniform strode by, cutting through the square to get to the parks office. He slowed, gave us a curious glance. "Morning, folks."

I nodded to him. "Good morning."

Billy Lee scowled and waited for the man to get gone. He wasn't finished with me. "That's another thing." He jerked his head toward the retreating employee's back. "You county workers think you can get away with anything. Accusing people of all kinds of things. Riding around all over the county in taxpayer-bought cars. Using taxpayer-bought gas like it was water."

"Now that's not quite—"

"Why, the day that woman got killed, I met one of them green county cars coming out of the park. It 'bout run over me. I ask you, what the heck is a county employee doing, wasting county time setting around a state park during work hours and wasting county gas to get there?"

He shook a finger, big as a cucumber, in my face. "You better remember, tax lady, we voted you in and we can vote you out just as easy."

Actually, I hadn't been voted in, but I understood his meaning. "I'm sure it's frustrating."

Somewhat mollified, he yanked up his jeans that had drooped another notch. "You don't know the half of it. That Sam Blanken's a damfool, running around setting up crummy trailers when I told him I had a perfectly good building I'd be happy to rent the county for offices. Did he bother to look at the building? No. Brings in that, that—" He waved toward my trailer, struggling to find the right word. "—that sardine can. It's a blight on the whole town. And now they're setting up another one on the other end of the square for the clerk. Whole place is gonna look like a dadgummed trailer park."

So Sam wouldn't rent a building from Billy Lee? Aha. Personal grudge here. That explained Billy Lee's outspoken contempt.

Not until after he'd left and I was back in the tax trailer did I reflect on what he'd said about a county car being at the park the day of Barbara's murder.

If the car was exiting the park as Billy Lee was going in, assuming Billy Lee had dropped his girls off at three-fifteen or so, that put his car sighting around three-thirty. Could someone in a county vehicle have used the park as access to Barbara's house before then?

No. I was connecting dots on different lines.

That didn't stop me from mentally listing who had county cars, though.

The assessors had two SUVs that could be considered cars. So did planning and zoning. Parks and recreation had trucks, maintenance had trucks, water had several trucks, but also a car for the department manager. That was all except for the county manager who drove a county car. Oh, and so did the commission chairman. That came to a total of…

Let me see. I counted on my fingers. Two, four, five, six, seven. Seven county cars if you counted SUVs.

One of the assessors or someone from planning and zoning might have been looking at property in the area and decided to take a break. That could be true of the water department manager, too.

Wild Honeysuckle State Park was a Georgia park, so our county park and rec people had no legitimate work business being in it. And there was no reason I could think of for the county manager or the commission chairman to be down that way, either.

I wondered if Billy Lee had mentioned the county car to Sheriff Duval. If he hadn't, did I dare get him in more trouble by mentioning it to Ethan?

More to the point, could I keep him from finding out I was the one who blabbed?

Chapter Twelve

SATURDAY AFTER LUNCH I went into the office to finish balancing payments and get the bank deposits ready. Then I spent some time trying to figure out how to disburse the money we'd collected to the State, the schools and the county. The computer did the State portion automatically, but the other parts fell on me. That is, I had to make sure the millages for county and school authorities were correct so the distribution was correct.

This behind-the-scenes stuff in the tax office was for the birds. I did not enjoy having my Saturdays taken over for piled up work that office hours left no time for, but was work that had to get done, one way or another.

When I left about four, I hesitated before opening the Hyundai's door.

All night I'd chewed over Billy Lee's words regarding a county car seen at the park. I bet he'd never said a word about that car to Sheriff Duval. Billy Lee didn't admit anything to anybody unless he was forced to. He didn't want to be connected to Barbara Prestotten's murder, not by having his dog rampaging around her back yard or by witnessing a county car in the same vicinity on the day of her death. But he might not have a choice.

I doubted a county employee had killed her, but whoever drove the county car might have seen something over toward Barbara's house when he first got to the park.

Mightn't he?

Darn. I *so* did not want to tattle on Billy Lee again.

Desire to keep my mouth shut wrestled with conscience. Conscience won. My shoulders slumped. "Rats."

The tax office trailer was across the street from the sheriff's office and jail. No cars were coming so I crossed without going to the corner crosswalk.

That was the nice thing about small towns. Not much traffic.

At the jail, in a small front area beside an electronically locked steel door, a hard-bitten receptionist sat glued to her computer.

I cleared my throat.

She didn't look up. "Visiting hours are over for today. Anyway, you have to have an appointment. That's assuming the prisoner is allowed visitors. Call next week and make an appointment."

My hackles rose. Did I look like someone coming to see a miscreant in jail? *I don't think so!* "I'm not here to visit a prisoner. I was wondering if Sheriff Duval is in his office."

"Sheriff Duval isn't in on Saturdays." Her fingers clicked on the keys. Unblinking eyes didn't move off the screen.

"Oh." I waited for her to look at me like my recent class on customer service said a good employee should do.

I waited in vain. She didn't so much as turn her head my way.

"What time does he usually get here during the week?"

The mouse moved, but nothing else. "Try nine o'clock. You may get lucky."

With a mumbled thanks, I left. No wonder Billy Lee and half our customers were so down on county employees. Some of us gave a pretty bad impression to the public.

As I exited, footsteps sounded behind me. One deputy and then another hotfooted it past, nearly knocking me down in their haste to get to patrol cars in the jail parking lot.

I recognized the woman who chased after them.

"Rayla. What's going on?"

She didn't stop. "Domestic situation. Gotta run."

I watched them peel off before crossing over to my car. Though curious as to what husband and wife were getting into it and whether I knew either of them and what kind of weapons were involved, I was also tired and wanted mostly to go home. The fracas would be all over the news next week, anyway.

Maybe Daddy would be grilling hamburgers. He was in charge of supper tonight, thank goodness, since Momma had gone to work at lunch today. Momma used to be a good cook whenever she had time to get in the kitchen, but lately she'd been experimenting with tofu and goat cheese and weird things like that.

Okay for some folks, but Daddy and I were plain meat and veggie types.

So I was driving along, minding my own business, getting kind of hungry, remembering I needed to take a book back to the library next week before it went overdue, reminding myself to talk to Fred Bauers and see how the digest was coming...

Oh, I also needed to tell Fred about Billy Lee's concerns that he'd been assessed too high. Mustn't forget to do that Monday.

Went back to wondering what Daddy was fixing for supper.

Nothing different from the usual trip home.

Until a naked man brandishing some kind of big gun ran out in the road in front of me and jumped up and down.

I braked, stopping before I ran smack into him and his, um, his *thingie* flapping at me.

Gray-bearded and wild-eyed, he waved the gun back and forth across his scrawny chest, screaming at the top of his lungs. "I got me a gun! I'm gonna shoot it!"

At me? Shoot at me? Why me? Who was this crazy person?

When my heart started beating again, my wits came back, too. I recognized Bert Macroff, our carpenter known for his weekend drinking sprees that landed him in jail and enabled the county to get fine carpentry done for free.

According to Daddy, Bert was basically harmless and had never hurt anyone.

Except a few times when somebody had confronted him aggressively when he was drunk.

Maybe I could go around him, or maybe I should back up the Hyundai.

Or maybe I should run over him.

No, no, I couldn't run over him.

What should I do?

Bert leaned against my window. "Roll it down!" he hollered. "Hee, hee, hee! Roll both of them front glasses down! I'm gonna put a shot right through 'em!"

Should I do what he said? Should I reverse? Should I step on the gas and hit him? Should I get out and run? Should I...?

He tapped the gun's barrel against my side window. Hard.

I let the glass down. Promptly.

"The other one too, missy. I'm gonna see if I can hit that sign over there on the other side of the road through 'em."

I hoped Daddy was right about Bert not being a bad person. "Um, Bert, you might hit me if you shoot through the car windows."

"Oh. Yeah." He scratched his head, and then brightened. "Get out, then."

Don't argue. Don't argue. Arguing was what riled him up and got him in trouble for jumping on people. Again according to Daddy, but no sense in my taking a chance. And no sense in staying in the car with him shooting at it. I opened the door.

"Let that other window down first!"

I let it down and scooted out. Fast. By that time sirens had started wailing in the distance.

Bert heard them, too. "Aw, don't pay no nevermind to them. They been over to the house 'cause my wife called 'em when she tried to take my gun and I wouldn't let her, but I left so's I wasn't home when they come. Hee, hee, hee! I'm *here!*"

Right. Too bad he wasn't alone. "You sure put one over on 'em, Bert."

He pointed the gun, longer than Dirty Harry's, toward the Hyundai and tried to aim.

He swayed. "Make it stay still. Its motor's running."

"No, I turned the key off. See?" I held up the key. "It's nervous."

"Aw, shucks, no need to be. I ain't gonna hurt it."

"It doesn't know that."

"Stay still, dagnab it." He swayed some more, managed to remain upright. "Aha! Got you now."

My hands clapped my ears barely in time.

The gun boomed loud and clear.

Then a second boom.

Hmmm. Two explosions meant the gun held more than one shot. Thinking about it, the barrel seemed pretty thick, like it had two. And it had a stock. A rifle or shotgun?

While one part of my mind came to this alarming conclusion, the other part of my mind hoped the deputies out searching for Bert would find us soon. It was too late for my poor little car. Pellet holes dotted the areas around the window.

"Bert, you've shot up my car." I tried to sound non-confrontational but authoritative.

Or would sounding sympathetic and pitiful be better?

Didn't matter. Bert was too busy pulling out a box of shells to care. "These come with the gun. Lessee if they fit." He pulled out a couple of shells.

Definitely a short shotgun. Aiighhh. "Bert, those things scatter pellets. You'll make more holes in my car. You don't want to do that, do you?"

"Naw. I'll put the sucker through the windows this time. I know where to aim now."

What? One shot and you've got it down? I don't think so.

Patrol cars with flashing lights rushed up to within several yards of us as Bert fumbled with his weapon. By the time they braked and took cover behind their cars, he had reloaded both barrels.

"Bert, we have company."

"The more the merrier. All rightie, tightie now. We're all set." He winked at me, a drunken kind of conspiratorial wink. "Lessus try again."

Talking to him was hopeless. My Hyundai was doomed. Besides the first shot drilling holes in the side, stray pellets had cracked the front windshield. More shots would finish it off. One last try. "Bert, don't you think that since—?"

"Bert Macroff!" blared a loudspeaker. "Put down your gun and come out with your hands up!"

Wheeling, I saw somebody who looked like Rayla. She was pulling on the arm of the guy wielding the bullhorn. My heart sank to my toes when I recognized the bullhorn holder.

Tim the Skinhead, not real helpful but gung-ho on going by the book and using lots of force. He hadn't been too great as a bodyguard and from the looks of things, he wouldn't be much better as a negotiator.

Snatches of murmured conversation drifted out from beyond the patrol cars.

"God help us!" The words rose loud and clear from the growing knot of deputies. "He's got a hostage!"

I hid my face in my hands. This was all Bert needed to go ballistic. What I knew about law enforcement tactics could fit into a thimble, but any ignoramus could see they had to be going about this all wrong.

Sure enough, their busy buzzing stirred Bert up. He scratched his head. "What they doing?"

"I don't know. Maybe you should go over and see."

"I b'leeve they're plotting. Look at 'em all huddled up. I ain't gonna fall for it."

He tried to hop up on my car's hood. After a couple of failed attempts, he managed to throw himself across it and clamber upright. Standing there like a tottering figurehead, he waved the gun. "Come and get me, coppers!" And to me, "I allus wanted to say that, hee hee hee."

"Bert! Put down the gun and put up your hands," blared the loudspeaker.

I covered my ears as Bert let loose one barrel toward the Dangerous Curve Ahead sign across the road near the patrol cars, Then I covered my eyes. I didn't want to see this.

Yes, I did. Peeking out from between my fingers, I glimpsed blue uniforms scattering.

Taking cover, the cowards. Sure. Now that they'd made it impossible for me to talk sense into Bert.

Bert himself was having a field day, jumping around on

my little Hyundai, whooping and hollering like the drunken madman he was. This had to end.

I went up to the car. "Bert," I called in what I hoped was a composed but forceful tone. "Bert, you've upset the deputies. They think you're going to hurt somebody. Give me the gun, please."

He turned his bleary gaze toward me. "What? Oh, you're the tax lady. Whatcha doing here?"

"That's my car you're standing on."

Looking down, he studied his perch. "Your car? I'm standing on your car? I thought it was a stray car out here by itself."

"No. It's my car. I got out of it a few minutes ago, remember? Can you get down? Do you need some help?"

"Naw."

About that time, the loudspeaker boomed again. "Bert Macroff, we know who you are. Let your hostage go and we'll talk about the situation. We're willing to negotiate."

Bert looked over his shoulder at the circled patrol cars. "What they talking about? What hostage? What situation? What they mean, negotiate?"

This was useless. "I have no idea."

Walking to the side of the road, I found a smooth boulder, sat down, put my hands on my knees, and waited for the inevitable.

Hey, I wasn't a teetotaler. I enjoyed an occasional beer or glass of wine as much as the next person. But this drunken farce along with the Athens debacle was enough to put me off alcohol for life.

About that time the sheriff's car raced up. Sheriff Duval's long form unfolded and was immediately engulfed by his jabbering staff.

He made an emphatic gesture that cut them off and made them fall back, then started talking. Slammed his Smokey hat down on the ground. Shook his finger at them.

He must be blessing them out.

I hoped he was.

Especially Tim.

In a minute, he came striding over.

"Bert, what the heck d'you think you're doing?" Sheriff Duval sounded calm, not mad or excited at all.

I approved.

Bert scratched his head, still clutching the shotgun. "Duke? That you? Why're your boys yelling at me?"

"They think you're gonna hurt yourself or..." The sheriff noticed me sitting on the roadside boulder. "Corrie? What are you doing in the middle of this?"

"I was on my way home and stopped to see whether anyone was serving ice cream."

He gave me a funny look.

I lost it. "This nutcase—that is, Bert here, jumped out in front of me. I had to stop to keep from running over him. Now he's shot holes all in my car."

Bert's mouth made an O of surprise. "No, I didn't. I shot through them front windows."

"With a shotgun," I snarled.

Bert took a step back on scrawny legs, almost fell off the Hyundai but recovered his balance. His *thingie* bounced. So did his big balls.

I tried not to look. His thin hairy chest and stick hairy legs made me nauseous enough without focusing on his dangling hairy junk.

"Pellets went everywhere including my car," I complained. The body shop with its big bill loomed. Again.

"Well, uh..." Bert looked around sheepishly. Then he leaned around the windshield, trying to peer at the side door without falling.

But he quickly recovered his drunken aplomb. "Well, they're itty bitty holes. Prob'ly nobody'll notice 'em."

Sheriff Duval strolled toward him. "Let me give you a hand down, Bert. You're liable to fall off if you aren't careful."

Bert immediately grabbed the sheriff's arm and half-climbed, half-fell down.

Sheriff Duval helped him steady himself. "What you got there? A shotgun? You're not a hunter. Where in the world did you get a shotgun? And a sawed-off one at that."

"This here?" Bert looked at the gun and concentrated, swaying. "Lemme think."

Sheriff Duval kept a firm grip on his elbow.

Bert pondered a few minutes. "Behind the restrooms in the park. Stuck up in a hollow black walnut tree. Box of shells, too."

"What park you talking about?"

"You know. The one close to the house. The state park. Honeysuckle."

"What were you doing behind the restrooms?"

"M'wife found my bottle of Jack and poured it down the drain this morning so I dug up the home brew I been saving for emergencies and went out to the park to drink. I figure I can't get in any trouble out in the woods, you know?"

"Yeah, I know." Sheriff Duval nodded like he understood perfectly. "So you found this gun in the woods."

"Uh huh. I set down right under it and commenced drinking." Bert looked at the gun. "When I stood up, I was kinda dizzy so I stumbled and fell. I was laying there on my back, trying to catch my breath, when I saw the stock poking out of the tree. I took it home but Neva wanted to throw it away. She's crazy. Don't know why I married her."

"She was worried you'd shoot yourself," the sheriff said.

"Huh. She's more likely to shoot me herself. She's mean." Bert held out the gun. "You know whose it is, Duke? They shouldn't of left it in a tree. It'll get all rusty and mildewed."

"No, they shouldn't have left it in a tree." Sheriff Duval took the gun with two fingers. "Somebody less responsible than you might have found it. I'll see who it belongs to and fuss at 'em. Why don't you let me carry you into town and find you a bed."

"Okay." Bert nodded, perfectly agreeable despite his defiant display moments before.

Sheriff Duval turned toward his people and beckoned. Skinhead Tim rushed out with a blanket.

The sheriff gave Tim the gun before taking the blanket and turning back. Bert allowed the sheriff to wrap up his nakedness.

Tim made off with the gun. Sheriff Duval took Bert away, his adventure over for the evening. My mind churned.

A shotgun. In woods not far from Barbara Prestotten's house.

When I got home and parked my Hyundai in its little side yard shed that my parents make me use ever since I accidentally drove my car through the back of the garage, Daddy was staring dispiritedly at something on the kitchen counter.

I went over to help him stare. "What is it?"

He sighed. A long-suffering, drawn-out sigh. "Casserole. Your momma made it this morning. It's got tofu and brussels sprouts and I'm not sure what else in it. She said to stick it in the oven for thirty minutes or so at three hundred fifty degrees and it'll be ready to eat."

"That looks skanky." I picked up the pan.

Daddy sighed again, miserable. "I don't dare not cook it, after she went to all the trouble of—"

Thoughts of Bert shooting my car made me throw the pan on the floor so violently that the casserole bounced on Bill's food bowl before it landed upside down. "Oops. Sorry. That won't be fit to eat, will it? Especially after getting cat hair all in it. I better get the mop."

Daddy perked up. "I'll run out to the Tastee Totem."

After he got back and we were munching burgers and fries, he said, "I heard Bert Macroff got all lickered up and got hold of a shotgun and took some fool hostage a while ago over on Crown Way. It was all over the Tastee Totem."

Great. I took a big swallow of Diet Coke. "Did they say who the hostage was?"

"No. Somebody driving by stupid enough to stop for him. That's the road you take home sometimes, isn't it?"

"Not any more."

Chapter Thirteen

ON MONDAY, I dropped my Hyundai off at the body shop and Momma drove me to rent a car. I got out and waved goodbye with visions of a nice new Infiniti or BMW, or failing that maybe a sporty SUV. Maybe even a convertible like Momma's.

The only vehicle the rental place had left was a Smart Car.

"Gets good gas mileage," the clerk told me. "Fifty on the road."

"I'm sure." I've never seen myself as a Smart Car type, but saving on gas sounded good. And I had to admit it was cute. "I've heard they don't go very fast. What's the top speed?"

The clerk assured me it would go up to ninety miles an hour.

"Hmm." When I circled it, it kind of flirted with me.

I signed the paperwork and, gritting my teeth, gave the clerk my strained credit card.

How long would it take me to pay this latest fiasco off? Would my auto insurance go up? It wasn't my fault, so maybe it wouldn't. If my insurance did go up, how much would it go up? If it did go up, would the insurance company go after Bert? If I had to wait for him to cough up repair fees, I'd be old and gray. His work record wasn't all that great since he was in jail most of the time and doing work for the county for sub-par wages.

Getting out on the highway and up to speed in the little

car took a few minutes, but the road was clear and the money saved in gas made any slight inconvenience worthwhile.

I got to the office late, but it didn't matter. All the weirdos waited to show up till I was on counter duty anyway. They must have lurked outside until Lucy and Kayleena left for lunch and Miss Ruby got busy with a customer needing eleven tag renewals and two title changes. Then they all trooped in to converge on me.

The line finally dwindled. Slowly. Despite drooping inside, I smiled at the last person before me and tried to sound sympathetic.

"I'm sorry. As I said, this title was assigned to someone else. You can either get J.M. Baccus to title it in his name and sign his new title over to you, or you can go back to the original owner, this Daphne DuBoise, and see if she'll sign an affidavit of correction saying she sold the car to the wrong person."

The forty-something skank spilling out of her tight tank top and tighter jeans took a deep breath. Looked like she was containing a scream by sheer air pressure. "The guy I got it from left town and I don't know this Daphne U. Boysie. All I need is a tag. So sell me a g.d. tag."

My smile felt pasted on. "I can't sell you a tag until you get the title changed. You can do a title bond, but it will be much cheaper to get the original owner to do an affidavit or find Mr. Baccus. Have him title it in his name and he can sign the new title over to you."

She steamed. "They don't do things this way in Michigan."

"I'm sure each state has its own rules."

"No, I mean they're smart up there. I told my husband when he got transferred down here I didn't want to come," she hissed. "I told him there was nothing but a bunch of ignorant hillbillies down here straight out of *Deliverance*. But did he listen? No."

Her tirade wasn't a first.

A lot of out-of-state people move into Ocosawnee County and they're accustomed to different rules and regulations. I always try to be pleasant. "I'm sure it's hard to learn—"

"Ha! I'm fed up with you stupid people. I'm leaving him and moving back home. What do you think of that?"

"If that's what you want, I think that's fine. I hope you'll be very happy." *And maybe your husband will be, too.*

She left muttering, a not-unusual circumstance.

I put my head down on the counter. This being tax commissioner wasn't any better than being a tag clerk. When did I get to hand off this job to someone else the way Mr. Jethro had done? Not till I got someone trained enough to take up the slack and unfortunately, training took time.

The next half hour kept bringing on more of the same.

Then Ethan strutted in. "Want to go to lunch at Joanie's Vittles?"

This would be a great opportunity to tell him about the county car Billy Lee had seen coming out of the park. "Sure, soon as Lucy and Kayleena get back."

Joanie's Vittles was still crowded even though it was after one o'clock by the time Ethan and I sat down. When we ordered our drinks and the Monday special—chicken and dressing, yum!—I immediately started prying.

"Was the shotgun Bert Macruff found the same one that killed Barbara Prestotten?"

Ethan, busy deciding what he wanted to eat, forgot he wasn't supposed to be talking about a case. "Don't know for sure. Can't tell 'cause shotgun shells aren't like bullets. Sheriff thinks it probably is since it was in the woods in the park behind the crime scene. He already sent the pellets to the lab for analysis, but even if they figure out the shell brand that killed Barbara and it's the same, it still won't prove anything."

"Could they lift any fingerprints?"

He shook his head. "None except Bert's. Shell box was clean, too." He suddenly caught on and looked at me with a guilty expression. "I'm, uh, I'm not supposed to talk about this. How'd your conference go last week?"

"Fine. Really peachy. Had a ball." *Lucky I didn't land in jail.*

Seeing I wouldn't get any more info from him, I told him about the county car.

He didn't understand its significance. "Yeah, those cars are hard to miss. Pretty ugly color, that moss green. On trucks it don't much matter but—"

"This car was in the park, Ethan. The park behind Barbara's house."

He looked blank. "So?"

Geez, did I have to spell out everything? "Well, I checked with Fred this morning and found out he works assessments in that half of the county, but he wasn't anywhere near the park that day. I also checked with the planning guys. One said he was in the office all that day, and the other was on vacation the whole week. And Sheila said the water department's car got back today after being in the shop for two weeks."

Ethan put on his disapproving face. "Don't you have anything to do but go around asking dumb questions? I swear, Corrie—"

Lucky for him, the waitress slapped our plates down and kept me from getting up and leaving.

After tackling the dressing, I debated whether imparting my information was more important than dealing with his stupidity.

Yeah, the sheriff needed to know. Still smoldering, I said between chomping chicken, "Let me connect the dots for the slower people among us. If Billy Lee saw a county car at the park the day Barbara Prestotten was murdered, it belonged to either the county manager or Dick Beaufort."

"Dick Beaufort?" Comprehending—Ethan's always been quick, if you consider having his face stuck in the truth for ten minutes before picking up on it, quick—his fresh-faced Huck Finn features lit up. He leaned over the table. "I heard he was upset over Barbara running for his seat next year."

"Yeah, I heard that, too. And it might be his car Billy Lee saw. But the county manager has a county car, too. We need to find out which one of them was in the park that day."

"I'll handle it." Ethan started gulping his food.

I opened my mouth, closed it. "Okay. Let me know which one was out there, huh?"

"Oh, sure." His eyes shifted away.

I decided I'd better develop some more sources of information. Maybe chat up Rayla.

***

TUESDAY MORNING, IT occurred to me that May was basically over and we were almost at June.

By law the tax assessors had to have assessments done and homestead applications entered in time to turn the digest data over to the tax commissioner by July first.

This meant they had another month to get everything together.

They might be on schedule, but they might not.

I trotted across the street where the assessors were stuck along with parks and rec in an old corner storefront that had once housed a barber shop. The assessors' portion was smaller than my trailer.

Like our tax computer backups, theirs were always stored offsite. Because of that, we only had to recreate one day of collections and they lost one day of appraisals due to the fire. Not bad, considering. Once both offices had a place to work and the computers came up, business went on as usual.

Sunny-tempered Fred Bauers, buried in new sets of maps and plats and other paperwork that made this office look much like the old, assured me that pretty much all the property returns, including homestead applications, had been worked up. "Oh, heck, yeah, we've done all the field work. We can start compiling the digest data June 1 and make sure it's all in order."

"And then I get it?"

His smiley-face mouth straightened into a worried line. He slicked back his thinning hair. "Assuming we can get Dyson to work on it. We're ready for him now but every time he comes by, he says he'll get started soon. Then we don't see him again."

"I'll talk to him."

Taking my cute little car, I chased Dyson down at the old Piggly Wiggly that now housed the commissioners and other offices. He sat with his feet up on Sheila's desk shooting the breeze and keeping her from working. She looked grateful for my interruption.

I sniffed.

Dyson didn't emit any kind of odor so maybe he hadn't yet hit the weed today.

"Fred says they're done putting data in their system. So when can you start working it up?"

His bloodshot eyes looked around and focused on a plain metal file cabinet before moving to a battered bookcase. He didn't take his feet off Sheila's gray metal desk.

Sheila, a mere secretary who took care of things like keep track of the commissioners' appointments and type all their memos and answer their phones and remind them of birthdays and speeches and set up meetings and manage all those other odd jobs men don't want to be bothered with and so foist them off on women, didn't rate a nice wooden desk and new furniture like the men. In fact, what she got looked like the discards stored out at the county barn to be auctioned off.

After Dyson looked around for several minutes, he decided I was talking to him.

He yawned and stretched. "Oh, I'll get started in the next week or so. Don't worry. You'll get it July first. Right now, I got data lines to run for the clerk's doublewide. The commissioners been hounding me night and day about getting 'em finished."

I didn't care about the clerk's problems. I cared about the digest.

After some close questioning, Dyson reluctantly communicated that the assessors had to cut off the current year's digest, meaning no more changes to land parcels could be made on their system. Once cut off, Dyson would run calculations and other analytic tools to find whether any errors or mistakes had been made on existing parcels, or whether all the new parcels had been picked up since last year's digest.

Then, when the analysis was done and any errors in, or omissions of, data corrected, he'd be ready to download the assessors' data to the tax system.

Then we'd have it all to do over again on our system because the two systems did not interact.

My head was spinning by the time he finished.

"It won't take long once we get started," he assured me.

Right. I knew from the three years I'd worked under Mr. Jethro that Dyson always said this. And he always drove Mr. Jethro crazy because getting the data downloaded to our system never turned out as simple as Dyson expected because unforeseen difficulties kept cropping up.

I also knew any mistakes the assessors didn't find in their data would have to be corrected in the tax office. Fred would give written corrections and then we would have to change the faulty data in our system.

Manually.

Delores Kineely had always worked on the corrections, but she was gone. That meant this year it'd fall on me. And I hadn't the slightest idea what to do.

"It appears to me the quicker you get started, the more mistakes you can find and the less errors I'll have to fix," I told Dyson. That would also give me time to figure out how to correct stuff, not to mention a better chance of getting a clean digest to the State on time.

Dyson put his hand inside his golf shirt collar and twisted it around his neck. "I'll get on it soon as I can. After the assessors cut off. They got to cut off first."

I got back in the Smart Car and drove back to the assessors' office. Inside its depressing space, Fred's diminutive form stood in front of a county map he was mutilating with stick pins. He turned at my entrance.

"Dyson says you need to cut off the data."

He huffed and drew himself up in his prissy way. His smiley-face grin turned down. "We've already cut off, Corrie. We stopped inputting data Friday because the school board's after us for the digest figures. They want to get it before they set their millage so we're getting everything together as quick as we can. That's why I said once Dyson runs our reports and we get all the data cleaned up, you can have it. But Dyson's got to run the analysis first."

"Whenever he gets around to it, you mean? That won't

work. I refuse to have a late digest for my first year. I need that data ASAP."

"And I'd like to give it to you. We've cut off and we got the upfront stuff done. Soon as Dyson does his part, we can get the errors cleaned up and you can have it." He shook his head. "Right now, we've done all we can. You might try prodding him if you want it early."

I drove back to the old Piggly Wiggly, but Dyson had fled.

Sheila sent me to the water department temporarily located at the water plant outside town, but he'd left there, too. A meter reader said the voter registrar was having computer problems, so I chased Dyson back to the old Piggly Wiggly.

The registrar's clerk said I was ten minutes too late to catch him and sent me to parks and rec. They were in the building with the assessors, and I caught him fiddling with a computer in the park director's office.

Dyson was sizzling with annoyance. "Look, Buster, if you can't learn the difference between deleting a document and deleting a file, you don't need to be using delete at all. You got to know what you're doing."

Buster didn't like being told he was basically an idiot. "But it asked—"

"It asked, DO YOU WANT TO DELETE ALL FILES! It was talking about the running files, too. You know. The ones that make your machine work. Now I'll hafta take it back to IT and install programs. It's gonna have to be set up from scratch. Dude, you gotta think."

Like Dyson took his own advice regarding thinking.

As soon as he got Buster's computer packed up, I stepped between him and the door. "Fred says the current digest data's been cut off. Fred says you have to go through it for errors and then you can download the data to our computers. So when do I get it?"

"When will you bring my computer back?" Buster asked plaintively.

"Soon's I can, dude." Stocky figure still bent over computer case, Dyson didn't bother to turn toward me but did wave a hand in my direction. "The commissioners want me to hook up the clerk's computers before I tackle the digest, Corrie. I got to do that first. Anyway, by law, you don't have to have it till July."

"I got to have my computer back by next Monday," Buster persisted.

Dyson started to look harried. "Can't promise anything, dude."

"If I don't get my computer, I can't get my summer ball schedules updated for—"

I raised my voice. "If I don't get my digest figures, you may as well forget your softball, soccer, and any other schedules, Buster. Because you won't have any money to run them with." I walked around and planted myself between the two men. "The data's ready now, Dyson. I want the digest now."

Mr. Jethro would have been proud of me.

The recalcitrant Dyson finally deigned to look up "Law says you don't have to have it till July first."

I stared back at him. "I want it now."

He turned his beady, red-rimmed eyes away first. "No use talking to me. I got my orders. Talk to the commissioners."

I gritted my teeth. "I will."

"My computer—" Buster's voice floated out behind me.

Steaming, I trotted out to the Smart Car and called Sheila to see if any of the commissioners were planning to show up at their offices that day. Since they're part-time, they come in and out whenever they feel like it and you can't always catch them.

It so happened that Dick Beaufort, the chairman, was in.

I drove back over to the old Piggly Wiggly serving as commission headquarters and waved at Sheila before barging into Dick's office. He half jumped out of his seat, spilling a jar of peanuts all over his desk.

I took a step back. "My entrance doesn't usually throw people into a state of panic."

"Oh." Dick made a stab at projecting composure by raking up peanuts. "Corrie. You startled me. How are you?" He threw most of them into the trash.

I bit back any demands of reassigning Dyson. This pallid man was not the oily county commission chairman I knew. His normal arrogance had disappeared along with the careful grooming and smarmy air. When he picked up a pen, it twisted around and around in twitchy fingers because no paper lay on his desk to write on.

He looked like a man having a nervous breakdown, right down to a noticeable tic over one eye.

"What's wrong?" I asked.

His quick answer was unconvincing. "Nothing. Why do you think something's wrong?"

"You seem…" I couldn't say he looked scared out of his britches. "Um, you look like you don't feel well."

"No, no. Just tired. It's been a long few weeks since the fire and all. Trying to get us all situated, I mean. Wouldn't believe what a job it is, trying to find places for everyone. I've been working too hard."

Though we chatted awhile, nothing more came out so I broached my reason for the visit.

He nodded vaguely as I poured out grievances against Dyson.

"—weeks to get the digest data and then it may take longer than usual for me to get it to the State since this is my first time compiling it. We don't want to be penalized by the State. Dyson needs to understand that and get busy. No reason to delay since the assessors have cut off."

Dick cleared his throat. His fingers kept working. The pen kept twisting. No paper magically appeared. "The clerk is anxious to get his systems up, too. We got your computers up right away so we need to work with him now. That's fair. I'm sure we have plenty of time to get the digest in before it's due."

We!

I saw I'd have to spell out the consequences so I put my hands on my hips like Momma. "Okeydokey. Let me put it to you another way. Do you want the tax bills to go out on time so the county can start putting money in the bank? Or do you want them to go out late and have the county pay to borrow money to operate?"

He blinked. "Well, we certainly don't—"

"You'd better talk to your accountant and the school's accountant, too, to see how long the county and schools can last without new tax money coming in. Because if this digest is late getting to the State, that means we can't send out bills and that means—"

His pen flew out of his hand and fell on the floor. "No, no, we don't want the digest to be late. I'll tell Dyson." He pushed his chair back and got under his desk to retrieve it. "I'll tell him," was the last thing I heard.

As I left in triumph, Sheila threw a harried glance at me from where she sat typing. Secretary to the commissioners and other people including the personnel manager and the accountant, she held the place together.

"What's going on?" I asked in a low voice. "He was jumpy as a dog with a cat on his back."

"The sheriff was here," she whispered, looking back over her shoulder toward Dick's office. "I'm not sure, but I overheard something about Dick's county car being seen near Barbara Prestotten's house the day she was murdered."

Aha. Ethan had told the sheriff what Billy Lee told me.

"Was Dick in it?"

She shrugged with an *I don't know* expression. She glanced back again to make sure Dick wasn't coming out before leaning over to murmur, "He was in the office the morning she died and I heard him call her. I think he planned to meet her at her house, but I don't know for sure. He took off about lunch and didn't come back that day."

No doubt my rounded mouth convinced her she'd confided too much. She swiveled back to her computer and tried to retrench. "Of course, the commissioners come and go all the time. I'm sure Dick had something else going on that day that kept him away from the office. It isn't at all unusual for him or any of the others to pop in and pop out. Why, sometimes they don't show up at all."

"Of course."

Sheila started typing furiously, a clear signal for me to leave her alone.

No wonder Dick looked worried. Had he actually been

at Barbara's house the day she died? That'd put him on top of the suspects list, wouldn't it?

Chapter Fourteen

LUCY AND I had signed up at the gym the past week, but not until Wednesday after our half-day of work could we get together to start our sessions. By the time we arrived, it was after one thirty.

First person we saw as we went into the big room was a perspiring Rayla Cothrew, slinging her arms around and striding on some kind of machine.

"Hi, Rayla," I called.

She looked up from under her sweat band. "Oh, hi. What you doing here, Corrie? Hi, Lucy. Did you two join up?"

"Yeah."

Lucy added, "We decided we needed some exercise."

"Do you good, but it's hard. I got to keep in shape since I'm a full deputy now, but man, it's work." Rayla labored to breathe. "I hate this darned elliptical machine but not as much as the weights."

This seemed a good time to start cultivating. I got on one of the treadmills beside her while Lucy climbed on the other. I started to pump Rayla about Dick Beaufort but about that time, Ike Hansfeldt appeared from the changing room area.

Lucy kept walking but waved at him. I did, too, but he didn't notice me for ogling Lucy.

She wasn't beautiful, but she exuded sex appeal. Something about her laidback air and sultry smile attracted all kinds of males. I'd known her long enough by now to realize she didn't intend to have that effect on men, that it came naturally.

Ike shifted his duffel bag and detoured across the room toward us. Smelling nice and clean, with his wet hair slicked back—he must have had a shower—and neatly dressed in khaki pants and a dark green Izod shirt, he looked pretty darned good to be the son-of-a-gun who'd made me stay flat on the cruddy sidewalk till the paramedics arrived, and who'd insisted I go to the ER.

I showed none of my resentment. I was in politics now. I even smiled at the meddling know-it-all while holding onto the treadmill bar and treading.

When Rayla, puffing away, said, "Hi, Ike." I did the same.

"Hey, Rayla, hey, uh…"

"Corrie."

"Corrie. How y'all doing?" he greeted us pleasantly.

We all allowed we were very well. Rayla, to whom any male over twenty was fair game, stuck her augmented chest out. "Haven't seen you in a while."

"'Cause you weren't here last Wednesday," he said.

"I was working. But I was here Wednesday before that and didn't see you," she said. "I missed you, too."

"Aw, ain't you sweet. Had a sore tendon."

The day the tags fell on me.

Sore tendon, right. But that didn't keep you from coming to town to pay your water bill, did it? Sheesh. I bit my tongue.

Ike abandoned Rayla to focus on Lucy. "Say, Luce, your car doing okay after the oil change?"

Annoyance with Ike fled. My instinct from the other day could be good. He and Lucy might be a perfect match. He was the right age, he was fairly well off, and he looked pretty darned good. Well, I reflected as I remembered the plaid shorts, except for his ugly bird-legs and knees.

Since it was kind of my fault her husband had died—I'd sent her home with a poisoned cookie bar meant for me— I'd feel a lot better if Lucy could find a boyfriend to go around with. It might be too soon now, but maybe in a month or two she'd be ready.

Lucy, going to town on her treadmill, didn't flirt with Ike but she chatted with him in her usual friendly way. "I'm glad you found another attorney, Ike. It must have been terrible losing Barbara that way, right in the middle of Arvin Smelting suing you."

"Yeah, but she'd done all the groundwork for countersuing and everything. Her husband agreed to let Bishop take her files on the case once the sheriff got through with 'em. I went ahead and took my copies over yesterday morning so he could start."

No reason Professor Random couldn't retrieve copies of his files, too, then. I made a mental note to find out if he already knew.

Lucy kept walking. "Lawsuits are scary."

Ike shrugged. "Not this one. I'm sure I'll win. Barbara Prestotten was sure, too. In fact, she called me the same day she was killed and said she had new information that would prove my case."

"That's good," Lucy said.

"I guess it would be if we had some idea what the information was. Unfortunately, the latest entries in her files are a couple of weeks back. The others are missing, so we still don't know what she found out."

Arvin Smelting. The connection immediately popped into my mind. She must have found out something about Arvin Smelting since he was suing Ike. Before I thought, I blurted out, "Do you think whoever murdered her stole the information in her files, Ike?"

His round blue eyes turned my way. "Could be. I don't know."

"Did you tell Sheriff Duval about it?"

"Sure."

As if reading my mind, Rayla, face aglow with perspiration, put in, "Sheriff's already questioned Arvin." She worked the machine like she was battling for her life.

I remembered what Sherry had told me about the sheriff staying a long time in Arvin's office. Now I thought I could guess why. Because Barbara had uncovered something proving Arvin had no case against Ike.

"Does Arvin have an alibi?" I asked Rayla.

"Of sorts."

Ike, Lucy, and I swiveled our necks toward her simultaneously, but Lucy was the first to ask, "What do you mean, of sorts?"

"He was collecting rents that day. Jamil Ogarty's still checking the tenants out and working up a timetable." She sounded like she knew what she was talking about, but she spoiled it by adding, "Whatever that means. Seems to me Jamil wastes a lot of time hanging around different places and making up a lot of charts."

Arvin had rental property all over the county. If he owned some in the area of Barbara's house, could he have bopped over and shot her?

I mentally slapped myself. *Not my concern. The sheriff will be on top of it.*

Anyway, maybe I could help Professor Random out since Ike had mentioned his new attorney. "Say, Ike." *Puff, puff.* This treadmill business was wearing me out. "Barbara Prestotten was representing a friend of mine." Good grief, I was breathing like I'd run ten miles. "In a, um, civil matter."

I needed to catch my breath. Maybe I'd better stop walking while I found out about Ike's new lawyer for the professor. Careful not to fall, I put my feet on each side of the walking belt where metal lined the moving part. "I gather you've got somebody else to take on your case?"

I concentrated on sucking air into my lungs.

As for Ike, he couldn't tear his eyes away from Lucy. Her curvy figure did look nice in the navy jogging shorts and pink exercise top and he seemed to be memorizing it. Yep, they'd make a cute couple.

"Somebody else?" he repeated, mind obviously still on Lucy. "Uh, yeah. Bishop Benton and I've come to an agreement."

"Bishop Benton." I committed the name to memory.

"He's got an office on the old Clareford Road outside town," Rayla added, unasked.

Ike nodded. "Uh huh. That's him."

I thought out loud. "Hopefully, Bishop won't charge so

much since Barbara did most of your work." What that would portend for the professor, I didn't know. "Since Professor Random is looking for an attorney now, too, do you care if I give him Bishop's name?"

Rayla perked up. "Jeff needs an attorney?"

Uh-oh. Bad move, Corrie. Rayla liked the professor. A lot. Despite him being her polar opposite. While he was shy and soft-spoken and retiring, Rayla was vivacious and blunt and outgoing. She didn't try to hide her interest in him, but he showed no signs of retaliating, er, reciprocating. So far.

"What's the prof need a lawyer for?"

I wasn't about to gossip about the professor's search for his father. "The usual stuff, I guess. Property deeds. Wills. I doubt he can afford an expensive lawyer, though."

Ike made a rueful face. "Neither can I, but right now guess it doesn't matter. I'll pay whatever Bishop charges if he can get this thing with Arvin Smelting settled so I can close on that acreage. It'll be worth whatever it costs not to have this thing dragging on."

"You must be getting a good price for your land," Lucy said. She'd worked up a sheen.

He laughed. "You might say so. I'll be a millionaire if everything works out and the government doesn't take it all."

"No way!" Rayla's eyes widened. "Well, you just better remember your friends when you're in the money."

"What, like free oil changes for everyone?"

He bantered with us a few more minutes before leaving.

A millionaire, eh? Yep, Ike was definitely a good candidate for Lucy's future dating life.

I went back to treading. Lucy kept on since she'd never quit.

I surreptitiously looked at my watch.

"Fifteen lousy minutes," I muttered.

Rayla sniffed. "And at least five of them spent standing still, talking to Ike."

I moaned. Oh, well, this was a good time to quiz Rayla. "I heard Dick Beaufort was over at Barbara Prestotten's when she got killed."

Rayla wasn't closemouthed like Ethan had recently become. "Yeah, that's what's going around the jail."

Lucy gasped. "The commission chairman? He was there?"

"Yep. According to him, Barbara was already dead. Also according to him, he was so traumatized he turned around and left without calling for help." She made a sound of disgust.

I puffed. "So did he go to the park before or after he was at her house?"

Rayla didn't ask how I knew he was at the park. She kept on swinging her arms and legs. "After. Says he was so sick after seeing all the gore, he had to stop somewhere to compose himself. Didn't help, though. He barfed. Ethan talked to the groundskeeper and he confirmed they had to clean up the men's room at the park after somebody got sick in it that day."

I probed. "But still, he was at her house about the time she died and didn't notify anybody. That's kind of suspicious, isn't it? Does the sheriff think he killed her?"

Rayla shrugged as best she could with her limbs all in motion. "Who knows what Duke thinks? But Dick certainly could have killed her, got blood all over him, stopped by the park and cleaned himself up. And barfed while he was doing it. Seems logical, doesn't it?"

Lucy asked, "Why would Dick kill Barbara?"

Forgetting to move my feet, I would have hit the bar except for hopping off the belt at the last minute.

Rayla smirked. "Barbara *was* running for his seat. Some people think she might have won." She cocked an eye at me. "You better walk if you want that machine to do any good."

I stepped back on. "That's kind of a weak motive to kill someone, thinking she was going to win the election."

Rayla's laugh turned into a gasp. "You think so? After what happened to you?"

"That was different," Lucy put in. "Dick Beaufort isn't a certified crazy."

Rayla shook her head. "People have been killed for less reason. Problem is we can't find that Dick ever owned that shotgun we found. Or any gun for that matter. Claims he doesn't know how to shoot."

I treaded in silence. Maybe that was true. Some men didn't care for guns on principle, and Dick always seemed more like the tennis-playing, golfing type. "I guess the sheriff's ruled Billy Lee out."

Rayla stopped long enough to indulge in a long swig from a water bottle perched on her machine's shelf. "Jamil Ogarty checked out Billy Lee's alibi. It holds up. Billy Lee picked up his daughters from school right before three, took them by McDonald's for ice cream, and left them at their dance class before it started at three thirty."

"Yeah, but what was he doing around noon?"

"Cutting hay with some of the Hispanics at his farm. They corroborated it in separate interviews. He knocked off about one and went home to have lunch with his wife. She told us what she fixed him—she has him on a diet."

No wonder Billy Lee was so grouchy.

"Then he got cleaned up and left in time to pick up his daughters. No way he had enough time to get all the way across the county and kill Barbara. Besides, he doesn't have a motive." She staggered off the elliptical machine. "That's my hour, thank you, Lord. See you later."

Lucy and I sweated another fifteen minutes before we left. I went home and collapsed.

***

LATER THAT WEEK, I found out from Sam Blanken why Dick had gone to see Barbara in the first place. He was trying to hire her to handle all his legal business pertaining to shopping centers and other investments.

"I thought his attorneys were Baker, Johnsfield, and Kulquarrin. Johnsfield is his uncle or cousin or something, isn't he?"

"Brother-in-law." Sam looked shifty. "Well, Dick figured if Barbara was busy doing most of his work, she wouldn't have time to run for commissioner."

My jaw dropped. "He was trying to bribe her?"

"No, no. Not bribe. I wouldn't say that at all." Sam got quite agitated. His potbelly bounced. "No sir. No bribing about it. He wanted to talk to her about doing some of his legal work. That's all."

So Dick was trying to bribe her. Wonder how Barbara felt about that? Would she have been angry, threatened to expose him? Would Dick have given way to anger if she turned his offer down? But he'd still have needed a shotgun handy.

***

FRIDAY NIGHT, BILL and I were napping on the ratty den sofa when the doorbell rang. Bill lifted his head, meowed at the unwelcome interruption, and lay back down.

I stumbled to the door. Bodie stood there, a plastic bag in his hand. I hadn't seen him since Athens when he'd told me he was dating Maura Czerny and...

Meeting his sky blue gaze and smelling his Bodie scent took my breath away.

I recovered quickly. "That better not be ice cream."

He smiled, teeth glinting white against his dark face. He claimed he had some Cherokee in him way back on his daddy's side and his cheekbones backed it up. "Pecan Cream Pralines."

"Darn it, Bodie. I spent two hours at the gym this week."

His eyes grew round and so did his luscious mouth. "Intentionally?"

Stupid. Don't get involved with him again. Remember what happened.

The promise of ice cream was irresistible. I stood back and let him in.

He took his bag into the kitchen while I ambled along behind him, admiring the fit of his jeans across his lean backside. Ike's butt might look good, but Bodie's took first place with no contest. Even if I wasn't about to get cozy with the man again, I had to admit that Bodie looked sexier than any other male I knew.

"Okay, what do you want?" I asked, getting out bowls.

"Want?" He radiated surprise.

I knew him well enough to know he was faking it, and he knew I knew it.

He grinned. "Nothing. Honest. I'm meeting your dad here. Promised to help him put up a webpage."

"A webpage. What kind of a webpage?"

Bodie shrugged. "Dunno. He didn't say. He asked and I hated to turn him down."

Not that I'd even wondered whether he'd come to see me.

Once we filled our bowls and got spoons, we settled down on the empty den sofa—Bill must have been taking a bathroom break—and rested our feet on the coffee table.

I took a bite. "Oh. Oh. Ohmmm." I closed my eyes in bliss.

"You sound like you're having an orgasm."

I let it slide. "No, this is better than sex. Oh, oh, oh. I can't believe I'm eating this."

"Nothing's better than sex. And a little ice cream never hurt anybody. You've always been too thin, anyway."

The way to a woman's heart is to call her too thin. Except we weren't going through *that* again. No way.

A safe subject, that's what was called for. "So did you find a job?"

"Uh huh." He licked ice cream off his spoon.

I watched the tip of his tongue till I realized what I was doing and dug out another bite to cool down.

Bill poked his head around the hall door opening, spotted the ice cream bowls, and strolled on into the den. After casually stretching and yawning, he ambled over to sit by Bodie's feet and pretended to groom his raggedy fur. He ostentatiously ignored us.

Bodie spooned up another glob of ice cream. "Caleb hired me to help him."

"At the car lot?" I couldn't see Bodie with his education working at a car dealership.

Bill made a jump for the sofa cushion between us. I fended him off with an elbow. He fell back down to the floor and glowered before resuming his grooming.

Bodie paid no attention. "Uh huh. I know cars and Caleb's been so busy lately he needs somebody to kind of look after things. Besides, he says my Spanish will help him with his workers. He's got a bunch of Mexicans on his crews to clean and drive and all."

"Doesn't sound like your kind of job."

Bill sprang up on Bodie's side of the sofa.

Bodie didn't swat the little rascal off. He finished his ice cream and let Bill lick the spoon. "It'll do till I find something better. Besides, I'm tired of having to use my brain so much. I'm ready to do anything I don't have to think about or do tons of paperwork for."

I told him ice cream would make Bill throw up, but Bodie grinned and let Bill have at his emptied bowl. We kept talking as I finished eating, his company easier to take by the minute. He didn't say anything about his kissing me in Athens and neither did I.

Best not open that can of worms.

By the time Daddy got home, we had progressed to starting supper together, almost like old times.

Daddy came straight into the kitchen, looked at me, looked at Bodie.

He didn't say anything.

I figured he was surprised at Bodie and me being in the same room without fighting.

Then I noticed his expression. I stopped pouring rice into the waiting bowl. "Daddy?"

He shook his head, opened his mouth, closed it, and opened it again. "I've got to go to California."

"California?" The suspended rice pot sagged. "What for?"

Bodie put down the cantaloupe he'd been slicing. "California?"

Daddy nodded. "My cousin called because Dad called him when he couldn't get me. Mom—my mother got put in jail up in Oregon."

I gasped. "MeeMaw? MeeMaw got arrested?"

My grandparents had set off in March for an extended trip across the country. They started by dipping down into Florida, then headed west through Alabama, Mississippi, Louisiana, and Texas where they stopped in San Antonio for several weeks to visit one of MeeMaw's sisters. After that, they went on to Albuquerque where they stayed a while with one of PawPaw's cousins.

Last week, they'd made it as far as Las Vegas where, during one of their calls to check in, I'd overheard Daddy cautioning them to put a certain amount aside for gambling since they were sure to lose, and not go over it. (He'd been disgruntled a few days later to learn they'd accidentally hit a jackpot for nearly a hundred thousand dollars on their last night.)

Anyway, they'd left Las Vegas for a relative's home in San Francisco. And now they were—

"In jail," Bodie repeated. "Why?"

"I'm not sure." Daddy pondered. "All I know is that they got her for not having a carry permit."

"But PawPaw does," I said.

"Yes, but MeeMaw was evidently the one who shot the man."

The saucepan of rice I held clattered on the counter. "Shot what man?"

I guess I shrieked because Daddy patted my shoulder. "I don't know exactly, chickadee," he said in his most soothing manner. "That's why I've got to go out there and find out what's going on. My cousin's gonna pick me up in Sacramento and take me up to Oregon. He knows a lawyer up there, too, so... I've talked to your momma. She's calling her niece who works at the Atlanta airport, trying to get me a flight out tonight."

I picked up the saucepan, luckily still full of rice, and set it on a trivet. For once, I was speechless.

Bodie wasn't. "Do you need me to run you down to the airport, Mr. C.?"

"No." Daddy rethought his answer. "Maybe. My oil needs changing. Darn it, I set up with Ike to get it changed tomorrow morning. He's open half a day Saturday, and I don't like to go over three thousand miles before changing it."

I gathered my wits. "Bodie can take you to the airport whenever you need to go. I'll take care of getting your oil changed."

Daddy nodded. "That'll work. I got to go up and get my stuff together."

Bodie and I watched him amble out of the kitchen.

"I didn't know your grandmother packed," Bodie said.

"She doesn't." Not quite true. I amended, "Well, she does keep a little snub nose Colt in her knitting bag. A thirty-eight Special. Just in case."

"In case of what?"

"Hey, they're old. There're lots of scuzzy people thinking they can take advantage of old people like them."

He looked at me.

After a minute, I bristled up. "If MeeMaw wants to carry a gun in her knitting bag, she's got a perfect right to do so."

"I didn't say anything."

"You were thinking it."

"My God, Corrie, can you read my mind now?" He started laughing. "I wouldn't have guessed your grandmother would know how to pick up a gun, much less shoot one."

So far as I knew, MeeMaw had never shot any kind of gun in her life. I didn't tell him that because it wasn't any of his business.

Smart ass.

He ate broiled salmon with us, but left as soon as we finished since Daddy didn't have time to work on any webpage.

I was kind of sorry to see him go. I wouldn't date him again, not after what had passed between us, but he was comfortable to be around. And he never made snide remarks about my accidents or my weight like Ethan did.

"What kind of webpage are you trying to put up?" I asked Daddy later as he wandered into the kitchen looking for his pillboxes.

"What?" He pulled his pills out of the cabinet. His mind was in Oregon. I could see him visibly coming back to the present. "I'm thinking about doing one of them blog things."

"A blog?" I stopped loading dishes into the dishwasher. My daddy with a blog. Beyond belief. "What are you going to blog about?"

"Oh, I dunno. Maybe talk about my fishing and hunting a little. Mostly fishing, though. Thought I'd put some pictures of fish and all on it. Tell how to tie some flies."

"Daddy, do you even know what a blog is?"

He didn't answer but went on back to his room to pack up his pills.

Chapter Fifteen

THE NEXT MORNING, I took Daddy's truck to Ike Hansfeldt to get its oil changed as I'd promised. I didn't like the idea of patronizing the business of the man responsible for all the awful pictures of me plastered through the newspaper— me lying on the sidewalk, wobbling drunkenly, being thrown on a stretcher. People already thought I was weird; now because of Ike, they probably thought I was an alcoholic, too.

But Ike was who Daddy had the appointment with.

I squared my shoulders and set off.

Driving Daddy's gas-guzzling, ten-year-old truck was like driving a tank.

After dealing with my sweet little Smart Car, I floundered all over the road. Keeping it in the right lane took a lot of focus.

Normally, Daddy takes care of oil changes and all that for Momma and me, but I'd gone with him enough times to know the basics. Drive it in, sit down, read some magazines, pay, and drive it out.

When I got to Quick Change Alley, I parked and slipped inside to find Ike in earnest conversation with a thin-faced woman dressed in black tank top, white capri pants, and white sandals. Neither noticed me.

I understood Ike's scowl. The woman, a few years older than me, shoved her purse in front of herself defensively, held her sharp chin up and put on one of those holier-than-thou faces that make you want to slap it. Her voice sounded self-righteous, too. "All I'm saying is that it could be bad for you."

"Oh, is that what you're saying?" Ike's words were clipped. "I must of misunderstood."

"Take it any way you like. If I were you, I'd think about it before—" She noticed me and broke off abruptly.

Ike looked over at me, too, wiping his hands on an oil rag. "We can talk about it later, Jasmine. I'll, uh, see what I can do." He moved toward me. "Hi, Corrie."

"Hi, Ike. Daddy has an appointment for an oil change. He got called out of town so I brought his truck in for him."

The woman straightened her top over her hips, lips tight and eyes hard. She didn't like being dismissed. When she put her bag over her shoulder, it looked like the Salvatore Ferragamo tote my sister who'd married money owned. Not a cheapie if it was real.

Ike ignored her. "Okay, Corrie. Let me do some paperwork and I'll get Juan started on it."

The woman started toward the door. "I'll be back later, Ike."

"All right, Jasmine."

I examined her bag as she sailed past me. It sure did look real, though how a Medder Rose denizen could afford or even aspire to a high-priced bag like that was debatable. Had to be a knock-off.

Jasmine. The name rang a bell but I couldn't immediately place it. Then the light bulb came on. "Ike, was that Barbara Prestotten's secretary?"

Ike nodded, busy writing on his clipboard. "Yeah." He shook his head. "Wants me to roll her odometer back. Can you believe it? And she works—worked—in a law office, too."

Roll back the mileage? "You'd think she'd know better."

"Huh." He curled a lip. "You'd be surprised how many people turn out to be a lot different in private than they let on in public."

I laughed, thinking of the tag customers. "No, I wouldn't. You're right on target about that."

"It's hard telling a good customer no, but sometimes…" He shook his head.

"Yeah, you'd be in big trouble if you diddled with the mileage."

He snorted. "You better believe it. I'm not going to prison for nobody. No sir, that's a fact."

When he went to the back with his clipboard, I sat down on a soft chair upholstered in stain-resistant fabric and picked up a *People* magazine and thought about what Ike had said.

So Jasmine wasn't against breaking the law. Maybe that was a real designer bag that cost a couple thousand dollars. If so, she couldn't afford it on a legal secretary's pay. Maybe she had a little something going on the side. Could Barbara have discovered her secretary doing something illegal that made Jasmine turn nasty enough to—?

I slapped myself mentally. *Stop it, Corrie!*

Figuring out why Barbara Prestotten got killed was not my business. I had enough on my plate, trying to get Dyson started on my digest and worrying about MeeMaw and PawPaw.

That sure did look like a genuine Salvatore Ferragamo bag, though.

***

EVEN THOUGH HE'D gotten MeeMaw out of jail, Daddy wasn't going to be happy until he'd persuaded her and PawPaw to come home.

I answered the home phone when Daddy called to say he'd elected to stay over at his cousin's house in California past the weekend. "I bonded MeeMaw out, but I think with another day or so, I can talk them into cutting short their trip. It's too darned dangerous out here for them to be traipsing around."

"What happened? How'd MeeMaw get arrested?"

Daddy groaned. "They were traveling up the coastal highway and stopped at a scenic overlook or something to watch the sun set over the Pacific. There was another man stopped, too, but they figured him for another tourist."

Short story, the would-be robber attacked PawPaw with

a baseball bat. MeeMaw ran to the car, got her gun and shot the assailant. Must have shot him a couple of times because she hit both legs. The assailant was in custody, but PawPaw spent a night in the hospital with bad bruising, though no broken bones. MeeMaw got stuck in jail.

"And to beat it all," Daddy complained over the phone, "they're being pigheaded fools and say they intend to go right on up through Washington State. I hope after they think about what could have happened they'll change their mind."

I wished Daddy good luck in convincing them, but I doubted they'd budge. I knew them pretty well. Hardheaded, both of them.

***

MONDAY I WENT in to find Kayleena missing from her workspace. She sometimes ran a few minutes late so I didn't worry, not till eight forty-five came and went.

At nine she called, boohooing. "Georgie got picked up last night by the sheriff." She snuffled loudly. "I'm over at the d-d-detention center, trying to get the bail paperwork done. I d-doubt I'll be in today, but I'll try to make it tomorrow."

"Picked up? For what?" That sounded as nosy as Miss Ruby so I softened my voice a bit. "Is he all right? Are you all right?"

"I'm fine. We're both fine except h-he's locked up." She broke down completely and started blubbering incoherently.

The most obvious reason was driving and drinking. "Did he get picked up for DUI? He didn't have an accident, did he?"

"No, n-nothing like that. I'll talk to you about it l-later." She hung up before I could ask anything else.

Lucy, Miss Ruby, and I were all dying with curiosity about why Georgie got picked up, but Monday's early influx of customers meant we couldn't find out anything till later that morning.

The first time we got the tag line caught up, Miss Ruby volunteered to call Rayla.

"We shouldn't be so nosy," Lucy said.

"We shouldn't use the county phone on personal business," I said. "And what if a taxpayer comes in and sees us on a personal call? Go back to the vault room."

Lucy and I both offered our cells. Miss Ruby had her own Jitterbug and toddled off to hide from customers.

"Rayla," we heard her drawl out before going on in her painstaking way, "You know that Kayleena girl who works here… Yeah, that's the one. She says her boyfriend got arrested and we were wondering what for. Do you know?"

Miss Ruby believed in getting right to the point.

"Uh huh. Is that right."

A tag customer came in. Lucy muttered something under her breath before summoning a bright smile and taking his paperwork.

I kept listening.

"My goodness gracious. You don't mean it." Miss Ruby's one-key nasal voice betrayed no shock or other emotion.

I should have made Miss Ruby turn on the speakerphone. If a Jitterbug had a speakerphone.

No, she couldn't turn it on with customers in earshot.

"Well, don't that beat the devil. So the whole bunch got picked up and took to jail." No expression at all varied her deadpan delivery, but I could tell Miss Ruby was excited from the way her north Georgia twang kicked in. "I bet you that Billy Lee don't like that overmuch."

A spate of dialogue squawked over the wires that I could hear from outside the vault room although Miss Ruby's words hadn't seemed incendiary in the least. I moved closer.

"My, my, my. You don't say. I cain't blame you one bit." Miss Ruby still used the same flat monotone, but she peeked around at me with her eyes gleaming. "He ort to be locked up, too, that Billy Lee. He's a scamp, that'un is. I'll talk at you later."

She closed her phone without ado and came out as Lucy's customer took his car tag decal and left.

Lucy and I zeroed in on her as she sat down. "Well?"

Miss Ruby took a deep breath. "You know all them Hispanics Billy Lee uses on his farm."

"Yes. What's that got to do with Kayleena's boyfriend?"

"Kayleena's boyfriend is friends with them. His name's Hore-hay or something like that, according to Rayla. He works for Caleb." White brows knit. "Don't know where Kayleena gets the Georgie from."

Lucy and I looked at one another.

"It must be spelled J-O-R-G-E," I guessed. "With the J pronounced like an H. He's Americanized it to Georgie."

We looked back at Miss Ruby. "What did he get picked up for?"

"That's what I'm a-telling you." Miss Ruby didn't appreciate being interrupted. "Billy Lee had a bunch of them working on his cattle barn till late Saturday night, and afterward, they decided to throw a party over at Hore-hay's place. They got a pig and a goat from somewhere and roasted them. They had beer and liquor, too, Rayla said. Anyways, Hore-hay and some more of them got into a fist fight and a knife got pulled and one of them's in the hospital, and Hore-hay and some more of 'em's in jail. Billy Lee's been over at the sheriff's office all morning, too, raising Cain about somebody stealing one of his prize hogs. Rayla thinks it's connected."

Duh.

Miss Ruby, having imparted her news flash without further interruptions, sat back to await reactions.

Lucy's mouth softened with pity. "Poor Kayleena."

"Georgie's the one locked up," I pointed out.

"Billy Lee ought to of offered them a pig to roast," Miss Ruby opined.

***

TUESDAY, DYSON DOWNLOADED the digest from the assessors' system. Fred and Dyson stood in my crowded so-called office, looking over my shoulder as I ran reports. Then Fred and I tried to match up our figures.

Our system had to show the same amount of parcels and values as the assessors' system. Both reports had to have the same amount of residential, commercial, industrial, and tax-exempt properties. Both systems had to agree on the same number of regular homestead exemptions, special exemptions, and school exemptions.

If anything didn't match, we had to find a valid reason.

Of course, nothing matched and we couldn't figure out why. That meant spending several days trying to work out why the data on our computer came up different from the assessors.

Dyson was no help. Luckily, Fred knew what to look for since I had no idea of how to reconcile the two digests.

Friday, after poring over the figures every day, we had reconciled the homestead exemptions, special exemptions, and school exemptions. We still hadn't made all the residential, commercial, industrial, and tax-exempt parcels agree.

By five, I felt my eyes crossing. "Do we need to work on it tomorrow?" I asked Fred.

"I can't. Got a family reunion up in Blue Ridge." Fred ran fingers through what was left of his hair. "Besides, we got time before it's due anyway, since you made Dyson download early. It won't take us that long to get the discrepancies settled."

"So long as it's done before August 1," I said grimly. "I do not intend to have my first digest be late."

Not until he'd left did I remember I had never told him about Billy Lee's concerns regarding his appraisal.

Darn.

"I'll ask him about it next week," I muttered as I turned off the lights and locked up.

When I got outside, my cute rental car sat in the middle of a commotion. A large form wagging his large finger confronted a tall stocky man in overalls. Both of them were shouting and both of them were red-faced and growling, but I could make out a few words.

"—my hog—" bellowed Billy Lee.

"—should have kept him inside your fence—" retorted the other man.

"—owe me stud fees—"

"—ought to sue for rape—"

I couldn't get to my car. I tried to get around them, but every time I went one way, they turned and blocked me.

"Um, excuse me," I said. "Please let me by?"

They ignored me except to get louder so they could talk over me.

Billy Lee's large fist waved. "I'll have you know people pay two hundred a dose—"

The other man's arms crossed. "Rape is rape—"

"—come back to his pen so tuckered out he can't—"

"—iffun you can't keep him penned up, you deserve—"

I squeezed between a trash can and bench on the edge of the sidewalk and made it to my car door. Once open, I hurled myself inside and fled. The two men were still going at it.

Evidently, Billy Lee's hog had been out sowing his wild oats instead of being eaten by Kayleena's boyfriend.

That was good. Maybe Georgie would soon get out of jail so that Kayleena would quit mooning around. She'd made several title typos in the past few days.

I got home to find Daddy back without MeeMaw and PawPaw.

Well, *that* was bound to happen.

Daddy wasn't happy they refused to cut their trip short, but he was glad to be back and starving for real food.

Momma was working, so he and I went out to the Tastee Totem for supper, to celebrate his return.

"Salads," he kept telling me as we downed one of their big hamburgers and onion ring baskets. "That's all my cousin out there eats. And the restaurants they took me to don't serve real food. Just things like sushi and bean sprouts. Or tofu, and these dang health foods. Oh, it was awful, chickadee. You just don't know. I bet I lost ten pounds."

"You're home now, Daddy. You need to let go of the bad stuff."

He shuddered, clearly unnerved at his memories of the food out in California. I could tell he would be reliving the horrors of his trip for days.

Chapter Sixteen

SATURDAY MORNING THE beginning of "I Fall To Pieces" woke me from a dream about Bodie scooping ice cream over my boobs and letting it melt while he licked it off with slow, tantalizing tongue strokes.

What the heck was I doing, letting that snake-in-the-grass near me?

Then my eyes opened.

Bill, feet busy softening me up, looked at me from where he'd sucked on my T-shirt till it was sopping wet. I threw him off so I could reach my cell on the nightstand.

"Hello." I tried to pretend I was awake and alert, but ended up sounding grumpy.

"Corrie," Sherry's voice came over the line, "what're you doing tonight?"

"Tonight? Tonight." I had to think. "Nothing."

"A group of us are going over to that new club near the college tonight. Want to go?"

"Sure." Then I sensed a trap. Bodie was working with Caleb now. "Who's going besides you and Caleb?"

"Ethan."

"Is Rayla going?"

"No, she's working."

"Who else?"

"Um."

I knew at once she didn't want to tell me. If she thought I'd go out with Bodie, even in a group, she was sadly mistaken. "Who else, Sherry?"

"Well... Uh, Vic Kendlin."

Not Bodie. Okay, no reason to feel let down. "So who's Vic Kendlin?"

"He's this dealer down in Atlanta. He came up last night to look at a Corvette Caleb got in one of his clients might want. He got divorced last year, and he seemed kind of down, and Caleb thought maybe if we took him out to—"

"No blind dates."

"He's got to be at least forty, silly. And Ethan's coming, too. How can it be a blind date?"

"You remember what I told you the last time you tried to fix me up? One more fix-up like that and we would be former friends."

The guy she'd pushed off on me was an Alabama supporter and we went out to an American Legion dance after Alabama won a football game over Clemson. He not only drank too much, he kept yelling, "Roll Tide!" and stuff like that all night long. I ended up getting my purse and calling a friend to come pick me up. Last I saw of him, he was reeling around the dance floor still shouting and making a general nuisance of himself.

Sherry huffed. "I keep telling you this isn't a date. There'll be five of us, maybe six if Joe decides to go with us."

My antennae went up again. "Who's Joe?"

"One of Caleb's auto clean-up crew. He's not real bright even if he is a hunk. But I know you aren't interested so I'll shut up about how hot he is. Anyway, he may meet us there."

"Nobody else?"

"No, but Caleb's Esplanade will hold seven comfortably. If you can think of anyone else that might like to go, we've got room."

"No. Oh, wait. How about Lucy?"

"Oh, good idea. Will you call her?"

"Sure." So no Bodie. I didn't know whether to be glad or sad.

Lucy turned down the invitation. "Not ready yet," she said. "Maybe later."

I told her I understood and after spending the day washing my car and cutting the grass and washing up clothes, I went to Sherry's house by myself where everyone was meeting.

The guys I didn't know seemed amiable enough as we started out.

Vic, with no hint of middle-aged spread and a head of well-cut hair, emitted an amused air that said, *hey you look good enough to eat but if you don't want to play, that's okay.* His nose was snub, his clothes preppie, his smile dazzling.

Like Sherry said, he was too old for me. A shame Lucy hadn't wanted to come. She was nearer his age.

Joe, from Guatemala, was well-built with a striking olive complexion and curly dark hair a lot of women would love to have. Unfortunately, despite his coloring, he reminded me of nothing so much as a male blond ditz. To be fair, that might be because he didn't understand English very well.

Okay by me. No need to make small talk with him.

When we got to the new club, it looked like any other sports bar and grill, with neon signs and four big TVs and a miniscule dance floor. The band, playing when we came in, had a lead guitar who was great and a so-so vocalist.

When we walked in, Joe, Vic and Ethan turned the heads of every woman in the club. Joe might be the hunk, but Vic's prep clothes on a toned body went over pretty well, too. And if I didn't know Ethan, I might have given him a second glance, too.

The music was loud and so were the conversations around us. We couldn't talk much because we had to yell to be heard, but we danced and boy, did Vic like to dance. He didn't seem too sad to me, either, despite his divorce. He talked a lot, though. I don't trust people who talk constantly, even while dancing. Especially while dancing.

He and I were out on the postage stamp dance floor, pressed in by about ten other couples, when Bodie came in.

He wasn't alone. Maura Czerny, dressed in a low-cut black blouse with cap sleeves and a stylish black skirt, held tight to his arm. With crystal drops in her ears and a tiny butterfly tattoo on one exposed shoulder, she looked sophisticated as all get-out. I'd thought my wispy skirt and sleeveless turtleneck flattered me till I saw her.

I hate feeling frumpy.

Bodie spotted Sherry and Caleb at our table, and bent down to say something to Maura. They went around past the dance floor, his hand on the small of her back the way it used to rest on mine.

I smiled brightly at Vic, still talking about his home in north Atlanta and his second home on Lake Lanier where he docked his thirty foot cruiser. I think maybe he also mentioned an airplane hangared somewhere or other and a sailboat at another house in the Tortugas. "You need to come down and we'll take it out," he ended.

"Sounds like fun," I said over the music, not sure whether I was half-way agreeing to go out on a boat or up in an airplane. One thing for sure, I wasn't going to foreign parts with some old guy I'd just met.

While we danced, Bodie pulled out chairs beside Caleb for himself and Maura. A waitress, dressed kind of like a Dallas Cowboy Cheerleader—the club was called The Dallas Cheerline; real original—brought over a beer and a glass of wine.

When the music stopped, Vic took my arm. "If I'd known women like you lived up here in the sticks, I'd have come up to see Caleb more often."

"Hmmm." I didn't care for his taking my arm. Going back to our group didn't sound good either, but I couldn't bolt and run, darn it. My car was at Sherry's. I steeled myself to face Bodie and his date.

At the table, Vic looked put out when I sat back down between Ethan and Sherry. Sherry recognized my expression and bent over to whisper, "I didn't know they were coming. I swear I didn't. Caleb never said a word about Bodie coming."

I shrugged. "Don't worry about it. Doesn't bother me."

I was lying and she knew it, but like a good friend, she did her best to cover.

From exchanged pleasantries, it seemed like Bodie and Maura already knew Vic, but Bodie introduced Maura to the rest of us.

She grasped my hand and sounded sincere. "I'm so glad to meet you. I've heard a lot about you." The sincerity part got tarnished when she added, "How's your head?" and looked at my forehead like she was trying to envision how bad it had been.

"Fine, thanks." *Would have been a lot better if you hadn't spread all those pictures in the paper for everyone and his brother to see.*

"That was such a freak accident." She didn't stop staring at my temple.

"Oh, Corrie's all the time having weird things happen to her," Ethan put in. "She beats all I ever saw."

I turned sideways in my chair and gave him my coldest glare.

He didn't notice. "She got her toe caught in a refrigerator grate one time. Like to cut it off. Had to go to ER for it."

Beside me, Sherry kicked at her husband.

"And then one time this bald eagle went through her windshield. She had to get stitches then, too. Killed the eagle. Thought the feds were going to get her for that one."

Caleb hopped up. "Uh, do you want to dance, honey?"

"No, dear, why don't you ask Maura?" Sherry said sweetly.

He looked confused but game. "Bodie, you don't mind, do you?"

"No. Oh, no. Maura loves to dance, don't you, Maura?" Bodie had the strained expression on his face that meant he was trying to control laughter.

Maura put down her wineglass. "Sure," she said to Caleb, and got up.

"Come on, Vic. I saw you're good on the dance floor." Sherry grabbed him and they went off, too.

Ethan didn't dance and apparently neither did Joe. They watched the couples for a few minutes. Then, when his attempts at conversation were met with monosyllables, Ethan livened up when 'pool game' broke through Joe's indecipherable English. They got up to wander over to an adjoining room where blaring TVs and pool tables lured the non-dancers.

I was left, seething, with Bodie.

"Ethan doesn't mean anything by it," he ventured.

"I haven't the slightest bit of interest in what Ethan does or doesn't mean," I said icily.

He slid into Ethan's chair beside me. "Okay. Listen, Corrie." He hesitated, serious.

I waited a beat. "I'm listening."

"How well do you know Vic Kendlin?"

"Vic?" I turned to look at him full face. "Exactly what does Vic have to do with it?"

"With what?"

"With—with—" With us, I wanted to say. "With anything. Oh, forget it. Why are you asking me about Vic?"

"I was wondering how well you knew him. I saw you dancing and… I heard some stuff about him."

"What kind of stuff?"

He shrugged, drank from his bottle. "Stuff that's not so nice. Wanted to make sure you knew before you got all involved with him. Save you the trouble of finding out later."

"Involved with—"

I almost blew. Did he think I was so desperate I'd grab any man who came along? Instead of screaming at him, I scrunched my eyes closed and counted to ten.

Then, very calmly, I said, "Let me think. Haven't we decided before that you have no right to tell me what to do?"

"Look, Corrie, I'm trying to save you some grief. I don't want to see you—"

I stood up. "I've got to go pee."

When I went by the dance floor, Sherry reached out and grabbed my arm. "You aren't leaving?"

"It'd be kind of hard without a car."

"You've done it before."

"Because I was desperate and I found a ride." I relented under her sympathetic gaze. "I'm okay. Honest. I'm going to the little girls' room."

"Oh." Her relief showed. "Well, it's tiny. If there's a line, keep going down the hall to the family restroom at the very end. It's kind of hidden so it was empty when I went."

The ladies room was indeed tiny, with stalls that struggled to accommodate two people. Since two people were washing their hands and four more people were waiting for the stalls, no one could move.

I made my way down the hall as Sherry had instructed. The family restroom could accommodate a wheelchair and had a changing table and, as predicted by Sherry, was empty.

After using the toilet, I washed my hands and splashed some water on my hot face as well. "Darn him. Darn him."

Why was it Bodie Fairhurst could make me feel like a cranky five-year-old? Why was it that at times, I—

Because I still loved him?

"You idiot." The woman in the mirror looked back at me with wide eyes. "So what if you do? It isn't going to change a thing. He's moved on. Now you have to, too."

I started to put on some lip gloss before realizing my purse and its contents were at the table. With a sigh, I brushed my fingers through my hair, flicked it back and started out.

The doorknob came off in my hand.

I stared at it a moment. "Oh, geez. What next?" I tried to put it back.

It slid on but wouldn't turn.

After a few fruitless tries, I took off the knob and tried to turn the pin with my fingers.

That didn't work either.

I labored for a few minutes before realizing someone would have to turn the knob from the other side or maybe get a tool to open the door.

And that wouldn't happen till someone discovered me locked in.

"Help," I said tentatively.

This was ridiculous. What kind of ignoramus allowed a doorknob on a bar restroom to get loose? For that matter, what kind of ignoramus got locked in a bar restroom?

I tried a louder voice. "Help!"

No one answered. I started slapping the door, and then progressed to beating with both fists and screaming.

No one came.

Okay, silly, get your cellphone and dial...

Who? Call 911 and tell them my situation? Didn't matter,

couldn't use it anyway. Not since it was in my purse at the table.

I banged my head on the door molding. *Think, Corrie.*

The restrooms were off to themselves down a corridor behind the kitchen, and this one was at the end of the hall. Inside my jail, I listened to the hearty bustle and laughter going in and out of the other restrooms. My spirits sank. Yelling and pounding wouldn't make a dint in that noise. I'd have to wait till someone needed these facilities, then shout and bang.

Thank goodness this toilet had a lid that looked half-way clean. I lowered it and sat down.

After maybe ten minutes, someone rattled the door. "Oh for the love of—" A woman's whiskey-hoarse voice barely came through.

I leaped up. "I'm locked in."

"Never mind."

"No, I'm locked in!"

"Someone came out of the men's room. I'll go in there."

What? She was going to use the men's room? "No, you can come in here! I'd love for you to come in here! I'm locked in! Hey, come back!"

Nothing.

It took twenty minutes for Sherry to realize something was wrong and come looking for me. Through the door, I told her I was locked in.

"Well, unlock the door, silly."

"Sherry, that's the whole point. I can't. I tell you I'm locked in."

Silence. "You've tried undoing the lock?"

"The doorknob's off. It fell off."

"How'd you manage that?"

"I started to open the door and it fell off. I can't put it back. When I do, it still won't turn. Get me out!"

It took another fifteen minutes for her to find the manager and another five for him to pry the remnants of the knob mechanism out so I could escape.

By that time, I was ready to call it an evening.

To top it all off, another person had been added to our

already long table. I saw her when Sherry and I circled around the dance floor.

Seductive in a shiny red tank top and short skirt with black fishnet stockings, the thin-faced woman sat on the end beside an attentive Vic and Joe's empty chair. Across the table, an animated Maura Czerny leaned over to talk to her. Bodie had his chair propped back, looking bored and drinking a longneck.

I won't deny a little *frisson* of satisfaction ran through my body when I saw he watched the band rather than his date. A *frisson* quickly brought under control.

Nothing he did concerned me in the least.

I muttered to Sherry, walking in front of me, "Isn't that Barbara Prestotten's secretary sitting by Vic?"

Sherry looked. "Ooh, it is. Jasmine Musselman. Caleb must have asked her to come." She didn't sound pleased. "She's been talking to him about trading for one of his cars."

Caleb, it turned out, had little to do with Jasmine's appearance in our group. Jasmine had recognized him after she walked in and come over of her own accord.

"She got stood up," Caleb told us when we'd sat down. He looked warily at Sherry. "I told her to join us so she wouldn't have to sit at the bar by herself."

Sherry smiled brightly, but kept her lips pressed together. "Sure thing." Sherry believed in discouraging wandering eyes of husbands, however faithful that husband might be.

Jasmine might have noticed the slight coldness. "Yeah, Trish Bradford and I usually meet here every Saturday, but she bailed on me," she said breathily.

She didn't sound at all prim tonight, the way she'd come across at Ike's oil change place. In fact, she sounded downright giddy. She twisted a dangling red earring. "Trish didn't get a hold of me to say she couldn't come till I pulled into the parking lot. I'm glad I found someone I knew here. I hate coming to places like this by myself."

I bet. Despite being on her own, she looked to be in a good mood. Or maybe she'd been enjoying the pink drink she held. An empty glass sat in front of her, too.

"Corrie. There you are." Ethan came over from the bar and sat down beside me. "Someone said you must've gone home but since we all rode over with Caleb, I figured you had to be here somewhere. Where you been?"

Locked in a small dingy space sitting on a toilet top.

Still frazzled from my experience, I said curtly, "Don't ask."

Down the table, I saw Bodie try not to grin.

Ethan held his head back in his disapproving way before noticing Jasmine across the table. "Oh, hey, Jasmine. Didn't know you were here."

"So, Jasmine," Maura went on, ignoring Sherry's and my return to continue her tête-a- tête with Barbara Prestotten's secretary, "you don't know what was in the package Barbara got?"

"I didn't say that." Jasmine smiled tipsily. "Guess my confidentiality agreement doesn't matter now since she's dead and I'm out of a job. What the heck. Actually, I do know. It was papers concerning Arvin Smelting's lawsuit against Ike."

Maura looked like a cat about to pounce. "Proof that Arvin didn't have a case?"

Jasmine leaned over, giving Ethan and me a firsthand view of her cleavage. "I wouldn't know that, would I? It was addressed to Barbara," she said demurely.

"So you didn't open it."

"Oh, no." Her answer was too quick. "Barbara didn't like me to open things that might have evidence in them." She drained the pink fizzy drink.

Wow, Barbara had actually received a package regarding Arvin's case against Ike the day she was killed. No wonder the sheriff had been questioning Arvin.

Ethan, Boy Scout that he was, realized Maura was interrogating Jasmine. "Jasmine, I don't know that you need to be talking about a murder investigation here in public."

Jasmine smirked at him. "Nobody's told me not to talk. I guess I'll say whatever I like."

Maura gave a sidelong glance toward Ethan and leaned back in her chair. Huh, she wasn't much of a reporter.

When Jasmine started snapping her fingers and shrugging her shoulders to the music, I jumped in. "Jasmine, how'd you know the package had to do with Arvin Smelting's lawsuit if you didn't open it?"

Maura sat forward. Hmm, had she been hoping someone else would take the blame if Jasmine talked out of turn?

Jasmine waved her empty glass at one of the Dallas Cheerleader clones. "The return address, silly. It was somewhere in Texas and I knew she'd been talking to people there about some old papers dealing with Ike's land."

Maura ignored Ethan's glower. "But you don't know for sure it had anything to do with Arvin Smelting, do you?"

Jasmine rolled her eyes as the server came over. "One more like this one," she told the perky cowgirl hat, then turned back to Maura. "Listen, honey, right after Barbara opened it, she talked to Ike Hansfeldt on the phone. Then she called Arvin Smelting and made an appointment to meet him the very next day. You do the math on why she'd talk to Ike and then arrange a meeting with Arvin. Had to concern Arvin's case against Ike."

I inhaled with a gusting sound. So that corroborated what Ike had said about Barbara telling him she'd found new proof Arvin's claim was bogus.

Maura opened her mouth, but Vic pushed his chair back and said to Jasmine, "Dance?" With him holding her round the waist—her five-inch red heels weren't the entire cause of her unsteadiness—they went onto the dance floor.

With a rueful glance at me, Maura shrugged and watched them go.

I wished I knew what she was about to say to Jasmine, but I wasn't going to ask. I turned my back as she pulled Bodie up to dance.

It wasn't that great a night.

Chapter Seventeen

FRED AND I started off the next week poring over the digest reports again.

We found two industrial parcels that had been coded residential in error, but that was all the progress we made on Monday.

I did tell Fred about Billy Lee's concerns that his property was rated too high.

Fred puffed up like a little banty hen. "Serves him right. Let him appeal like everybody else."

"He did."

"Then the board of assessors will look at his appeal. Doubt the assessment will change, though. His property's worth a whole lot more than he claims and he knows it. Aw, he likes to appeal for the heck of it. He does it every year."

Fred was normally very laidback and easygoing and fair, but the mention of Billy Lee brought out a vindictive streak I'd never seen and never suspected he possessed. His frank eyes glittered, his breathing quickened, and his whole shrimp-sized body jiggled with tension.

Billy Lee never should have punched him in the nose.

On Tuesday as Kayleena left to go to lunch, Arvin Smelting came into the office.

The old saying, "He'd take the pennies off a dead man's eyes," applied to Arvin, according to my daddy. Nobody in the county liked him. The only people he could socialize with were people new to the area that haven't yet learned he'd stab them in the back at the first opportunity.

When Arvin pushed through the door, I was going from the coffeepot at the other end of the trailer back to my tiny office where Fred still labored over the digest reports. I tried to duck out of sight. Unfortunately, a small metal box doesn't leave much room to hide.

"I need my tag number," he boomed without preamble. He swept off his straw panama and fanned himself. Garbed in a white summer suit and white goatee, his portly figure reminded me of Colonel Sanders from KFC fame.

My grandparents had met the Colonel one time when they were visiting New Orleans and even had their picture made with him. It still sits on the buffet in their dining room. From listening to MeeMaw's fond reminiscences, I think meeting Colonel Sanders was the high point of that particular trip.

The kindly southern gentleman image, however, belied Arvin. He was not known for politeness. "I need it right away," he said, when Lucy and Miss Ruby kept working with their customers. He glared at me. "My tag number. Need it. Right away."

"Okay." I set down my coffee cup and came back to my computer.

When I typed his name, several vehicles popped up. "Are we talking about the BMW convertible, the Infiniti sedan, the Lexus hybrid or—"

"My red GMC pickup," he snapped. "The two-year-old red GMC pickup. The only truck I own. It's been stolen and that witch in the sheriff's office won't put in a report till I get the tag number."

He fanned his hat harder, looking off to the side and mumbling something about county employees not earning their money and hardworking folk like him paying taxes up the kazoo so they could give him sass.

I remembered the disinterested woman at the computer the day I went in looking for the sheriff. She had to be the one who wouldn't take Arvin's information without his tag number. The way he was grumbling, maybe he'd report her to the sheriff.

Enthused at such optimistic imaginings, I put on my

most sympathetic expression. Arvin Smelting wouldn't leave the tax office complaining about his service here.

"Stolen! I am so-o-o sorry, Mr. Smelting." Sugar wouldn't have melted in my mouth. I printed out a copy of his tag receipt. "There you are, sir. All your information's right here. That'll be a dollar, please."

His hand stopped halfway to taking the receipt. His mouth gaped. "You're charging me for my own tag receipt?" Veins popped out in his forehead. "You mean to tell me you people are so cheap you won't give me a copy of my own tag receipt?"

The other two customers turned to frown in disapproval.

"Not us," I muttered, heat rising up my neck. Darn it, I was blushing. I thought I'd outgrown that. "The State puts on the fee. It all goes to the State. Every penny. All of it."

The other customers *tsked, tsked.* I thought Arvin would have apoplexy. My heat blush faded as his anger flush grew.

Grumbling, he fished in his pocket and threw three quarters, two dimes and five pennies on the counter. One of the pennies rolled off and I had to climb down to get it, all the while listening to him grumble. "Blasted state. If the county don't take everything a man makes, the state does. And what they don't get, the feds get. This country used to be free but now look at where it is. I tell you, it's going to the dogs. We ain't had a good president since Eisenhower."

I popped back on my stool and tried to change the subject. *Show an interest in what the customer's saying,* my customer service class in Athens had stressed. *Understand his concerns and assure him you will do all you can to help resolve the problem.* "So, Mr. Smelting, when was your truck stolen?"

"How the hell should I know?" His face got redder. He might have a heart attack in my office! "I left it to get the oil changed last week. When I went to pick it up this morning, it was gone. Can't trust anybody to do their job anymore."

Not my problem but I could be sympathetic. "My goodness. Did nobody realize it was gone?"

He pouted. "Of course not. Ike thought I'd taken it, stupid ass. He said he figured I had a spare key and came by to get it over the weekend." He waved his hat impotently.

"I ask you. Why would I take my truck and not pick up the key I left with him?" As an afterthought, he added, "And still owing him for changing the oil, too. Does he think I'm that careless?"

I managed not to snort, all the while thinking, *he thought you sneaked your truck out to keep from paying him for the oil change.*

After a while, Arvin calmed down enough to take his tag receipt and leave.

"Poor Ike," Lucy said when her customer left. "That Arvin Smelting sure is a mean old grouch. I bet he wasn't shy about blaming the whole thing on Ike."

"Don't you know it. I'm kind of surprised he'd use Ike with the lawsuit and all."

Miss Ruby cut her eyes at me. "Ike's the cheapest place in town," she said like that explained everything.

I guess it did as far as Arvin was concerned.

***

ON WEDNESDAY, I met Lucy at Trim With Fitness for our workout. So far Wednesday had been the only day we'd been able to go, but we intended to pick up the pace soon by going after work a couple of nights.

Maybe next week. Or the next.

Once inside, we saw Rayla and Ethan. They were busy walking on side-by-side treadmills and talking about retrieval efforts of a car from the lake.

"Somebody went in the lake?" Lucy asked, taking the treadmill next to Ethan.

I took the one next to her and pressed ON. "Who?"

"Hah," Ethan scoffed. "How should we know? Hey, bring out your crystal ball, Rayla, and tell us whose car it was."

Rayla pretended to hold something in her hand. "Wooo wooo wooo, crystal ball, tell me whooo whooo whooo."

They burst out laughing. I ignored them. "But you do know a car went in? Where?"

I started to tread.

"They think a vehicle went off Mercy Bridge."

"Mercy Bridge?"

The long bridge went over the channel that marked the

county line. I hated driving over it because deep waters lay a hundred feet below and could be seen clearly through the metal meshlike span the car drove over. Two people had died jumping off it.

Bodie could have been a third.

People in town still talked with awe about his jump when he was seventeen. He'd made a bet with two friends. The friends chickened out, but Bodie didn't. He admitted himself, once he got older and developed some sense (and maybe sobered up, though he never would own up to it), that it was a wonder he hadn't killed himself.

Caleb had driven us across that bridge to the night club last night, then back across it bringing us home.

"What happened?" I asked.

Ethan shrugged. "Patrol car saw the metal railing was busted like maybe a car coming from the college went right through it."

"So they think somebody went in."

Rayla said, "They organized a dragging crew Monday and started yesterday afternoon. Didn't find anything yet but maybe they will."

Ethan had stopped to check his watch. "Whew, that's my half hour. I'm good to go. You ready, Rayla?" He looked past her. "Hey, Ike, you all finished, too?"

Ike came up, toting his little duffel with his gym stuff. "Yeah, going on home. Got to pressure wash the deck."

As before, Ike looked freshly scrubbed in khakis and open neck knit shirt. If he bathed before washing his deck, he must be some kind of clean freak.

Now, Corrie, there can be a lot worse things for Lucy to worry about in a man than him being too clean. Or knobby knees.

Rayla pushed her chest out toward Ike but as before, he detoured over to talk to Lucy. Scented soap permeated the air from several feet away. Or maybe it came from his cologne.

Smelled pretty good.

"So you don't know for sure anybody went in," I said to Ethan.

"No way they couldn't of gone in, the way that rail

looks. Doesn't mean we'll find them though. You know how deep that water is under that bridge."

I shivered, imagining being inside a car going down in the cold lake waters. Rayla, seeing she couldn't garner Ike's attention, got off her treadmill. She and Ethan started packing their stuff to leave.

"—but that Arvin Smelting sure seemed upset," I heard Lucy saying to Ike, talking about the stolen truck.

Ike shrugged and made a face. "Believe me, I heard way more about that dumb truck that I wanted to. I don't know what I could have done, though. The key was in the office after the truck got gone, hanging on the board right where I put it after I parked his truck."

"So nobody'd stolen it."

"Heck, no. I gave it back to him when he came in yelling and carrying on. And I told him flat, all I know is if he hadn't come got his truck, somebody else with a key must have."

"You think somebody else had a key?" Ethan asked, putting a sweaty towel round his neck.

Ike turned wide eyes on Ethan. "Like I told Duke, that truck was in my parking lot and the key was in my office when I left Friday. And when I came in Monday, the truck was gone and the key was still there. I figured Arvin had a spare."

"If I'd been you, I'd have figured he might be trying to get out of paying," I murmured.

Ike grinned. "Yep. That, too."

"Somebody must of hotwired it," Rayla said. She twisted open a bottle of flavored water. "Personally, I wouldn't care if Arvin Smelting ever finds it except he'll figure out a way to get the insurance to pay for another one if it doesn't turn up. He'll wangle him a new one, wait and see."

Ike and Ethan chortled, and even Lucy smiled. Arvin was not Mr. Popular.

"Maybe somebody stole it and drove it into the lake," I suggested. "Maybe through the bridge rail."

Ethan looked surprised. "That might be. Bet nobody's thought about Arvin's truck busting the rail."

"Boy," Ike said. "That'll make Arvin *really* mad if his truck turns up in the lake."

"Oh, I don't know," said Lucy. "He'd have a better case to make the insurance company replace it."

Our grins turned to groans.

***

THE NEXT DAY, another candidate for the vehicle smashing the bridge rail came to light. One of our customers brought in rumors about Barbara Prestotten's secretary. "She's gone missing," he said.

"Missing! Reckon she's taking a vacation?" Miss Ruby asked.

He shook his head. "Nope. Jasmine's roommate says she didn't come in Saturday night. None of her friends or family heard from her all weekend. Her sister was asking me if I'd seen her Sunday since she goes to my church. But she didn't show up." He added after some silent consideration, "Though I must say she doesn't always show up."

I remembered how tipsy Jasmine had been Saturday night. She probably couldn't have made it to church with a hangover.

But she and Joe seemed to be hitting it off. "Maybe she's off with a, um, a boyfriend."

Miss Ruby's customer shook his head as she handed him his tag renewal decal. "Nope. Sister says they talk every day and she can't get a hold of her no matter how many times she calls. She's been over to her place, but no sign of her or her car. Lilac's right worried, she is."

After he left, Miss Ruby grunted. "That woman. Bet you anything she's off with her latest married man somewhere."

Lucy turned to look at her. "She goes with married men?"

Miss Ruby didn't normally gossip or say bad things about people. This last had evidently slipped out because she put her lips together and looked away and refused to say more despite our coaxing.

Behind her back, Lucy and I exchanged knowing glances. We both believed Jasmine was definitely the kind of woman who went after married men.

On the other hand, there was that broken rail on the bridge.

Sherry heard the rumors about Jasmine being gone and called me to see what I knew. "We saw her at the club Saturday night. As much as she had to drink, do you think she would have driven herself home?"

I repeated what our customer said and Sherry voiced what I hated to think. "If she thought she was sober enough to drive, she would have had to come back over Mercy Bridge. You don't think she could have gone off the bridge, do you?"

"No. Of course not. Arvin Smelting had a truck stolen. I'd say joy riders were more likely to run it off the bridge deliberately than someone accidentally driving a car off. And besides, we don't know for sure a car went in. Right now all you've got is a broken rail."

On the other hand, the possibility of Jasmine's car being in the lake loomed large.

They found the car in the lake Friday, but didn't get it hoisted out till dawn Saturday. Sherry called me before I was awake.

This time, I looked at the caller ID before I answered. "Will you please stop calling me at ungodly times of the morning? I don't get up on weekends till nine. You know that. What in—"

"They found a car under the bridge last night but didn't get it pulled out till about an hour ago. Jasmine Musselman was inside."

I quieted. "She was?"

"Uh huh. It must have happened when she was coming back home after we saw her Saturday night. Caleb gets up early, and he heard on his scanner they'd located a vehicle. He called to see if they needed his tow truck but they already had one. They pulled the car out when it got light enough to see. She still had her seat belt on."

I felt sick. First Barbara, and now Jasmine. "How awful. She seemed so happy Saturday night."

"There's more."

"What?"

"The paint on her car looked like it'd been sideswiped."

My chest tightened. "Like somebody ran her off the bridge?"

"Uh huh. It's not far from us so Caleb went over. He got to talking to the tow truck driver and found out about the paint. I thought maybe you could pump Ethan."

"At seven in the morning?" My barely awakened state refused to take in Jasmine being dead and her car being sideswiped. I tried to pull myself together. "Besides, even if Ethan knows something, he won't tell me. He's turned into Mr. Clam. I think the sheriff must have written him up for talking out of turn."

"Oh." Disappointment came through the cell. "Go back to sleep then. I'll try somebody else."

But I couldn't go back to sleep. If Jasmine's car had been sideswiped, was it because she knew something about Barbara's murder? Or was it an accident? Maybe someone had run into her car earlier and left the marks and they didn't have anything to do with her going off the bridge at all.

It was an accident. Had to be. Jasmine was well on her way to being sloshed when we left, so it was logical she drove off the bridge all by herself.

Sure. Too bad I couldn't completely believe it.

I got up, fed the demanding Bill and cleaned his litter box. Put the used litter and empty cat food can in the trash and saw another empty can on top of used coffee grounds and filter.

Daddy had already fed the stinking cat before he left for wherever he was headed on his day off.

"You sorry liar," I told Bill, who looked extremely innocent. "Just like a male. It's a wonder you don't weigh twenty pounds."

His answer was to begin grooming himself, a hopeless cause since he's so scarred and his fur so tatty.

The coffeepot was still warm so I poured myself a cup and sat down to think about the situation.

Jasmine had wanted Ike to roll back her odometer. That meant she wasn't the upright person a legal secretary ought to be. The more I thought about it, the more it seemed that, if she was sideswiped, her death wasn't coincidental.

If Jasmine knew or suspected who'd murdered Barbara, and if the murderer suspected she knew, he or she could have wanted to keep Jasmine from telling. Why would Jasmine have been foolish enough to let a murderer know she knew his or her identity?

One reason stood out.

Maybe became she was blackmailing him or her. Would Jasmine stoop to blackmail? Was she that type of person?

Hey, if she was the type of person to date married men and roll back her odometer, she was the type of person who could blackmail someone.

Okay, so who would she be blackmailing? I'd seen her arguing with Ike. They'd obviously been at odds when I came in on them last week. Could she be blackmailing him? Why? Maybe something to do with Barbara's murder? But Ike had no reason to kill Barbara. Barbara thought Ike's case was so strong that she defied Arvin Smelting and threatened to sue him for slander when he accused her of malpractice.

No, Jasmine's argument with Ike must have been related to his refusal to tamper with her odometer.

Okay, so who else could Jasmine be blackmailing?

Dick Beaufort? Jasmine naturally knew him through her work with Barbara. And Dick had admitted he was at the murder scene. If he was lying about Barbara being dead when he got there, Jasmine might know somehow. But how? Had she been at Barbara's herself?

Or, remembering Miss Ruby's unintentional slip, was Dick one of the married men Jasmine dated? That might be more likely.

I sighed, trying to consider other suspects. Billy Lee immediately came to mind, but he had an alibi, according to Rayla. Hmmm.

Billy Lee always seemed to be in the vicinity whenever something bad happened. But he always seemed to have alibis. And he always managed to come out shining like a new penny.

Still, an alibi was an alibi and made it hard to blame him. Not that I wanted to. I did owe him for saving my life, even if he was a horse's ass.

How about Arvin Smelting? Sounded like he had a darned good reason to kill Barbara. I was sure the sheriff had checked on his whereabouts thoroughly, but I still wondered what he was doing when Barbara died. After all, alibis could be fabricated, according to the mysteries I read.

My head hurt. I needed to leave this to the sheriff.

Chapter Eighteen

MONDAY, FRED WENT back and fixed some errors on the assessors' digest data.

After I won a short wrangle with Dyson who looked unusually bleary-eyed, he pouted ungraciously but finally began downloading the corrected version of the assessors digest data to our system.

The download took all night but Tuesday morning, I started printing tax reports to compare to Fred's assessor reports. The numbers in both systems had to be the same.

Some things had changed so that they balanced, but most remained disparate.

Fred and I worked all that day and Wednesday. "We're definitely getting closer to a digest," Fred said as we got ready to leave. His little smiley face looked hopeful. "We'll get there."

Right. Like we hadn't been wrestling two weeks with the stupid data and still couldn't get everything to balance.

"You think?"

"Oh, yeah."

"By the way, did you check on Billy Lee's assessments?"

His face clouded. He gave a drawn-out sigh. I could see his inner struggle. "It looks like we may have been a little on the high side for his farm," he grudgingly said. "Looks like maybe Calvin went up on it because of the way prices were increasing a few years back. Looks like he didn't take into account the current market."

"So you'll reassess?"

He gave a tight smile. "Calvin will. I won't be responsible for what I do if I get around Billy Lee."

As if poor little Fred would have a chance against huge, pugnacious Billy Lee Woodhallen.

***

BY THE END of the week, we'd found more errors in the data and Fred started correcting them on the assessors' side.

The school board's accountant called on Friday. "We need some preliminary digest figures. We need to plan our budget for next year."

"We're working on them."

"We need them as soon as possible."

"We're working on them."

He harrumphed importantly. "We can't decide on a school millage till we know what to base it on. We need those figures right away."

"I can't pull them out of thin air."

He turned whiny. "Give me an estimate. A ballpark figure. That's all we need here."

I got irritable. "Look, I don't have one. And I can't work on getting one with you harassing me. Why don't you use last year's figures?"

He squawked.

I hung up on him.

Fred, sitting beside my table that served as a desk, looked sympathetic. "He's been after me, too. I don't answer when I see his number come up. Guess that's why he's bugging you."

I decided Fred's solution might be best and started looking at the caller ID screen. After the county accountant called a couple of times, I stopped taking her calls, too.

That led to the county manager barging in. Not knowing I didn't want to talk to him, Lucy let him back behind the counter. Teague Longbottom was a meek man with a weak chin and a prominent Adam's apple. He reminded me of a clumsy puppy. When he came into the office, crowded as it was, he knocked over a half-full box of college tag plates on a shelf beside the door. I caught it before it hit the keyboard but not before the corner pressed some keys down.

Fred gasped.

I looked to see what he was gasping at.

To my horror, the digest figures on the screen were going haywire. No, they were disappearing!

Teague Longbottom didn't notice. "I need to know when we can expect a preliminary digest," he said apologetically. "Remonica says you won't answer her calls when she's trying to find out when we'll get the figures and we need to know. We've got to work on our budget."

"Yeah, that's right. I've stopped answering her calls. And the school accountant's, too." I shifted my glare from the screen to him. "And your guess as to when we'll have the figures ready is as good as mine."

"What?" He tried to puff up, but he didn't have enough self-esteem to pull it off. "We need those figures. We can't work out a millage till we get those figures. When are you going to have them ready?"

"Well, since you just deleted the entire digest by pushing that tag box down on the delete key and we're going to have to start all over, your guess really is as good as mine." I pointed to the computer.

"What?" He looked at the screen.

"Don't you know any other words besides *what?*"

"What?" He stared at me like I was crazy. "You—you—we need those figures."

"Yeah, and I need that data you just deleted, too."

He drew himself up and stared at me as if not believing what I'd said.

I glared. "The. Data. You. Deleted."

He looked at the screen one more time before he left, muttering.

"Never mind," Fred said placidly. "I've got the printout here of the errors I need to fix. Dyson's going to have to download it again anyway after I fix them."

But a problem arose. Dyson had taken the Friday off—probably for one of his pot parties—and so it would be Monday before he'd be available to start the download again. "Next week's the last week of June. You're supposed to get me the digest by July first."

Fred nodded. "And it's almost ready. Once we get these errors corrected, you should be good to go. Not much else for you to do once we get it balanced." He beamed. "Usually with Mr. Jethro, we worked right down to the digest due date and here we are a whole month ahead. You're doing great, Corrie."

Right. This digest thing was taking forever. I never before appreciated how much work it was.

Bill and Sherry let me sleep late Saturday. When I came down to breakfast in my shabby housecoat that had once been white until I'd washed red boxers with it, Bodie was eating breakfast with Momma and Daddy.

I did a U-turn to go back upstairs and get dressed in shorts and enhanced bra that showed off my curves in a sleeveless knit shirt. A little mascara and blush didn't go amiss, either.

I needed all the confidence I had to face Bodie. Hanging out with my family the way he used to do before he jilted me. Eating breakfast with them like before he'd left me at the altar. I could still see all those shocked faces as he strode up the aisle alone, while the preacher flailed in the baptismal pond—he'd stepped back when I bristled at Bodie and fallen in—and I stood watching Bodie's back disappear. That was the most humiliating moment of my entire life.

When I returned to the kitchen, he and Daddy were gone, and Momma was taking dishes out of the dishwasher.

I got a cup of coffee. "So what are Daddy and Bodie up to?" I asked casually.

Momma sent a speculative glance my way. "Bodie's helping your daddy with some computer stuff."

I tasted the coffee and started to feel human. "Not a blog. Is that what they're working on? Tell me it isn't."

Momma shrugged. "How should I know? I don't do computers, you know that. They're down in the basement is all they said." She eyed a pan she was holding. "Do you know how this dent got in my good casserole pan?"

I recognized the pan that had held the awful casserole I'd dropped on the floor. "I don't cook."

"It looks like someone took and bent it deliberately."

She tried to straighten it on a corner of the counter.

I prudently left the kitchen but didn't go downstairs. I wasn't interested in what Bodie did or didn't do, but it'd be nice if he left my daddy out of his plans, the dog.

Later as I started clothes to wash, Daddy and Bodie emerged from the basement through the utility room.

Daddy's face beamed. "—put the picture of that eight-pointer up and some of them fish from our deep sea trip. Oh, it's gonna be great."

I started the machine going. "Daddy, you aren't doing a blog, are you?"

Bodie laughed, dark lashes narrowing so they looked like black caterpillars.

I tried not to melt.

"Right now it's a website." Daddy led us back into the kitchen. "I'm putting pictures and stuff up on it. Bodie says I ought to work out how to keep that part up before I start blogging."

"O-ka-ay."

Daddy pulled a couple of beers out of the fridge and handed one to Bodie. "The website looks real good. Bodie knows all about stuff like that."

"I bet. Isn't it a little early for drinking?"

He looked at his watch. "It's lunchtime."

Sure enough, it was.

When Daddy sought the bathroom, Bodie brought up Vic.

"Who?" I had to think before I remembered. "Oh, Vic. Actually, he's giving a housewarming party this weekend at his new lake house. He called and asked me to drop by."

Bodie knew when to hold back. "I see." He narrowed those steady blue eyes into slits between black fringes.

I started to tell him I was going. But I never can lie convincingly and I always feel guilty afterward which is irritating in situations like this when I desperately want to lie convincingly. Goaded, I said, "Don't look at me like that. I'm not going."

He let out his breath.

"Not because you told me not to get mixed up with him,

either. When he called, I already had plans." Lucy, Rayla and I were going to a movie over in the next county, but Bodie didn't need to know that. "So don't think I won't go another time."

"Vic's bad news, Corrie. He's a...a bad man." Worry lines creased his forehead.

"Seemed nice enough to me." There might have been an undercurrent about the man I didn't care for, but no sense in telling Bodie that. I'd learned a long time ago to trust my instincts about people. Sometimes they were right and sometimes they weren't, but they were a good indicator of whether I wanted to know somebody better or not.

Bodie, for instance. I'd known right away he was somebody I wanted to go out with.

Yeah, and look how that turned out. Some instincts.

"Anyway, thanks for the warning, Bodie, but you can keep your opinion to yourself. I'll make up my own mind."

He smiled faintly. "I'm sure you will."

***

SUNDAY, RAYLA, LUCY, and I went to the movies in the next county.

I drove. Since my little Hyundai was still in the body shop, Momma let me borrow her convertible.

We put the top down and played her oldie music loud like we were three hot babes. We even sang "Fun, Fun, Fun" along with the Beach Boys, substituting "her momma's car" for "her daddy's car," till we got tired and started talking.

Rayla told about the investigation into Jasmine's death. "They're checking to see if Arvin's truck is the one that sideswiped her car."

I couldn't risk a look to see if she was joking. No way was I going to dent Momma's car.

Lucy inhaled. "Arvin's truck that was stolen?"

Rayla wasn't joking. "Uh huh. Some kids found it in the park behind Barbara Prestotten's house, hid in the woods. It has a navy blue streak on its fender and side, like it might of hit something."

"What color is Jasmine's car?" I asked.

"Navy."

I clutched the wheel, realized I was clutching the wheel, and loosened my grip. "Could Arvin have done it?"

Rayla shrugged. "Last time anyone saw Jasmine was at that new nightclub. Arvin says he was at home all weekend, but Jamil Ogarty can't find anybody to vouch for him."

So either Arvin had picked up his truck and run Jasmine off the road or someone had stolen it and run her off the road. I went over the conversation that night, when Jasmine talked about the mail Barbara got regarding Arvin's lawsuit.

"Rayla, has anyone got in touch with those people in Texas? The ones who sent that packet of papers to Barbara? Jasmine said something about them at the club."

"Oh, yeah. Jamil checked on them first thing. Jasmine threw the mailing label away but he talked to the post office and traced it back that way. When he talked to the Texas people, they said all they sent was a bunch of old, falling-apart papers. Duke thinks they may be connected but we don't know because we didn't find any papers like that in Barbara's house or office."

"Can you get copies?"

She snorted. "The dumb clucks sent the originals. They said they'd been cleaning out their attic and were about to throw them out when Barbara Prestotten called and asked for 'em. They said there wasn't anything important in them. Nothing but a bunch of old deeds and letters and things they didn't need and didn't see any reason to keep."

"Dumb clucks is right," I muttered.

"That sounds like stuff that would confirm Ike's case," Lucy said from the back, though the rear seat was so close to the front she could almost have been sitting with us. "Ike said Barbara called him the morning before she was murdered, told him not to worry, she had evidence proving he owned that land free and clear. You remember?"

"Guess his new lawyer'll have to start all over," said Rayla. "May be hard without those originals. Sure will help Arvin out in his lawsuit."

We all grunted. Not a one of us didn't think Arvin had murdered Barbara and Jasmine.

I couldn't stop mulling it over. "Jasmine said she didn't know what was in the package. Why would Arvin—why would anybody want to kill her?"

We drove quietly for a few minutes.

"Unless," Lucy said hesitantly, "Jasmine lied and she saw what was in the papers. And if she saw them, maybe the murderer found out she knew what they were, what they proved."

"He would sure have found out if she'd been blackmailing him," I finished grimly. In the cold light of the new facts, what little I'd learned about Jasmine meant blackmail definitely fit in with her character. Or lack of it.

"Duke's looking at that possibility," Rayla said. "On the other hand, Dick Beaufort was having an affair with her. She might have known something about his visit to Barbara's house that Dick wanted to cover up. Or Dick might have wanted to kill Jasmine for something as simple as her threatening to tell his wife he was doing her."

Lucy and I both gasped. The Mustang wobbled.

Lucy stuttered, "D-Dick was having an affair with Jasmine?"

A memory of seeing Dick when I was at the tax conference came back out of the blue. The woman with fishnet stockings pressed up against him. Jasmine's fishnet stockings at the club the other night. "*That's* who I saw him with in Athens!"

"Watch the road, Corrie. Yep, Dick and Jasmine were getting it on. Real hot and heavy. Gossip's already started going round," Rayla said. "Everybody in town that don't know about it will pretty soon."

I kept the convertible in its lane. "Dick hasn't been cleared of Barbara's murder, then?"

"Corrie, Corrie." Good grief, Rayla was as patronizing as Ethan. "He admits he was in her house though he claims it was later than when they think she was murdered. But he has a motive, weak as it might be. Yeah, Duke's still looking at him, too."

I let her snarkiness pass. "But how would Dick have got Arvin's truck keys?"

Out of the corner of my eye, I saw her shrug.

"The keys aren't locked up in Ike's shop," Lucy said from right behind my ear. "There's a big board by the front desk where he hangs them. When I picked up my car, all he had to do was go into the office and get the key. So during the daytime, when he's out to lunch or changing oil in the garage area, anybody could have sneaked it out, made a copy, and brought it back."

"We know all that already. We got it all under control," Rayla said complacently.

She was starting to sound as know-it-all as Ethan. Must be the job.

***

ON MONDAY AFTERNOON, Lucy and I went by the gym after work. I didn't want to go so late, but Lucy's enthusiasm carried the day. "I'm already seeing progress," she said. "I've lost three pounds since we joined. If we start going twice a week, I'll lose more."

"Um." If anything was worse than someone flaunting the amount of weight they've lost, I don't know what it would be. Especially when my own scales refused to show any change.

Rayla wasn't at the gym, but Ethan was. He and another deputy, a little red-headed guy I'd met before who looked like he might be sixteen at most, were busy lifting weights. Ethan stopped when we came in and intercepted us. "You headed for the treadmills?"

"Yep."

He made a face. "You need to do some weightlifting to get your muscles toned. Walking's okay, but if you want to get in shape you need to use the weights. I'd say you need to start off slow and build up over a couple of weeks. Jim over there's the weight trainer. Get him to help you."

I have no idea why I ever dated Ethan. He grows more obnoxious every time I see him. "Maybe later." Yeah, like next year. Or in ten years.

I stepped on the treadmill and pushed the ON button.

Nothing happened. "Oh, shoot. Now what?" I punched the ON several times. Still nothing happened.

Just my luck. Maybe a blown circuit?

I scratched my head, then leaned over to look at the bottom of the handle bar where a reset button poked out. I pushed it.

Nothing happened.

"Huh. That ought to make it start if it got offline. I wonder why—"

A sudden lurch knocked me forward.

"Somebody unplugged it," Ethan said from the side. "I plugged it back. It's good to go now."

Still stumbling, I snagged a handle to break my fall, but landed face down on the belt anyway. Lucky it was an easy landing. Except for...

"Hey! Hey! Turn it off!"

"Good lord, Corrie. Can't you even stay standing up?"

Even through my squealing, I could hear Ethan's disapproval.

I barely noticed. I had a bigger problem. My hair was being pulled out by the roots. "Stop this thing!"

Lucy saw my dilemma. "Corrie! Help her, Ethan! Unplug it, unplug it!"

He did, but too late. My hair was well and truly caught.

Lying half on and half off the belt, I gingerly moved my limbs.

Nothing seemed broken, although my position, partly on my side and partly on my stomach, was more than uncomfortable.

My head wouldn't move. When I tried a gentle tug to free my hair, an involuntary *oww* came out.

This must be how being scalped feels.

"It's okay, the machine's stopped." Ethan's voice sounded far away. "You can get up now."

"Easy for you to say." I tried to grab hold of enough hair to take some pressure off my head and free myself but there wasn't room to grab. I couldn't get my fingers between the conveyor belt opening and my head.

Lucy saw me trying to work my hair loose. She bent down and started to help.

"Eeeeeek!"

She stopped and bit her lip. "It's no use. We're going to have to cut you loose."

Cut me loose? "Aigghhhh! No-o-o-o!"

Lucy ignored my screams. "We need scissors. Ethan, run down to the beauty shop and see if they have some scissors they can loan you."

Ethan protested. "Why don't we give it a good yank and see—?"

"No!" My scalp was already on fire.

"Ethan! Her hair's already being pulled out of her head." Lucy pushed him. "Go."

"Oh, all right. Seems to me we could do this without involving half the people in the gym, though. This is downright embarrassing," he mumbled as he walked away.

Lucy leaned over again. I could see her face, but behind her, the legs and hands of other people were visible. A lot of legs and hands. Everyone was gathering to view the spectacle.

No time to worry about them. Bigger problems loomed. "Don't let Ethan cut my hair," I told Lucy.

"No, no. I'll do it. Better yet, maybe one of the beauticians can do it. They'll do a better job." She tried another gentle tug.

"Owwww!"

"Sorry," she said, and then screamed over my head, "Hurry up with those scissors! Bring a beautician, too!"

"Lucy, don't worry." Plaid shorts covering skinny legs appeared at the front of all the legs blocking my view. "I've called nine one one."

Déjà vu. No way! "I am not going to the emergency room! I am not! You better un-call nine one one right now, Ike Hansfeldt!"

The crowd edged closer.

"Is she scalped? I knew a man whose sister's hair got caught in one of those paper shredders and—"

"Why in the world did she put her head down there?"

"Lucky she wasn't skinned alive."

The next fifteen minutes were filled with more of the same. I closed my eyes and tried to pretend I was elsewhere.

About the same time Ethan returned with a hairdresser—

"Sorry to take so long. Rory here's working by herself tonight. She had to rinse out a perm before she could get away."—the EMTs arrived.

One took charge. "Let's have a look." He saw my face and staggered backward. "Oh. Oh, my."

"What's wrong, Charlie?" the other one said.

"It's her again."

I closed my eyes and wished I could be swallowed up by one of the machines.

While the EMTs oh'ed and ah'ed and inspected my head, the beautician pushed to the front of the crowd. I opened my eyes to see scissors flashing. *Not my hair!* "No, no, please! I'm sure there's some other way."

"Looks like cutting it all off is the only way you're gonna get loose," Charlie said. "Boy, I never seen anything like this. How'd you manage to get it caught? What were you doing laying down on the belt anyway?"

The scissors neared. I grew desperate. "I'm sure there's something—"

"Don't worry, hon." The beautician bent over. "I style short 'dos for lots of my customers. It'll be fine."

Oh, lord, please, no. Not a beautician who works in a beauty shop inside a gym. No, no, no, please.

In a few minutes she had me freed. I managed to sit up and lean back against the treadmill, sore but mostly intact. I put my hand up to gauge the missing parts and froze.

"Now now, hon," Rory said, accurately evaluating my reaction. "It's not as bad as it feels. I just had to cut the one side that short. We can work it out. You come down to the shop when you're more composed and I'll get you all fixed up. These asymmetrical 'dos are all the rage in places."

I felt hysterics welling. "Get me fixed up? With what? A wig? Or will you shave the rest of my hair so I look like Sinead O'Connor? Ohhhh." I put my head between my knees.

"Get the stretcher," Charlie told the other EMT in an aside I wasn't meant to hear. "She's fainting. I think she needs checking out by a doctor."

I raised my head, the rage inside me threatening to set

me on fire and incinerate anyone foolish enough to stand too close.

"Are you out of your mind? I will NOT get on your stretcher! I will NOT ride in your blooming ambulance! I will NOT go to the ER looking like this! I won't go anywhere with you, period!"

Cowed, the two EMTs stepped back. A murmur arose from the crowd. Fringe onlookers also moved back a pace or two.

"Now, now," Lucy intervened. "I don't think you're hurt that bad, are you, Corrie?"

"Better listen to the EMTs," Ike put in.

"You!" I managed to get to my feet. "You and your *Better go to the ER, you know what happened to that actress, take her away, boys!* You, you, you…meddler!" I grabbed him by his faded T-shirt with both hands. "I'll tell you what you can do with your advice, mister! You can stick it up your—"

"Ma'am." The fresh-faced deputy stepped in, making me release Ike's shirt. "There's no call for hysteria."

"I'm not hysterical!" I lunged for Ike again. "I'm gonna kill him!"

Ike prudently stepped back out of range.

The deputy gulped. "Now, ma'am, you don't mean…"

He fell back as I struggled for words.

Lucy put a hand on my shoulder to keep me from following Ike.

The crowd moved away from him, making him a path like they were afraid I'd come after him and go ballistic in their midst.

Ethan, the little prig, pursed his lips. "Look, Corrie, you ain't got no call to act like—"

I turned on him. "And you!" Saliva spewed from my mouth. A drop or two may have splattered his shirt. "I ought to sue you for damages! Plugging in a treadmill while I was on it! Knowing it was turned on! Knowing what would happen!"

He fell back as far as Ike. His brown Huckleberry Finn eyes got big. "I didn't—I never…"

Lucy cleared her throat.

"Come on, Corrie. Let me help you over to the beauty shop. Rory said she'd make it a point to work you in tonight before she closes up. I think the café has frozen yogurt, too. Let's get some and calm ourselves down. It'll be fine once Rory works on it, you'll see."

***

MOMMA WAS HOME when I got in. She and Daddy sat in their side by side recliners in front of the big TV, watching Daddy's favorite movie, *The Man From Snowy River*.

She glanced over, and then sat up so fast her recliner nearly popped her out. "What in the love of God happened to you?"

"I decided to get a haircut." I casually ran a hand through my new waif 'do, maybe an inch on top and not half an inch on the sides.

"Looks real good, too," Daddy said without turning away from the bunkroom fight.

"You haven't worn your hair that short since you were..." Momma thought a minute, still staring. "I don't think your hair's been that short since you were born."

I waved a hand and tried to bluff it out. "Time for a change. Long hair's out of style."

Momma looked doubtful.

"Looks real nice," Daddy said again, glued to his big TV.

As I turned to retreat upstairs, the last words I heard were, "Lose the bottle, Curly. I done it once and I'll do it again," from the screen.

If I'd had a bottle at the gym, I think I would have used it on Ethan.

Or Ike.

Chapter Nineteen

AT WORK THE next day, Miss Ruby gawked. "What in God's name did you do to your hair?"

I passed it off. She'd hear about my accident soon enough.

Kayleena called, said she wouldn't be in. I hoped it wasn't her boyfriend again.

With her out, Miss Ruby, Lucy and I stayed so busy I didn't have time to work on the digest with Fred. Just as well, since Dyson was evidently taking the day off, too.

About noon, after Lucy left for lunch, James Cleuny, one of the inept deputies who'd acted as my bodyguard when Mr. Jethro's murderer was trying to kill me, sauntered into the trailer. Middle-aged with a paunch but ever optimistic about attracting another wife, he stopped and put his thumbs in his belt. From in front of the door, he inspected the metal walls, then the counter barring his way.

"Boy, that's some nice cabinetry, ain't it? Ol' Bert does real good work. Shame they couldn't get you a bigger trailer for them pretty counters he made you."

Miss Ruby sniffed.

I asked coldly, "Do you need something?"

"Nah. I was heading to Joanie's for lunch and Ethan asked me to stop by." He noticed my hair and his forehead creased. "You got you a new haircut."

I showed my teeth. "Yes. Yes, as a matter of fact, I did. What did Ethan want?"

He nodded. "Thought so. I hear women like men noticing

things like that about 'em. I'm practicing, trying to get this lady who works at the sandwich shop to go out with me."

"Good approach. Maybe it'll work for you."

And maybe it won't. "Ethan asked you to come by?"

He pulled his eyes away from my hair. "Oh. Uh, yeah. He wanted me to let you know Kayleena's in custody."

What the heck did that mean? "Custody? What kind of custody? Kayleena's out today. She's sick. Why did Ethan say she's in custody?"

He looked around with interest. "Say, I bet you don't even have room for an office in here, do you? This is kind of like a submarine, ain't it? Course it's got windows. And it isn't under water but—"

I coughed. "What exactly did Ethan mean by *Kayleena's in custody?*"

"Huh?" His attention came back to me. "Oh. You know. Locked up. She's in jail."

"What?"

Miss Ruby's neck swiveled till she could gawk at James. "Locked up! Land sakes, you don't mean it."

James nodded. "Yeah. Caught her trying to throw packs of cigarettes over the back fence to an inmate."

I closed my mouth. "Georgie?"

James dropped his thumbs and looked around as if expecting Georgie to appear. "Nah, there ain't nobody coming in. Musta been a car parking out front."

"No. I mean, was the inmate her boyfriend Georgie?"

"Huh?" He turned away from the front door. "Whose boyfriend?"

I ground my teeth. "Was Kayleena trying to throw the cigarettes to her boyfriend Georgie? Or maybe you know him as Jorge," I added, giving it the Mexican pronunciation.

"Hore-hay. Yeah, that's the one."

I gathered my scattered wits. Kayleena was locked up and I needed a clerk. Okay, I didn't like the idea of her trying to slip cigarettes to a jail inmate, but I needed her. Bad. "When's she getting out?"

"Getting out?" He put his thumbs in his belt again and looked at me like I'd lost my mind.

"Surely to goodness throwing a box of cigarettes over the fence isn't a federal crime. Can't she bond out? I need her back at work."

"Ooh." He scratched his head. "Well, thing is, she'd hid a screwdriver in one cigarette box and a metal file in another. That makes it a felony. So you see—"

"Screwdriver? File? *Felony?*"

"Yeah. The grand jury'll arraign her and then she may be able to bond out till trial, but they caught her red-handed. Aiding and abetting a prisoner's escape is a felony and that means she's automatically fired from the county, no matter what sentence she gets."

I began to hyperventilate.

"My land," Miss Ruby breathed, eyes getting big. They gleamed when she reached for her phone to spread the news. "I allus knew that gal was trouble. All them tattoos and bad language and not a bit ashamed about chasing that man up here from Atlanta."

The rest of the week was spent dealing with Rick, the personnel manager. I had to go to him with my tail between my legs and beg for his assistance.

Once he got over his shock at my new hair-do, he turned out to be pretty helpful. According to him, James was right. I had no choice but to fire Kayleena. Which was fine since I didn't need a lawbreaker working in our office.

Even if she was knowledgeable about tags and had so much experience in salvage and vehicles imported from out of the country. Not to mention big trucks.

Oh, well. Regrets never changed anything.

Rick himself got Sheila to do the official letter sent out to Kayleena terminating her employment. He also did the paperwork so I could hire Dick Beaufort's cousin's daughter. I didn't want her, but with the fiasco my insisting on Kayleena had created, I took her. Especially when Rick said the last batch of applications could still be used, and we wouldn't have to re-advertise if I hired one of those applicants I'd already interviewed.

After my snippy behavior toward him a few weeks ago, he was nicer to me than I warranted. But then he was getting what he'd wanted all along: making me hire the commission chairman's relative.

A timid girl, she wasn't anything like Kayleena so she shouldn't turn out to be a felon.

And maybe she wouldn't turn out to be anything like Dick Beaufort.

I hoped she could learn tags.

As I left late that day, I confronted Dick himself.

He jumped like a scalded cat when we almost collided. He carried a suit and white shirt along with one of those leather shaving kits men tote their stuff around in. He tried to hide it behind the hanging clothes.

"Spending the night in your office?"

I was joking but he turned bright red. Too late, I remembered he'd been caught with his hand in the cookie jar. Maybe his wife had thrown him out.

My face heated up hot enough to match his.

"I, uh, I, uh…" His shoulders slumped. To my dismay, a tear rolled down one cheek. "What does it matter? Everyone's going to know soon enough. Tanya's… My wife and I…"

He shook his head, too distraught to go on.

"I'm so sorry," I said automatically. I couldn't stand to see anyone cry, even an arrogant, oily politician like Dick. Rummaging in my purse produced a wad of tissues. One looked clean. "Here."

He took it and blew his nose. "You may not have heard about Jasmine and me."

"Uh, well, I did hear something."

He groaned. "I guess everybody knows. When Tanya found out, she went ballistic."

A bruise on his jaw along with what looked like a scratch mark on his neck half concealed by his golf shirt's collar, made me wonder exactly how ballistic Tanya had gone.

"Anyway," he said, composing himself, "I decided I'd better stay out of her way for a while. So yes, I am spending the night here on the sofa in the break room." He hastened to add, "I've talked to the other commissioners and they say it's okay with them. And it's only temporary. Till Tanya takes me back."

He sniffed and wiped his eyes.

If Tanya took him back. I'd be for cleaning out his side of the closet and packing up his stuff if I were Tanya, but you never could tell about people. Maybe she'd cool down. "Sure. Well. I guess I better get back to the office. See you later."

He hadn't made one single remark about my hair. Maybe it wasn't as bad as I thought.

Or, more likely, he was too upset to take it in. Poor thing, he did look pretty sick. Too bad he didn't have any friends to bunk with. If he'd been nicer to...

Come on. Dick Beaufort's sleeping arrangements weren't my problem. Jasmine's death wasn't my problem, either, but Dick's admission started me mulling. If Tanya found out about Jasmine before Saturday, would she have been angry enough to kill her?

But Tanya hadn't known, not if she was just now throwing Dick out. Besides, how could she have gotten hold of Arvin's truck? No. Seemed to me either Dick or Arvin himself must have taken the truck and sideswiped Jasmine's car. Or someone else who knew it was there and who had a key.

One of Arvin's employees?

I mentally shook myself.

None of this was my problem. Duke Duval was competent. More than competent. He and that Ogarty suit-person would do the grunt work and doubtless arrest someone sooner or later. For both murders, Jasmine's and Barbara Prestotten's.

I believed the sheriff knew his business. I had to believe that because I sure couldn't take his job on. I had enough on my plate.

***

THE FIRST MONDAY in July, my Hyundai came out of the shop looking pretty good for what it'd been through. I thankfully turned in the Smart Car. It was cute but it did have drawbacks, like barely room for me and a bag of groceries.

At the office, Dick Beaufort's relative sat at the counter observing Miss Ruby and Lucy wait on customers. Zara

Distell had started work barely in time to claim holiday pay for the Fourth of July which was the next day.

Zara might look like a scared rabbit but she put on an upbeat air about becoming a tag clerk. "Lots better than flipping burgers," she said cheerfully.

Little did she know. She'd find herself another job when she started actually working the counter and dealing with our crazy customers.

Maybe not, my better self urged. *Don't be so negative. Give the girl a chance.*

It was hard to be optimistic, though. From her demeanor, Zara was way too shy to deal with the belligerent types coming through our office. I bet the first time someone said something nasty to her, she would burst into tears.

Stop it! No negativity, remember? No negativity!

I let Lucy start her on simple tag renewals while Fred and I pored over the digest data again.

Once he found two big errors and I found a typo, everything balanced: the residential parcels, the homestead exemptions, the special exemptions, the commercial parcels, the industrial parcels, the historical buildings, the agricultural parcels...

Our downloaded data had been successfully reconciled with the assessors' original data.

Search as he might, Fred couldn't find anything else that needed correcting. Ignorant as I was about the whole process, I made no attempt to look.

Fred got up and stretched, threatening to knock a box of college tags off the crammed shelf above him. "Yep, I think we'll be through when we fix these and Dyson does one last download," he said in his prissy way. "Then we should be able to put this thing to bed, Corrie. Anything else we find wrong should be small enough to correct on both our computer and yours."

He beamed.

I beamed.

A new employee, my car repaired, and the digest done.

I would have done a happy dance if there'd been enough room.

When we looked for Dyson, however, Sheila told us he'd taken the July 4th week for vacation.

Darn him, he knew we'd need him to download.

On the other hand, his absence meant Fred and I wouldn't have to work over the holiday to chaperone him. I'd be free to enjoy the festivities.

Chapter Twenty

OUR TOWN DOES the Fourth of July up in style. A band composed of volunteer members, many who are high school kids and others who participated in band one to fifty years in the past, march in the parade every year. Troops of Boy Scouts, Cub Scouts, Girl Scouts and Brownies show up to add enthusiasm, but the biggest highlight is a collection of classic cars owned by various Medder Rose citizens and others from as far away as Iowa.

Different businesses have floats and in election years, so do politicians. Then you have various other industries that get involved, too, like the plastics plant, the canning facility, the marble quarry and the apple orchards.

Oh, our county believes in going all out for the Fourth.

This year, at Sherry's urging, I had agreed to ride with her on a float Caleb sponsored, to help throw candy to the children who always lined the streets. The parade would start in the parking lot of the Fairhurst Plastics manufacturing plant west of town. From there the participants would wend a mile to the square, trek around the square, and stagger another mile to a middle school where the parade would disband.

I parked my Hyundai at the middle school so we'd have transport back to the starting point once the parade was over. Sherry followed me to drive me back over to the parade assembly site.

Other car dealers used convertibles or antique cars for their entries in the parade, but Sherry and Caleb had designed an entire float using a car carrier. With a little help from me the past Saturday, and a lot of help all week from Caleb's employees, the transformed Freightliner stood prepared for its day in the spotlight.

The behemoth carrier, its frame swathed in streamers, artificial flowers, and greenery, could carry five convertibles, all with their tops lowered. The two bottom ones would be without passengers, as would the BMW over the cab.

Sherry planned to sit with Caleb in the red Cadillac roadster on top while hunky-but-dumb-as-a-doorknob Joe and I would ride in the silver Lexus directly behind them at the rear. All five cars had banners proclaiming CALEB'S CAR CORRAL in easy-to-read letters as did the front and sides of the cab.

When Sherry and I arrived, candy boxes beside the carrier waited to be lifted into the two convertibles. Sorting through the goodies, I found a miniature Snickers bar to eat while I stared up at the convertibles.

The cars loaded on top were well over my head. I would be inside one. Way up in the air. Way up there above the ground. No way down.

Did I really want to be stuck that far up?

In the cold light of a bright July sun, Sherry's grand plan seemed ridiculous. This couldn't possibly be safe. The upper cars were much too high.

Were they securely fastened onto the frame? What if one rolled off backward with someone in it? Someone like me?

Someone could get hurt.

I could get hurt.

While I tried to decide if I wanted to be an occupant in the Lexus, someone came up behind me.

"Looks dangerous to me. You really gonna ride up there?" a familiar voice asked.

I spun around. "Bodie."

He wore denim shorts and a red, white and blue sleeveless tee that showed off his biceps. A baseball hat kept his dark curls in tow but his lashes extended as long and black as ever.

He jerked his head toward the top of the carrier but couldn't quite hide the twitch at the corner of one lip.

"Well? Are you?"

"Um, um…" I started to waffle.

Stick to your guns, girl, and stop thinking about his mouth! Don't you see he's trying to tell you what to do? As usual.

I squared my shoulders. "I certainly am."

He raised his brows. "With your track record, you may be asking for trouble. It's not hard to imagine you falling off. Considering your past and all."

"I don't value your opinion in the least so you may as well keep it to yourself."

He chuckled, and the low sexy sound evoked a warm syrupy feeling deep in my stomach.

I showed him my back but couldn't escape his cedar scent. "As soon as Sherry gets here, I'm climbing up."

"Suit yourself."

"Thank you. I will."

"I like your hair."

I had forgotten it but a hand went up involuntarily. I couldn't help but glance over my shoulder. "I, I, I guess you heard what happened."

"Caleb said something." He continued to eye my new 'do. "I like it, though. It suits you. Makes you kind of look like, um, that redheaded girl with Bruce Willis in that sci-fi flick."

"Not Bruce Willis?"

He laughed. "You got too many curves for that, Fluf—"

He stopped and we both pretended to study the car carrier and didn't realize that he'd started to call me Fluffball.

When Sherry came up, she greeted Bodie and turned to me. "I see you know."

"Know what?"

A coughing spell hit Bodie after which he became extremely interested in the next float.

Sherry made a moue. "Caleb didn't tell me till this morning that Joe left yesterday for Guatemala. He's going to visit his family."

"Guatemala? He's not here? So—" I narrowed my eyes.

"So Caleb asked Bodie to ride with us." Her expression pleaded with me to understand.

I opened my mouth to object but wavered.

I'd already told Bodie I was riding regardless of what he said.

Bodie understood my dilemma. "You girls can ride in the front car. Caleb and I can ride behind you."

Sherry's brow puckered. "Girls in one car and men in the other? Won't that seem a little, uh, strange?"

"You're both so gorgeous, nobody'll be looking past the two of you anyway."

Deflated, I pulled myself together. So what if Bodie didn't want to ride with me? Maybe he didn't want Maura to see me beside him. Maybe she was prone to jealousy.

Doesn't matter. Not my problem. "That'll work. Okay with you, Sherry?"

Sherry was smart enough to see the question was rhetorical. "Sure."

The car carrier was parked in line but since the parade wasn't ready to start, the three of us strolled around to check out the other floats. A lot of time and money had been spent on some of them. Others showed imagination.

Trudell's Pick-It-Yourself Farms, known mainly for its corn maze and mini-petting zoo, sponsored a flatbed truck with low stake sides. The bottom was strewn with loose hay. Random baskets of squash, watermelons, okra and tomatoes stood around a large cage that held baby goats, pigs, lambs, and a lone calf.

Hay bales behind the cab added atmosphere and would double as seats for the teenagers in cut-off overalls and straw hats hanging out in the street till time to load up. As the kids tacked banners on each side of the trailer, they made a lot of noise. A middle-aged man supervised. He wore a matching straw hat and looked familiar, but I couldn't place him.

As I tried to figure out where I'd seen him, Sherry poked me.

"Isn't that Billy Lee Woodhallen with some big black animal?"

I swiveled my head over to see where she was pointing. "Yeah. Him and his dog."

Sherry *tsked*. "Those two little girls in front of him have *got* to be his daughters. Poor things are shaped exactly like him."

The sequined pink costumes on Billy Lee's girls billowed.

"I don't know, Sherry. Could be those costumes they have on make them look a little plump."

"Huh. Look over at that trailer where they're heading. It must be a dance school float because those other girls have on the same costumes. *They* don't look chubby."

She was right, but it seemed unfair to blame Billy Lee's daughters. "The girls can't help it. Their mother's not that slim, either. They get the fat gene from both sides."

"You're so Pollyanna-ish," she said witheringly. "You always have an excuse for everybody."

"Not everybody," Bodie on her other side murmured.

I caught my breath. "Well," I finally said, sounding a little lame even to me, "I've met Billy Lee's wife in the tax office and she's nice. A lot nicer than him."

Sherry snorted and then waved. "Looks like Rayla out on the road stopping traffic. Bet she's enjoying throwing her weight around."

Rayla did seem pretty pleased with herself. Bodie and I waved, too, but she pretended not to see any of us. She was too busy bringing a big SUV to a screeching stop before sashaying over to the driver's side. From the waving of her arms and her militant posture, she was fussing at him. Maybe for going too fast though he couldn't have been speeding with all the traffic in front of him.

Do all deputies have such high opinions of themselves? I couldn't remember Rayla being so full of herself when she was a mere dispatcher in the sheriff's office.

A group of Cub Scouts scurried around us.

After a little more walking around and socializing, we started back toward our float. As we moved past the dance studio's entry again, little girls in pink tutus and tiaras practiced baton twirling in a close line.

One of Billy Lee's daughters accidentally hit another girl, a tiny blonde with hair up in a knot, on the head with one end of her baton. Luckily, the bun took the brunt of the blow, but the blonde ballerina still spun around, scowling.

Billy Lee's daughter was oblivious. She kept on twirling, dancing away on her plump little legs and swinging her plump little arms enthusiastically.

I could tell the abused dancer was struggling with herself about whether or not to lay into Billy Lee's daughter. Guess she decided it was better to stay quiet because after a moment she joined in the routine again. She kept looking daggers at the chubby twirler, though, as she moved a little further back.

Wise of her to keep her distance. Billy Lee's daughter had at least fifteen pounds on her.

Off to the side, a familiar figure skulked away from the farm truck. He looked to the left and then the right, and then tugged at Doc's leash as if anxious to be elsewhere.

What was Billy Lee up to? I wanted to wander over that way and see, but Sherry grabbed my arm. "Hurry up. The front floats are starting to move. We need to get in place. Where's Caleb?"

Bodie assured us Caleb was coming before he boosted me up and then Sherry. We both made the climb without incident. In triumph, I settled down in the comfort of the Cadillac.

If the sun hadn't been so hot, I'd have enjoyed my luxurious surroundings more; but Sherry brought out some personal misting fans for us to use so we didn't swelter too much.

In fact, our perch on top of the carrier offered a great view of horses and riders in western regalia and convertibles bearing beauty queens trailing a trolley decked out in patriotic colors to haul our local veterans.

Sherry pointed to a tow truck. "That's Ike Hansfeldt's truck. He must have volunteered to drag that smashed car for MADD. They asked to borrow Caleb's, but he'd sent it down to south Georgia to pick up a wrecked Corvette he wants to salvage for parts he can use in that one he's been restoring forever. Didn't you say Lucy kind of liked him?"

"Caleb? Oh. Ike. Uh huh. At least I think so."

Pausing before getting into the driver's seat, Ike looked fit and athletic in khaki shorts, flag T-shirt and a red baseball hat. The buttinski still annoyed me no end, even if Lucy did think he was nice. "She always talks to him when we're at the gym so I guess she likes him."

"He's cute. And he's always such a classy dresser."

I pooh-poohed that. "You wouldn't say so if he was wearing his plaid shorts today."

"Plaid shorts?"

"Yeah. You ought to see them. They're hideous."

Sherry raised a brow. "He usually wears his uniform when I meet him. Otherwise, it's khakis and Izods. I've never even seen him in blue jeans. Sometimes, like on Sundays, he wears a suit and tie."

She thought about it. "Plaid shorts, eh? Hard to believe. I've never known him to look less than preppy. Or is it yuppie?"

"I wouldn't describe him as either." I didn't care how snide I sounded. "Not with his knobby knees and those bird legs like two sticks. Haven't you noticed them?"

"No. Ooh, we can look right down on that marble. Isn't it pretty?"

Directly in front of us, a flatbed trailer from the quarry outside of town carried a huge chunk of marble that hung over the sides. It was at least twice as big as the convertible we rode in. Though the jutting quarry stone stood almost as high as our seats on top of the car carrier, we still got a good view.

Washed and lightly polished, the stone in its rough shape was beautiful. Beside it, we could see Arvin Smelting, who owned the quarry, talking to his driver. A huge banner draped the back.

I said, "I can't believe Arvin wasted money on a banner. Usually he goes with the quarry name already on the cab."

"Caleb said he traded the sign painter an engraved marble gravestone for the banner."

"A monument for the sign painter? How does Arvin know when the sign painter's going to die?"

"I don't know. Maybe he—Ooooh! That hurts!"

Sherry slapped her hands over her ears and I quickly followed suit.

The calliope in front of the marble float let off steam in a shrill piercing whistle.

"Where're those earplugs?" I shouted.

Sherry found them and gave me a pair.

Beyond the calliope, the flatbed for Trudell Farms held its place in line but the animals pushed and shoved in their cage. They had to be freaked out. If that steam whistle kept this up, they'd be ready to make a getaway.

The straw-hatted driver came around the back to yell at the calliope as Billy Lee happened by with his dog.

The two men would have bumped into each other except the driver stopped short. Billy Lee puffed up, but neither man backed down. They started wagging fingers at each other. I was pretty sure they weren't using sign language.

Their confrontation jarred my memory. "Hey, that farm truck driver's the man Billy Lee accused of, of, um, borrowing, his prize hog for stud duty."

"Hoooo boy," said Sherry.

We waited for fists to fly.

The farmer measured a good size but his girth was nothing compared to Billy Lee's bulk. They menaced each other for several minutes, trying to stare each other down. Then both turned and left in opposite directions. A few baleful glances over the shoulder ended the standoff peaceably.

"Guess Sheriff Duval can relax. No fight today," I murmured.

The old fashioned calliope's steam rose in a steady flow from its wood box. Soon the strains of "Take Me Out To the Ball Game," "Down By the Old Mill Stream," "The Band Played On," and a lot of other favorites from a generation long gone started filling the air.

I sighed.

MeeMaw loved that kind of music and could even sing all the words. A shame she and PawPaw were still touring the west coast. Not that they enjoyed the festivities when the heat was always so bad. The last time they came to the parade was to see me march in the band my senior year of high school.

Speaking of the band, they blared somewhere behind us,

but the calliope music was so loud, even with the marble truck between us, that it drowned everything else out.

Down below, Caleb had come up and was talking to the driver of the Freightliner. The driver got in, Caleb and Bodie hurried back, climbed into their Lexus behind us, and we were off.

Sherry and I didn't talk much as we tossed out candy to excited, screaming kids. We didn't hear much from Bodie and Caleb nor could we see them without turning halfway around and standing up in the seat, so we assumed they were doing their part. I aimed at the smallest kids and pretended not to see the adults begging us to throw some their way.

"Look at those grown people waving for us to throw them candy," I said to Sherry.

"Candy should be for kids."

I popped a melting Hershey miniature into my mouth. "Exactly."

In past years, if I didn't march in the band, I sat on the sidewalk by the bank where the town proper begins and watched everything go by as I collected my candy. Today, from my lofty position, the parade took on a whole new aspect.

We could look beyond the crowds and see the barbecue pit smoldering in the square and the watermelons ready for slicing in their tubs beneath awnings and the vendors setting up in the cordoned off streets and the people in lawn chairs lolling on the sidewalks.

Overall, it was pretty cool. Except for the heat.

After about an hour or so going through town at a snail's pace that allowed our body temperatures to get way too high despite our misting fans, our part of the parade reached the school grounds. We had to stop to wait for the floats in front of us to turn.

"Thank goodness we're almost done." I took a long swig from my water bottle. My arm was numb from all the throwing and waving and aiming mist at myself. "I have never been so hot and tired and sticky in my entire life."

"Me, too. Especially hot. If hell is like this, I hope I don't have to go," Sherry moaned. She stuck a piece of limp toffee in her mouth. "Not much candy left. Better have a piece."

"I'm saving myself for stew and homemade ice cream. What say we get off while we're stopped and head back to town where the food is? Caleb and Bodie can finish up with the float, can't they?"

"Sounds good to me. I'll tell Caleb." As she started to stand up in the seat so she could twist around and call back to her husband, her eyes widened in horror. "Oh, no-o-o-o!"

I looked to see what had upset her and, in the parking lot up ahead, witnessed the whole thing.

Although, afterward, I never could quite be sure exactly what I witnessed.

Everything happened so fast.

As the flatbed with the farm animals pulled to a stop inside the school grounds, the back gate lowered to let the teen riders off. About the same time, Doc, free from any restraints or leashes, bounded up.

He began to bark furiously.

The calliope behind the farm float finished its sweeping turn into the school and slowed.

As Doc jumped and barked, the frightened animals pressed against the cage door. It swung open. Piglets, lambs, baby goats, and the lone calf broke free.

Even over the calliope I could hear squealing and *baa*ing and *moo*ing.

The calf stood and looked over the edge of the trailer. The piglets ran down the ramp alongside the lambs. A couple of nimble goats jumped down from the side and made a run for it.

Doc, after looking from the calf to the piglets to the goats and back, made an executive decision and took off after the goats.

About that time, a bellowing Billy Lee, leash in hand, ran up and grabbed Doc's collar. Successful in fastening the leash, he relaxed.

But Doc had a mission. He yanked Billy Lee forward. Billy Lee stumbled and, with no choice in the matter, got dragged along behind Doc until a swing set on the nearby playground abruptly stopped his progress.

Doc, with Billy Lee enmeshed in the swing's chains, slowed. A few minutes saw Billy Lee get untangled, but that meant Doc was free to lunge forward. He nearly caught up to the goats.

The goats—no fools—climbed up the slide the wrong way and scampered down the steps. Doc tried to run up behind them but slid backward into Billy Lee, still being towed along behind. Doc's weight knocked Billy Lee down. He lay stunned while Doc trampled on him before scrambling back up the slide.

In the meanwhile, during the melee, the truck in front of ours that pulled the chunk of marble, started to make the turn into the school parking lot where the calliope had stopped.

A heretofore unseen SUV parked to the side started backing out between the calliope and the marble truck, but veered suddenly to avoid squealing piglets streaking across behind him.

The truck driver, deep into his left turn, couldn't go to the right because of the calliope. He tried to avoid a collision with the SUV by going further left.

He did avoid a fender bender, but the sharp turn meant disaster for the trailer with the rock being towed.

It tipped sideways.

The gigantic hunk of marble started to slide.

A nanosecond later, a huge thump rent the air as the stone landed on a car near where the SUV had been parked.

"Oh. My. Goodness," Sherry breathed.

The sight was a terrible one, but I couldn't spend time watching it.

I had to look back at the animal action.

A teenager, straw hat askew, corralled one wayward pig. Another teen guarded various animals already back in the cage. Several more kids chased the other piglet and the little lambs.

The goats on the playground had doubled back toward their truck and now raced up the ramp. The lone teen guarding it tried to keep the caged animals inside while enticing the goats in.

A shaken Billy Lee, Doc barely under control, looked right and left when he emerged from the playground. Then he turned tail and made a fast exit.

Uh huh. Getting as far away from the farm float as he could. Good choice.

Everything seemed to be getting back to normal except that the driver of the farm truck began stalking off in the direction Billy Lee had gone.

"I think everyone's all right," I said. "D'you reckon Billy Lee had something to do with those cages—"

"Ohhhhh, Corrieeee."

All my antennae rose. My head swiveled. Pity struggled with horror on Sherry's face.

"What's wrong?"

"Oh, Corrie. Wasn't your car parked over there somewhere?"

"My car?"

"Yeah. That big chunk of marble landed on a car and I think..." She bit her lip.

"Nooooo! Don't tell me! Don't you tell me that!" I gripped Sherry's arm. Hard. "Is the car white?"

She didn't have to say a word. Her expression said everything.

Chapter Twenty-One

MY POOR LITTLE Hyundai, its holes and paint barely repaired, was smashed flat as a pancake.

This time it was totaled. Lucy dropped me off Wednesday afternoon at the rental company where by now I was on a first-name basis with the sales clerk.

"Hoped I wouldn't see you again so soon," Harry said compassionately.

"Yeah."

"If it'd been Friday, I'd of had a choice for you. But we had a big run on everything Monday."

Once again, the Smart Car was the last rental left in the lot.

I sighed. It was cute, but it was also so…little.

He went on, "I don't know why so many are out. Maybe it being the Fourth and all. Course we generally don't keep but four or five car rentals on hand 'cause hardly nobody needs 'em what with the cost and everyone nowadays having two cars and relatives to borrow from and all. Still, business has been good lately and maybe with the holiday and—"

"Never mind. I don't plan on keeping it long. As soon as the insurance company comes up with the cash, I'm going shopping for a decent car."

Two more payments would pay off my Hyundai. With what the insurance allowed and my new improved salary as tax commissioner, maybe I could afford a new car this time. Maybe a cute little convertible like Momma's.

Hey, yeah!

I perked up. I think I even hummed as I drove out of the rental car lot. Looking at a possible showroom new car in my future made me forgive the lag time in acceleration.

At the tax office the rest of the week, Zara did okay. She had teeth leaning toward the bucked side which was one reason she reminded me of a rabbit, but she seemed determined to learn.

Maybe her eager attitude would hold. I still thought she wouldn't be able to take the stress of waiting on tag customers when she had to go live on the tag line, but I'd been wrong about people before.

On the following Monday, Dyson did his thing.

The digest got whipped into shape. Everything looked good.

That afternoon I called the State to get an appointment to take it down to the Department of Revenue for submission.

"July nineteenth," I told Fred and Dyson. I didn't much want to take Dyson with us but Mr. Jethro always had and I was afraid we might need him for some reason.

Although I couldn't imagine what that reason might be.

Lucy and I hadn't made it to the gym the past Wednesday, so she was determined to go today.

I waffled and tried to beg off. After my last experience, I never wanted to go back to the place again and told Lucy so.

She ducked her head and looked pathetic. "But it's helping us so much. I've lost weight and you're trimming up so nicely. Those pants aren't as tight on you as they were a couple of weeks ago, are they?"

Under her urging, I reluctantly agreed. After all, Lucy needed to keep getting out and not mope at home. If I didn't go to the gym, she wouldn't either.

About six o'clock, we reached Trim with Fitness. The redheaded sixteen-year-old deputy happened to be lifting weights. Tim the Skinhead, uniform on and bag in hand like he was about to leave, was talking to him.

The kid poked Tim and jerked his head toward us as we came in.

Tim looked our way and snickered.

It would take a long time to live down my hair getting caught in the treadmill.

And it was all Ethan's fault. Good thing he was absent today.

Ike Hansfeldt wasn't. On the other side of the deputies, he lay back on some kind of machine that stuck his legs up in the air and made him flap his arms.

If he knew what was good for him, he'd keep his distance. His meddling burned me up as much as Ethan's stupidity. No sir, Ike had no business trying to send me off to the ER again after the first time he'd butted in.

He saw us and waved at Lucy. After a little hesitation, he waved at me, too.

Lucy waved back.

I vacillated. Okay, Corrie, I told myself. Ike may irritate you no end but Lucy gets along with him pretty well and he looks okay except for his bird legs and knobby knees. If he sells that land, he'll be a good catch for some lucky girl. If it could happen to be Lucy, don't rock the boat.

Besides, you're a politician now.

So I stifled my annoyance with Ike's interfering habits and smiled and threw up my hand like we were the best of friends.

Relief spread all over his face.

He wore the same plaid shorts and grungy tee that he had on when the tag boxes knocked me down. Come to think of it, they were all I'd seen him wear at the gym.

I mentioned it to Lucy. "I wonder why he dresses so nice most of the time, but then turns up here in those awful shorts."

Lucy shrugged. "I don't know. He probably doesn't mind getting them dirty. Lots of old clothes are more comfortable than new workout stuff."

Ike's outfit looked pretty skanky to me even for gym wear but I didn't say more because, when he came over to flirt with Lucy, she livened up like she was getting attached to him.

***

ON WEDNESDAY, I got held up by a customer so Lucy went

on to the gym. Since I was near two o'clock getting there, she'd already changed and started on the treadmill. I followed suit but had barely been exercising for half an hour when Ike sauntered out in pressed khaki shorts and a neat golf shirt, smelling like a baby fresh from its bath.

He did use some fantastic cologne.

Lucy shot me a mischievous look when he stopped by to chat.

"Got a question for you, Ike," she said. "Corrie wants to know how come you wear such nice clothes all the time, except for here."

His back stiffened. "What do you mean?"

Lucy didn't notice. "Let's face it, those plaid shorts are so not you. Corrie wondered about them. I told her they must have some sentimental value or something. Do they?"

Ike's face turned bright red. I jumped in. "All I said, Ike, was that you have excellent taste in everything you wear. Except for your workout clothes."

He gave a brittle laugh. "They may be ratty but they're fine for a place like this. And they're clean. I wash 'em every time I wear 'em."

"Oh, I'm sure you do," I hastened to reassure him. "It's the color. You usually wear dark colors and the shorts are so...so bright."

His smile didn't reach his eyes. "They go back a long way. Had 'em since I was on the college golf team."

"Did you say you take them home and wash them every time you work out?" Lucy asked.

He turned from me. "Sure do."

Lucy, picking up on his touchiness, almost cooed. "I'm impressed, Ike. You have no idea. Most men aren't too careful about stuff like that. Bri—" Her face clouded at mention of her dead husband. "Briant never would have thought about washing any of his own clothes. I always took care of things like that for him. Oh, gosh…" Her voice broke and she turned off her machine. "I think I'm done for the day, Corrie. I'm kind of tired."

Ike and I watched her go. His expression was unreadable. Maybe it was because of the reference to Briant.

"She's not over her husband yet," I said. "It takes time."

"Sure. Must be hard to lose someone you love all of a sudden, the way she did."

I looked down. I hadn't killed Briant, but the poison that did was meant for me. I guess guilt would always be there for even the unintentional part I'd played in his death. "They hadn't been married all that long. Three years or so."

"Yeah." Ike took a deep breath and looked at me hard. "Any more questions about my clothes?"

Uh oh, my criticism of his taste had upset him. "Oh, gosh no. I never should have said anything to start with. Hey, I'm the last person to be a fashion arbiter."

I hoped he'd loosen up and laugh it off, but he left abruptly. I still felt a chill.

Moody interfering meddler.

What did it matter whether or not Ike disliked me? So I wouldn't get his vote. I still didn't know if I planned to run next year or not anyway.

It wasn't much fun treading by myself, but I dutifully finished out my hour, packed up my stuff, and left. Unlike Ike, I didn't change out of my workout clothes. I liked to clean up in my own bathroom.

Outside, as my women's protection course had advised, I got my keys out and hurried toward the Smart Car.

Something gripped my arm. "Go round to the passenger side," came a husky whisper.

"What...?" Something sharp poked me in the back.

I looked up into Ike Hansfeldt's face. He gripped my arm harshly. His grim face exuded determination. "The passenger side. Shut up and go on around. My knife is right at your throat. Understand?"

Knife!

"Ike?" Shock made me stumble.

He jerked me upright.

The knife point pricked my neck. "What're you doing?"

"You know what I'm doing. You figured out why I had on those shorts that day in town, didn't you?"

Shorts? What was he talking about? "No, I don't... What do you mean? What about your shorts? Are you talking about what I said? I didn't mean anything by it. I was just wondering—"

Why was he threatening me with a knife over a stupid remark I should have kept to myself? What kind of person got this mad over criticism of his clothes? "I thought those shorts were kind of loud for you, that's all I meant. You usually dress in khakis and look all preppy and they—"

"Don't give me that." The blade pricked again.

"Ouch! Ike, don't."

He pushed me around the car. "You got the keys. Open the door."

No one else was in sight. Yelling wouldn't help. No one inside the gym could hear. Maybe if I dropped the keys I'd have a chance...

My hand was already trembling. I held the key control out and pressed. The latches clicked open. The keys clanked against the pavement.

Ike pulled me up against the knife before I could move. The blade pricked.

"Owww!"

He forced me down on my knees. "Don't play with me. Pick up those keys."

When I retrieved them, he jerked me back up. "Get over here, dammit."

He didn't wait for my response but dragged me to the passenger side. "Go ahead. Open that door and get in."

Obediently, I took the handle and opened it.

He pushed me inside. The knife came up to my throat. "Move over to the driver's side."

Further away from the knife.

I scrambled to get over the console, and let me tell you, that was a tight squeeze. He slid in beside me. Something warm crept down my neck.

Blood, dripping from where he'd nicked me. Was my throat cut? Thank goodness I still had on the sloppy T-shirt; blood wouldn't hurt it.

I'm the one about to be hurt! Worry about important stuff!

Ike looked nervously behind us. "Where're your keys?"

If I told him, he'd make me drive away somewhere far

away from any help. As long as I stayed here, I could still have a chance.

"Keys!" He put his face against mine, the knife point gouging.

The sting brought tears. I held them up mutely. *He's gonna kill me.*

He allowed a couple of inches between us. "Okay. Start the car and drive."

I sniffled. "Where?"

He bit his lip.

He hasn't thought that far ahead.

Hope flickered. If this was a spur of the moment thing, he couldn't have planned this out enough to make my kidnapping go smooth. Although…Weren't most successful killings spur of the moment things? Had I read that somewhere? I remembered…

Stop thinking about stupid stuff like that and figure out what you're going to do!

I plucked up my nerve. "Someone's going to remember you left the gym right after me. And how are you going to explain your car being left here?" My arguments would have sounded better had my voice not quavered.

Ike gnawed his lip, thinking. Then, "I walked over like I do all the time so my car's at home. I live right across that field. Far as anyone'll ever know, I left first, you left later, and that'll be the last anyone saw of you. Nothing to do with me." He made a sudden decision. "Drive back toward the highway. We'll head for the park."

Behind Barbara's house.

My bones chilled. Maybe I could reason with him. "Listen, Ike, what's going on? Why are you doing this?"

"Why'm I…?" He freaked. "You know! You know damn well! When you got Lucy to ask me about those shorts, I could tell you knew! Don't you pretend, don't you, don't you… You better not… Drive, dammit, drive!"

What in heaven's name was going on? I used my calm voice, trying to soothe him, trying to figure out what he meant. "All I know is that you have bad taste in workout clothes. I don't—"

The knife pricked again. "Drive."

I started the car and drove out from the gym.

Just my luck. No traffic on the road. Not a vehicle in sight. The one time I needed people around, they were absent.

I would have to reason with him. "Ike, I don't know what's going on but—"

"Don't give me that." Coming to a decision had calmed him. "You know I put those shorts on after I killed Barbara because my clothes got bloody."

Bloody? Killed Barbara? I gasped. "No. No! I didn't know anything about—"

"Shut up and drive."

"That's crazy. You didn't have any reason to kill Barbara," I said in desperation.

"Hah." The sound was sarcastic. "I had every reason to kill her. The stupid cow dug up one of the freaking Adamses way out in Texas, and the old lady sent letters from her grandfather. He wrote that the right of way width he gave us on that one acre was limited to eight feet for a driveway. Once Barbara got that, she said there was no way in hell I could win against Arvin's lawsuit. And without being able to widen that driveway, I can't sell that property."

The pieces clicked into place. "We had it backward. Barbara wanted to talk to you first because she was giving *you* the bad news. Not Arvin."

"Yeah. I asked her to forget she'd ever seen those papers, but the dumb cow refused."

Amid my whirling thoughts, I latched on to that last. "She couldn't forget she'd got them, Ike. She knew the law."

"Sure she could have. But I came over to her house prepared. I had this old clunker left in my yard a few years back when the owner skipped town, see? With a sawed-off shotgun in it. Never thought I'd have a use for a shotgun, but I kept it anyway. So that day I brought it with me, thinking... I knew if it got traced back, it wouldn't be to me. If she wouldn't... I figured..." He stopped. "Doesn't matter. Turn here."

We got on the highway.

He'd killed Barbara when she refused to withhold evidence that he didn't own access to his acreage.

And I'm next.

My spinning brain tried to think of a plan.

A plan.

Okay, keep him talking. Wasn't that what they did in books? Didn't killers like to talk about their crimes?

"So you killed Barbara." I called on my customer service knowledge and used my most sympathetic tone. "Wasn't she suspicious of the gun when she let you in?"

"Had it under my jacket in the back of my pants. Tried to talk her one more time out of turning the letter over to Arvin but she wouldn't budge. Not even when I offered to split the money with her. Stubborn bitch."

Maybe we'll meet a car. Maybe I can ram it head-on or something.

"So you shot her and got blood all over your clothes." *That's right, speak soothingly.* "Then you changed to your shorts because they were in your truck. You always wash your workout clothes and put them back in the truck."

"Yeah. I figured if I went back to town and told everyone I'd just left work and run by the house to get my water bill, nobody'd suspect me. They'd never realize I had time to go by Barbara's if I showed up in town right away."

Okay, he's talking, so develop a rapport. Isn't that the thing to do in a situation like this?

"You didn't go home at all?"

"No. I skipped the gym that day 'cause she agreed to meet me at her house when she got home from work. After... It was lucky I had the water bill in the truck. Gave me an excuse to go to town."

"You must have got blood on you in other places, too." *Be understanding.*

"They said blood squirted everywhere. That must have been awful. Changing clothes wouldn't have hidden all of it."

"Had on coveralls and a jacket. Burned them later. I went by the park and washed off my hands before going on to town. Changed clothes in the park, too."

No wonder my questions about his shorts had stirred him up. "I didn't know, Ike. Honest."

"You do now, so I don't guess it matters."

I'm going to die.

A sob crinkled my throat, was conquered. "Did Jasmine know?"

"Jasmine." He groaned. "She was another stupid cow. She opened Barbara's mail so she saw the papers from the Adams woman when they came in. She knew what they meant. After Barbara... Afterward, she tried to blackmail me."

So that*'s what was going on that day in his shop with Jasmine. Odometer rollback, my foot.* "You killed her, too."

He swallowed hard, but the knife didn't move off my neck. "Used Arvin's truck to run her off into the lake. Thought that'd throw all the attention on him. And it was working. Is working. Without you asking questions, he'll be the one they think did it."

"But I didn't suspect anything! I was just carrying on with Lucy like we always do. You always dressed so nice and the shorts seem so unlike you..." This time, I couldn't hold back the snuffle. "You killed two women, Ike. All because you wanted to sell your land."

"And what else could I do?" He turned angry. Angry because Barbara wouldn't conceal the truth, because Jasmine tried to blackmail him, because I couldn't condone his actions. "Listen, they offered me near two million dollars for that land. You know how long it'd take me to make that much money changing oil?"

The road that led to the park lay ahead. A familiar black truck turned onto it.

My heart leaped. Billy Lee? I glanced at the dash clock. Yep, time for him and Doc to visit the park while the girls took their ballet lessons.

Maybe I could get his attention. He'd saved me once before. Maybe he could do it again.

If he can get me away from this knife, I promise I'll go over his assessments myself with a fine-tuned calculator. I promise I'll see they're no more than fair market value. I promise...

We reached the turn-off for the road that led to the park entrance. As the Smart Car followed the path of Billy Lee's truck, its rearview mirror reflected an old classic Mustang coming up behind us. I didn't pay much attention to it, even when a few minutes later it turned onto the road directly after us.

My mind was focused on the truck ahead. If I could get Billy Lee's attention, he might see what was going on.

Billy Lee showed no signs of slowing.

I risked a glance at Ike.

He didn't have his seat belt fastened. If I could run into a tree or something, he might be thrown forward and I might have a chance to escape.

What could I hit? Lots of trees around but they were too far from the road. Long before the Smart Car hit one, Ike would have the knife in my throat.

The truck ahead leisurely moved forward.

Inspiration struck. What if I rammed Billy Lee's truck from the rear?

Billy Lee would kill me.

Hah, Ike was about to kill me, and he was right beside me. Did I have a choice?

First I'd have to speed up. I gently accelerated.

The rearview mirror reflected the Mustang charging up fast. It better not get between me and Billy Lee. If it did, I'd swerve into it. Maybe Billy Lee would stop to see what was going on.

The Mustang stayed on my tail and didn't try to pass.

At least I'd have another witness and someone else to help if my plan worked.

Plan. Right.

Forlorn hope, more like.

The Smart Car hit forty, but took exception to the dilapidated road. We bumped and rattled. If I could overtake Billy Lee before he turned into the park, I would take a chance and ram his truck.

We hit a pothole. Hard. The knife bit my throat.

"What the hell are you doing?" Ike yelled. "Watch where you're driving!"

I swallowed. If I hit Billy Lee and the crash didn't shake Ike up, his knife would be through my throat.

Don't think about it.

Taking a big breath, I pressed on the throttle. Hard.

The Mustang kept up like the driver wanted to get around me.

No way. Not now. I was determined to have somebody else around if this worked.

Ike noticed my glances at the rear view mirror and turned in the seat. "What's going on with that car?"

"I don't know. He's following awful close."

Ike pressed the knife back to my throat.

He had to be getting tired, the way he had to hold the knife up like that.

"Ease off the gas." He didn't sound tired. "We're almost to the park."

Ahead of us, Billy Lee had slowed to turn. His right indicator blinked red.

Ike muttered, "Oh, hell, he's going into the park." The knife at my throat relaxed. "Forget the park. Go on straight."

"Straight?"

"Goddammit! Straight! Keep going!"

I had taken my foot off the accelerator to slow down, but now I gunned it.

Well, as much as I could gun a Smart Car.

We hit Billy Lee's truck before it finished its turn into the park entrance.

Ike, without a seatbelt, hurtled into the windshield. The knife fell between the seats.

The Mustang on my bumper nudged us. The little car was trapped like a book between bookends.

All I needed was for the air bags to explode.

They didn't, thank goodness. Prepared, I released my seat belt with one hand and opened the door with the other to scramble out.

Ike recovered and caught my ankle. "No, you don't!"

"Aiiiigh!" I started hopping on my free foot, the other still in the car. "Let me go! Let me go! Help!"

Billy Lee, climbing out to look at the damage to his truck, gawked at us.

"Billy Lee! Help!"

The driver of the Mustang also got out. He used a crutch because he had a cast on one leg.

Professor Random.

He recognized me. "Corrie?"

"Help me!"

Billy Lee started yelling. His approach wasn't friendly. "What the heck do you think you're doing? You ran slap dab into my truck!" He recognized me and stopped. "Aw, no. Not you again." He took off his baseball hat and threw it to the ground and stomped on it.

Ike wouldn't let hold of my ankle. In a moment, I'd be yanked back inside the car.

I caught the door frame and held it with one hand and beat at Ike's arm with the other. "Help! Help!"

Billy Lee finally realized something was wrong. He started toward us, but the professor was already hopping over. He used his crutch to poke Ike in the face.

Ike let me go to clutch at his eye. "Arghhh!"

I tumbled free and fell, scraping my knees on the pavement in the process.

Billy Lee noticed the professor for the first time. "What the hell! Why can't you leave me alone? If you don't stop stalking me, I'm gonna get a warrant and have you arrested. If I don't bust you in the face first."

Ike, still clutching his eye, jumped from the Smart Car and rushed to Billy Lee's truck.

I started screaming. "He's getting away! He killed Barbara Prestotten and Jasmine Musselman and he's getting away!" My phone was somewhere in the car. "Call for help, somebody!"

Pushing myself up off the pavement, I limped to the wrinkled car door.

I had to get my purse with its phone.

The professor already had his cell out, dialing. "Yes, this is Jeffrey Random and—"

I grabbed it from him and blathered something about

Ike murdering Barbara Prestotten and her secretary, and that he was getting away in Billy Lee's truck.

Billy Lee, standing bemused at our antics, heard that part and whirled. "My truck!" he yelled at Ike. "You get out of my truck!"

About that time, Ike's yells almost drowned Billy Lee's.

I looked in time to see him tumble out of the truck with Doc latched onto his arm. Ike, screaming, tried to push the dog off, but Doc wasn't about to let go.

By now Billy Lee was incensed. "Sic 'im, Doc!" he roared. "Good boy, Doc! Sic 'im!"

I don't know how hard Doc bit Ike, but he hung on for the entire six minutes it took for a deputy's car to drive up.

Tim the Skinhead saw me and did a double take. He started to amble over, trying not to grin.

"Hurry it up!" I waved toward Ike, rushing words together as I tried to get across Ike was a murderer who was about to get away.

When Tim finally understood, he reacted like a tough guy, pulling out some kind of loop device and rushing to take charge of Ike.

Except Doc wouldn't let go.

Tim tried to get his collar, but Doc growled and stretched a paw to bat Tim's legs from under him.

Billy Lee had to go over and calm down his dog.

When Ike got free of Doc's mouth, he started to make a run for it. By that time, Tim was back on his feet and grabbed him.

In two seconds flat, he had Ike's arm twisted up behind his back.

When Ike struggled, Tim slung him to the pavement—a lot harder than necessary, but under the circumstances I didn't complain—before he cuffed him with the plastic thingamajig and breathlessly started reciting the standard *you-have-the-right-to* stuff we always see on TV.

About that time, two more cars drove up. The sixteen-year-old kid got out of one and Tim barked at him to sort out the details about Billy Lee's truck and the Mustang and the Smart Car. James Cleuny, the other driver, stood shooting the bull with Billy Lee before Tim ordered him over to help with Ike.

"Okay," I told the wide-eyed kid as he got out his clipboard and started taking our accident reports. "It may have been my fault. But I had a good reason."

His eyes were wide. "I'm sure, ma'am."

He may have been young, but he turned out to be okay. When little black dots swirled before me and I started swaying, he helped me sit down on the pavement.

"Don't worry about a thing, ma'am. EMTs are on the way and I know CPR. You sit here and don't worry about a thing because we've got everything under control and as soon as..."

***

NATURALLY, I ENDED up in the emergency room with Dr. Bennigan, Momma, and Ethan crowded in beside the examining table. My one consolation was that my face didn't have a bruise, black eye, cut or bump for Dr. Bennigan's inspection.

"Looks good," Dr. Bennigan said when he'd sutured and bandaged my neck. "Hey, you can even hide this one with a high-collared shirt. We'll get Nancy to swab those knees and you'll be out of here."

"How's Ike?" I asked him as he started washing his hands. "He got shoved... Uh, he fell down pretty hard and I think he got bit, too."

"He's fine," Ethan answered. "Some cuts and bruises and teeth marks. He's already been picked up and taken over to the detention center. They should be charging him now."

So much for my idea of matching Lucy up with a nice guy.

"Has the professor gone, too?"

"He'll be here for a while longer," Dr. Bennigan answered.

"What for?"

He grinned at me. "Now, now, don't be so nosy. Privacy rights, remember?"

When he left, Momma helped me get down. "Is the professor okay?" I asked her.

"Dr. Bennigan called in his orthopedic surgeon to check his leg. He may have reinjured it."

"Oh, no! Poor Professor Random. Can we go by and see him before we leave, see if he needs us to do anything?"

"He doesn't need anything. He's got his boss or somebody already here," Ethan said. "She's hovering over him like a mother hen."

His boss. The same boss who'd taken him home and brought him meals when he first broke his arm and leg.

That woman had to be after him.

Like I cared. I wasn't feeling like tending to anyone besides myself. As we went through the waiting room, Sherry burst in. And with her, looking somber and maybe a tiny bit scared, Bodie.

Sherry threw her arms around me, squealing. "Caleb heard it over the scanner. I can't believe it. Ike Hansfeldt. Are you all right? How did he get you? What did he do to you? Are you all right?"

I pushed her away. "I'm fine, Sherry."

"They said you got cut," Bodie said.

"Yeah, but it's not bad. I'm fine."

And I was, until Bodie's hand touched the bandage at my neck and I smelled his cedar scent and saw the concern still on his face. Then I started crying.

"Hush, Fluff," he said. "If Mrs. C. won't stop and get you some Cold Churn Dash on the way home, I'll bring some over."

So I stopped crying and wiped my face on the front of his shirt. Momma handed me a tissue and I blew my nose. "Deal."

I was a big girl. I was the tax commissioner.

I was alive.

The End

If you enjoyed this book, please consider leaving a review to help others discover it. Several sites offer places for reader reviews such as

http://www.amazon.com

and

http://www.goodreads.com

among others.

If you do have the time and take the effort to leave a review, please accept my sincere appreciation and thanks.

www.cherylbdale.com
cherylbdale.blogspot.com
cherylbdale@hotmail.com

LOSING DAVID

By Cheryl B. Dale

A vintage mystery with romantic elements.

AVAILABLE 2014

"If *Losing David* were a film, it would blend parts of *Charade* and *To Catch a Thief* into an *Anastasia* set on a fictional barrier island off the southern coast."

LOSING DAVID by Cheryl B. Dale

Vintage fiction with mystery and romance elements, inspired by tobacco heir R.J. Reynolds' Sapelo Island.

1962. An era of rotary phones and clacking typewriters. Sleepy southern towns cling to tradition while determined blacks and soft-spoken women welcome change. Still, one constant remains: respectable people, like elderly attorney Lawrence Wykerton, prize integrity above everything.

All his life, Lawrence distinguishes right from wrong so confidently, a close friend called him the only honest lawyer in Georgia. Sadly, that same man died before a son/heir David vanished at sea in a boating accident.

For sixteen years, sole trustee Lawrence has safeguarded his friend's estate. Now he must turn it over to a dilettante, a man who'll dismantle and sell businesses. His friend would never have approved the destruction of the local economy, but Lawrence will do his duty however unpalatable. Until he learns the man murdered David.

His ethics fray. When he finds an unsavory actor who resembles David, they completely snap. He hires the actor to resurrect David, trap the killer, and save his friend's legacy.

But David's childhood playmate, as moral as Lawrence once was, appears. If she exposes the truth, Lawrence will forfeit everything—his career, his reputation, even his freedom. And David's murderer will go unpunished.

Available 2014 at Amazon and other booksellers

Other Fiction by Cheryl B. Dale

Romantic Suspense

Intimate Portraits
Treacherous Beauties
The Man in the Boat
Set Up

Paranormal Romance

The Warwicks of Slumber Mountain

Light Mystery

Taxed to the Max